QUEER BASHING

Tim Morrison

TP

ThunderPoint Publishing Ltd.

First Published in Great Britain in 2016 by
ThunderPoint Publishing Limited
Summit House
4-5 Mitchell Street
Edinburgh
Scotland EH6 7BD

ISBN: 978-0-9929768-9-7 (Paperback)
ISBN: 978-1-910946-06-0 (eBook)

www.thunderpoint.scot

CHAPTER 1

The first queerbasher McGillivray met was in the mirror. It was not an attractive mirror rimmed with gold and held up by semi draped angels, nor was it a magical mirror hidden away in some house of degradation in the back streets of Alexandria or Paris. No, it was a utility mirror bought after the war and hung on the back bedroom wall of a council house in Stromness which was, and is, a town on the west side of the Mainland of Orkney, second from the top and over to the right on any competent weather map of the British Isles.

For some that is exotic enough. Indeed McGillivray found, when he was older and busy in the bars of Soho, that an island accent was sufficient lure to bring home the bacon and put plenty of fat in the fire. His favourite accomplice on these fishing expeditions was a certain Raphael who knew well how to cast his nets over the waters and was more than happy to share his technique with McGillivray. Men over fifty were most likely to be entangled in his snare. By the time he had finished his drink he had always caught the eye of an attractive stranger, indeed one with a pulse, who would then return his smile, this alone sufficient to constitute a binding contract.

'There is an old friend over there, now what was his name? I must chat with him. Would you mind?'

McGillivray did not mind, indeed, he was relieved because he stood more chance of pulling when he was alone and Raphael already settled for the night. With his pint glass balanced cautiously on the top of the fruit machine he scanned the room looking for someone even more drunk and desperate than himself. To pass the time he ran his own parodies of Gaelic verse through his head and tried not to miss the peat fires of home. Ah, the glamour of the city life, the pleasures of depravity.

The two rapscallions drank most often in a bar where Grace

O'Malley, Raphael's partner, performed drag on the small stage she always called the Throne. The conventional roles of Garland and Minelli were far below her; much more to her tastes were the tragic queens of the 16th century. Her Elizabeth addressing the troops at Tilbury could raise patriotic feelings in the most Scottish of hearts and no one who saw it forgot her recitation of the last words of Anne Boleyn.

As a true sovereign, she was never that bothered about the petty infidelities of her man. 'It is nice to have a hobby,' she once said to McGillivray, umbrella from her drink crushed in her sharp little hand, 'he used to collect stamps and talked about his penny dreadfuls in bed. Nothing could be worse.'

Raphael's looks were sufficient to get him laid but McGillivray, being more gouache than oil painting, had to rely on his tongue. Those of the American persuasion were most susceptible to his charms. 'You are not from London,' Ben or Rock or Scott would say. 'I detect an accent, from where do you originate?' McGillivray would arrange an appropriate smile upon his face; 'originate' made him feel primordial. 'I come from the very North of Scotland, the islands, yes, further north than Inverness.'

'Gee, you are Scottish? I have Scottish ancestry!' Todd, or Marc – spelled with a 'c' – would enthuse as the bait took and the process of reeling in began. 'Yes,' McGillivray replied, 'from the Islands in the North,' and for further clarification if required, 'I was born in the Western Isles and grew up on the Mainland of Orkney. I have dual nationality.'

'How wonderful it must have been,' the young man, or men, so calculating to count how many, continued, after a slight laugh, 'to grow up there. Did you have to go to school in Edinburger? How on earth do you cope down here, why did you come, why did you leave such a beautiful place for this,' 'this London,' 'this Bexley Heath' or even, a hard day that one, 'this Clackton'?' By then, not even aware that their fate was already decided, they were flapping about on the dock.

'Yes,' McGillivray continued, as he sorted them out, those of the largest size, the tiddlers given to the waiting cats, 'being so close to the sea and the bones of our ancestors does indeed make us more spiritual. We are in tune with the elements, the movement of the sun and the dance of the moon. I,' he would continue with a small laugh, 'am descended from peaceful Viking traders.'

Most of it was true, well more or less. At least lies ran in the family, his 'clan' was Norse. 'We are,' he had heard it declaimed, 'the descendants of Luon swept ashore from a shipwreck one cold night. Her children and then their children took the driftwood that kept her alive as their badge. Her father was a King, one of the Olavs.' The little McGillivray had felt proud when he had first heard this. He was not descended from mere crofters but of royal descent. In the Western Isles, in the Golden Garden of the Hebrides, the ploughs are pulled by princesses and fishermen throw regal nets upon the waters. He was, he could almost see, typical of her line. It is unfortunate for the rest of the world that Lewis has never experienced a drought of words or the Word; its people are in love with the twin passions of sermonizing and story telling, poetry quarried from the Metrical Psalms bestowed on them by the graciousness of God in Gaelic.

Unaware of the gutting knife, the gleaming of the blade and the frying pan to come, Brad or Chuck would then go on to say, 'You must want to go home?'

'Yes.' McGillivray gave a slight sigh that always managed to appear unrehearsed. 'I would go home tomorrow.' The prospect sighed in turn imagining them both, united and full of years, tilling the soil and running a small tearoom.

McGillivray was greedy and a liar. He had no more intention of going back home than he did of going to the grave. Cock mattered far too much. Homosexuality was not the only issue: all islanders in London are hypocrites, they always whine on about how much they miss the sea, the pure air and the desolate consolation of watching the horizon from a long shore. Yet, should some benefactor give them a plane ticket, they will panic, 'I am busy this week, a hair appointment, my tailor, maybe next Friday.'

The South is easy and comfortable, the jobs more pleasant and vices more varied. Morality, for islanders, is solely determined by the probability of bumping into someone from home whilst in the middle of a wicked act. Mrs Cumlaquoy or

Andro of Foss were unlikely to wander into any of the bars that McGillivray frequented in the more dubious parts of London.

The sober truth that McGillivray coped through alcohol and the ingestion of a range of substances of varying legality did not seem appropriate to disclose. Never once did he say that he took the boat and train down from grace because of his peculiar appetites. Nor did he ever ask them about how wonderful it must have been to grow up near the Tower of London or the Natural History Museum. To do so would have meant going back to his little room in the outer edges of the London zones three to four on his ownio, alone, again.

Of course they were all correct, the queued admirers, especially those who were very cute. Orkney was and is a 'wonderful' place to grow up but only if one likes that sort of thing. Most places are full of wonder. To most children who have had parents who begat them in love and who continued to like each other, the world is a wonderful place; even in Croydon tables have the potential to become tabernacles and all staircases lead to delight. We are all exotic to someone.

And no, in turns of the next question, the big question, the one that people write books and fight campaigns over, 'What was it like for a gay man to grow up there?' McGillivray would laugh and tell pretty stories to divert attention away and to normalize. The islands were not as he would then explain, his hand edged along the North American's thigh, like those of the West where he was born. Although his own family had the theological infection bad, he had eventually escaped.

'My first cousin,' he would say, whilst savouring a long sip from a Guinness he had not paid for, 'was known as the Reverend Most High. This was because of his habit of lying down in front of the planes when they tried to arrive from Inverness in any week with the Sabbath in it, a harmless hobby that provided much work to the otherwise underemployed local constabulary who had to drag him out from under the flight path. Thank you. I would love another drink.'

In the time of his belief, McGillivray's faith had been founded upon the rock of good Orcadian sandstone rather than the igneous Hebridean rocks. Being sedimentary rather than volcanic it was prone to eventual erosion by the storms of reason and tides of common sense. His creed was a home-grown affair, a 'vernacular religion' that had evolved despite, not because of, the Kirk whose established clergy were mostly *ferryloupers*, non-natives who came off the ark that arrives several times a day in Stromness, season dependent. Their Clerical Southerness ensured that, as they were not part of the island tangle of relationships and so had no cousins that mattered, they were fit to perform the shamanistic rites of passage but little else. Mostly they were endured rather than appreciated. Island parishes were not that attractive to the brightest, the wisest, or the most interesting. These lustreless wind kirns and empty girnels responded with alacrity to any Pastoral Call after having given up hope of less remote charges. This 'Call' was no voice from on High, but rather a formal offering of the care of souls in a particular parish. In the preceding weeks the typed sheet of paper would be laid out in the vestry by the appointed elder to be signed by both members and adherents of the congregation, rather like the death warrant of Charles the First. Once completed with a short list of names it was put in an envelope, terms and conditions included, and then sent first class to its eager recipient, S.A.E.

When the new minister answered, simple curiosity ensured that all the groaning pews were well covered by the arses of those who had left, disaffected under the ancient regime. Their attendance would not last for long. We are born dissenters. Sooner or later, something about him, and in those days it was always a 'him', his doctrine, financial rectitude or way of life would cause sharp intakes of breath and a muttering to rise up with complaints that they, the People, were not being fed. They would rise up and cleave themselves yet again from the ungodly. No need to purify themselves in the tedious fire of conventicles on Sunday mornings, not for them the barren hillside; much more convenient to sing their songs and say their prayers on sofas in the front rooms of white bungalows with a little stone facing. After comfortable devotions, Temporal Mercies would be provided by the lady of the house on little plates with a floral design. These Meetings would continue until the Minister's departure and the appointment of his Successor enabled the redeemed to return to the familiar discomfort of their reclaimed pews. There they would sit for a blink until the new man in his turn offended and off they all trooped again. This love amongst the family of believers has always been the guarantor of the integrity of their faith. By their fruits, we do know them.

Clerics were, overall, imported. In McGillivray's youth, there was only one native born cleric in the Island. The Reverend Tommy Tait was beloved by most. He was an apple-cheeked minister who preached with anecdote and laughter. After his retirement he had a secondary career as a stand-up comedian at kirk socials and guild meetings.

> " 'I wiz in Stromness fur the Mairt and I
> met wan o' ma pairishoners, a fermer. I
> said tae him,
> 'John, yer luiking gey cheerful.'
> 'Aye,' he replied, 'a guid price fur the kye.'
> 'Weel beuy,' said I, 'hid'll be an eckstra five
> pund i' the plate come Sunday.'
> Quick as a flash he replied, 'Price o' sheep's
> doon.' "

Tait was wonderful. Honest. Funny. The only people who hated him were the enthusiasts. A proverb attributed to him is sufficient explanation, *Some call it living by faith; I call it scrounging.*

No wonder they doubted the soundness of his faith, the mirth and warm skepticism. Perhaps they thought he was making fun of them. He probably was, but they didn't get the joke. Despite their relative lack of numbers, they were skilled in making their disapproval felt. How strange it all seems now.

How could McGillivray explain all this to a man in a bar who has been blessed with a modern mind. His life is illuminated by nuclear power and the internet and so has no mechanism to appreciate these island passions. To the urban and urbane they are foreign but to us, who live far from their coffee shops and wine bars, they are more immediate. In large cities people move around in clumps of others like themselves, determined by taste, occupation, similarity of views. In the islands, we have no protection from our neighbours.

The reality of small community living means that we are indeed something more in touch with the basic structures of life and death. That awareness has nothing to do with an innate mysticism or us being closer to the elements. Death is all around us. Funeral notices appear in the window of the Paper Shop, the Florist and the Red Cross. Its nearness contributes to the fervour of those amongst us who have tasted Truth and become more careful in their ways. They have spoken to God directly. Within their hearts the joy of the Lord abides. The Spirit moves them and lo, we see their solemn smiles as they contemplate the fires of perdition awaiting the rest of us.

Often the numbers of believers decline as the weed killer of common sense removes the tendrils of credulity from young minds. As with dandelions, unless the root is removed, they will return. It seems to have started with one James Haldane. In 1797, he poured his spiritual blessings over a congregation of thousands at the agricultural show in Kirkwall. Every decade or so since then, the numbers of believers have been replenished by the Spirit rammaging over the Islands in Revivals that each raise a fresh stour of dissension that tears families and parishes apart. In the late 1840s green-faced missionaries with stern stomachs harried the fishing fleet all the way from Shetland down to the east coast of England. In 1870, under the Reverend Mister James Roy, two hundred were converted at mission meetings held over three weeks in the parish of Evie. It is reported that the island of Sanday became delirious with joy under the preaching of Mr. Matthew Armour.

Evangelical religion within that context was progressive. Believers were released from credulity; it is fashionable these days to imagine that magic was all illusion but the islands had been clarty with witchery since the 17th Century. No one doubted the efficacy of spells; if a spey wife crossed the road three times in front of a neighbour, death would occur; her spittle could take the profit from ale and butter kirn. The praise of a tinker was sufficiently lethal to kill a cow. In Rackwick, the tounship on Hoy famous for enchantment, the local witch was paid two lambs from each croft annually as protection. In addition, she could command a man to work a day for her at will. The fear of the woman was rational and evidence-based. The only time a crofter refused her commands, his house was ashes by the evening. No wonder, when Haldane came up from the South who said he served a greater power, the fishermen and farmers drank themselves stoshious on his Living Waters. He freed them from the fear of every tinker's curse and so gave them permission to be mean. To be cautious of the minister was no large price to pay; he was never more inconvenience than disturbance.

Consider too the tedium of the congregation in Stromness who before these revivals heard the only four sermons of their minister, Mr. Clouston, follow each other as the new moon followed the old, and he had a long ministry. The revivalists were at least interesting and sought not just to minister to spiritual but to social and political needs as well. Armour was a good man and a radical. He testified on behalf of the crofters at the Napier Commission and got a sentence of four days for disrupting the Tories when they held a meeting in his parish – one that cannot have used a big hall. The High Court of Session considered the prosecution nimious and the controversy was such that Questions were asked in the Lords. When the clerical felon's chains were removed and he was set free, the Presbytery presented him with an address and one can only assume much righteous backslapping.

Away from the Presbyterians, the strange passions of non-conformists flared up like burning kelp and were gone, and, according to Edwin Muir, leaving nothing but illegitimate babies in their wake. Pentecostalists met for a time in a chapel they built at the back of Hamnavoe. They did not last, their meeting place was sold off as a dwelling house, its baptistery drained and commemorated now by an electric fire.

Their more substantial kin, the Baptists and Brethren, found salvation in their own kirks, Gospel Halls and tabernacles. The Brethren, fishing and farming families mostly, worshipped without clergy; they believed that all men who had saving knowledge of the Lord were authorized to pray in public, to expound the Gospel and say the words over bread and wine. Trusting neither women nor the Moon, they practised equality and gender apartheid before the Lord. Hymns were sung from little red books that crinkled with damp to the accompaniment of a harmonium. Their preferred translation of Scripture was the Authorised Version. Good enough for Paul, it served them fine, sure and steadfast, their Anchor Held in the Storms of Life.

This was not ancient history to McGillivray. The legacy of these religious conflicts were still re-emerging about McGillivray as a boy. Old grudges live on. Christians seem to have a strange view of forgiveness and their ongoing strife meant that religion was always interesting. His parents took him each Sunday morning to the Kirk at the foot of the hill. The children were sent out during the second hymn to formal Sunday School sessions that were even to him a tad dull. He had heard most of the stories before. Much more fun was to be had at the Brethren Bible Classes at three o'clock each winter afternoon, D.V., the unpleasant abbreviation for the Latin 'God willing', if they were spared. No one made him go. The Grown Ups there had a genius for religious capitalism and were not afraid to pander to the unpleasant elements of the infant mindset if it got children through the pearly gates. They specialized in the wondrous gore of the Old Testament that embarrassed other adults and so fuelled his dreams of the Apocalypse with brazen serpents, talking donkeys, whole cities destroyed by brimstone and fire as well as the tender love of David and Jonathon.

The children learned that they were engaged in a thrilling war against sin, or as they sang it, Ssss.Iiii Nnnnn, 'a very little word that often spells dis-ahhster' and that the tangible Devil was prowling around them like a lion waiting for the moment to devour their souls. They had no need to be afraid though. Lamb blood washed, they were on the winning side and had the very best weapons. These they learned how to use in 'Sword Drill'. The rows of troops would bawl out at the tops of their voices, 'The Sword of the Spirit is the Word of God, EphesiansSixSevenTeen.' The General, the Grown Up who maintained order with ease, would then give out a verse reference followed by the barked command 'Sheath Swords', Bibles under the armpits; 'Draw Swords', held at full stretch above the head for an agonizingly tense time and then at the command to charge, the race to the reference. First person to find the correct place in Obadiah, Habakkuk or Philemon would win a point from an empty sweetie tin. Points were also awarded for coming to the meeting fully armed with a Bible, doing homework and answering catechetical questions correctly in the Quiz. These coloured disks were real currency. They would be saved up and used to purchase items from the 'shop', rubbers with scriptural texts, testaments and tracts. Greed was not sufficient to hold the children though. To sharpen the competition, the attendees were divided into two groups, 'Sure' and 'Steadfast'; the team that did best over the year would win a wooden shield and each member would earn a stake in a huge box of Quality Street.

Best of all were their solemn havocs, sober picnics followed by wild games on the West Shore beaches of Whaurbeth and Breckness. Fires were lit to keep the night at bay and sausages were eaten with red sauce in white rolls. That at least was good fun and idyllic, until sex, as it always does, buggers things up. How these Christians love each other.

CHAPTER 2

So how did McGillivray take a tumble from grace? How was it that he abandoned the sober pleasures of the Careful to go drinking in the fleshpots of Gomorrah and worship the golden calf of Sodom? How could one who had known the joy of the Son of God leave the body of the faithful? How indeed!

The story is sad and serves as a cautionary tale against the reading of books and the studying of religion. For the seeds of depravity were sown in this young Christian by a kind aunt who sent him a parcel of gay paper one Christmas. Little McGillivray undid the wrappings carefully and was thrilled to find the Book. He turned its pages to marvel at pictures of a garden and an angel with a sword made of fire and red gold from whom a partly clad man and woman ran in terror. One of their sons killed his brother instead of a lamb. In his infinite mercy, God drowned nearly all the people but saved two giraffes, rhinoceri and all the other animals save for the unicorn. It turned up late. That was a lesson to it, indeed.

In the second part of the wonderful book there were pictures of a man who had long fair hair and blue eyes like a Viking. Sometimes he wore no shirt and had nipples. He called the dark haired fishermen to follow him and take up with their cross, no mention of nails. McGillivray thought he was beautiful; with true devotion he experienced love for the first time. Such is the slipperiness of slopes. The Devil, our enemy, who roars and prowls around the island saw the chink in the little boy's spiritual armour and pounced. For no one had told young McGillivray that loving Jesus with all his heart did not mean loving him with the rest of his body. He would not be safe again for a very long time.

School was horrible at both the primary and secondary school levels. Children in inner city classrooms were no worse off than him; bullying and gangs were rife and few horrors have ever been so great as a Scottish 'playtime'. Even the children who were good at sport, beautiful and popular hated the place. McGillivray stood no chance; his crimes were manifold: he was bookish, bad at sport and even worse than having the wrong vowels, religious. This made him insufferable to his classmates, no blame to them. He had 'kick me' written on his nose. To add icing to the cake and cream to the cat, from the moment he was first aware of such things, he knew that he was gay. A worm had stirred in his Garden of Eden and caused the apple to rot.

McGillivray's sex education was a relatively liberal affair and many questions and blushes were pre-empted for teachers by the judicious screening of the ITV series, 'Living and Growing'. It depicted human reproduction with diagrams of the 'put tab A in slot A' variety. Mummies and daddies all loved each other very much but no one seemed to have any fun. The fruitful horror of reproduction was demonstrated in the last programme of the series. Stromness children whispered stories of a lassie in Kirkwall who fainted when the lady gave birth; this raised expectations to fever pitch but when their turn came to watch they were disappointed; it was gory rather than ghastly and not really plausible. McGillivray found the stork and the mulberry bush much more believable than the idea his parents had ever done anything like that. He had never seen a mulberry bush.

The local General Practitioners, a married couple, came in to the school on the hill to discuss certain medical matters with the Second Year pupils at the Academy each year, the sexes well segregated. McGillivray never found out what happened in the other room between the girls and the Lady Doctor. Some things are best left unsaid, but they were certain to have had more fun.

As homosexuality was considered a disorder by the head doctors of the United States until McGillivray was aged twelve, it would be irrational to have expected the doctor in the Islands to be enlightened but he was, after the fashion of his kind. He was a magnificent man and a true Socialist hero in the town.

Once they were alone together he showed the crimson-faced boys some alarming maps of human genitalia that bore more resemblance to the British Empire than any anatomical reality that they were likely to experience. Conquered territory was marked in pink. Masturbation, they were assured, was not a cause of hard hands or blindness and condoms should always be used on Saturday nights after the Harray Dance. Venereal diseases did not come from toilet seats, no matter what their older brothers or Tam o' Outer Quoys said. If anything strange happened down there they should come and see him, no nonsense, no questions asked.

To allow privacy, the doctor told the boys to write down personal questions on slips of paper that he would answer the following week. The guidance teacher, a chemist, gathered them up and placed them in sealed envelopes that were duly forwarded. The aim was to allow pupils the privacy to ask the questions they were too nervous to raise in class before their peers. How little the Southern teachers understood the island children. Stromness lads were not going to miss their only legitimate opportunity to demonstrate their knowledge of dirty words. Questions were masterpieces of obscenity, the triumphant work of giggling clacks. The doctor pronounced himself disappointed at their evident lack of maturity.

One slip was different and was read out carefully. Someone, somehow, had managed to get sufficient elbowroom to express a real anxiety; he was worried about finding boys Attractive and wondered what to do. Everyone looked around and tried to guess who the pervert was. Accusations, angry denials and pencils rebounded around the room. McGillivray blushed and tried to be invisible, convinced that his burning face would cause them all to think it was him, but he was desperate to know who it was, that there were others tempted even as he was. The old man imposed order with some difficulty. He suppressed the smirks and giggles under a kindly authority; he had clearly spent a long time considering his answer. The tone he chose was compassionate and forbade any further teasing.

'Everyone', the man of science said, 'goes through a homosexual phase before becoming normal. You should not be worried by those feelings. Some unfortunates seem to get stuck at a particular stage of development but this is unlikely to be you. And if it should happen you may well be very happy.'

This was the first time McGillivray had heard the word 'homosexual' and made the connection between it and the terrifying playground words of 'poof' and 'poofie' that were used to enforce common standards of masculinity. No one would define the words for him, yet everyone seemed to know what they meant. McGillivray tried to ask the grown ups what the words meant but they did not seem to want to answer. He was left to his own conclusions and surmised that somehow they covered playing with girls, coloured underpants and inappropriate hair. Interest in the opposite sex was discouraged. He was very afraid.

When he realised it was only fancying boys that was being disapproved of his by peers he was rather relieved. He certainly did not associate it with sin or the damnation of his soul. Grown-ups were always issuing warnings of the perils and snares of the opposite sex, and his desires seemed a loophole. He soon learned his error. The young minister who leant on the pulpit to play his ukulele told McGillivray that homosexuality was of the Devil and evidence of the Fall. Action was to be taken, the Barbarians were at the gates and threatening the morality of Scotland. It was proposed that the country should enter the modern age by bringing itself in line with the 1967 effect that entitled gay men to slightly less persecution. The minister was not pleased. He quoted the Epistle of Paul to the Romans, an Iron Age text that for him clinched the issue,

> 'For this reason God has given them up
> to the vileness of their own desires, and
> the consequent degradation of their
> bodies, because they have bartered away
> the truth of God for a lie, and have
> offered reference and worship to created
> things instead of to the Creator, who is
> blessed for ever; amen.'

Here the minister paused for full effect. He could see in front of him, not the blue woollen hats and upturned faces, but the idols, ideals and idylls of Rome, all judged and found wanting. His voice built up to a thunder as he delivered the sentence of

God on the fucking of men: indeed men fucking men was the punishment.

'In consequence, I say God has given them up to shameful passions. Their women have exchanged natural intercourse for unnatural, and their men in turn, giving up natural relations with women, burn with lust for one another; males behave indecently with males, and are paid in their own persons the fitting wage for such perversion.'

The Minister announced that a petition would be placed in the vestry on the very table that was used for the pastoral call. All should sign. McGillivray did. He entered his name in the Book of Life and became a hypocrite.

Oops.

Looking back, McGillivray could think of worse ways of spending eternity than being handed over to the lusts of men. But in those days, long ago, he was bending his back under the double blow of original sin and the unnatural perversions he had not yet learned to enjoy. Of course, all are damned alike; Calvin is nothing if not democratic but those with homosexual desires are more damnable than most. Salvation is for all who are saved. The way to claim it, repentance; a precise formula in stages: firstly, one has to acknowledge that one is a sinner and is powerless in the face of sin; then one has to accept that the innocent Christ bore the just punishment for all one Eastertide. Finally, solitary confession on one's knees and the invitation of the Saviour to dwell within, divine penetration. Only then one would experience the rapture of salvation, at one with Jesus.

A kist o' havers indeed. Unconditional love was never found by anyone in that false gospel. Its proclamation of salvation by works: that proper and efficacious repentance from sin was needed to ensure safe passage with Pilgrim to the Celestial City. No one, if they were honest, could be sure of their salvation. How could one know that one had done enough, used the right words? There would be no second chances after death. McGillivray's curse, his mental health problem, rose from the anxiety that he could never repent enough, trust enough, be saved enough to be healed and forgiven thoroughly. He would pray, feel clean and know he was freed forever but then later that night, every night, the tangible evidence of continuing sinful desire would present itself to him in his sweating sheets. One inevitable morning, he knew he would not wake into the day but instead feel the pitchforks tearing him apart in a literal and everlasting Hell. He would sleep with an unsheathed Bible in his bed.

McGillivray's anxiety manifested itself in a kind of spiritual compulsive disorder that involved a constant repenting until his adolescent soul was red raw and randering. His metaphorical flagellation and masochism were then followed by a euphoric release. Deep in the midweek prayer held in groups that gathered in devout bungalows he would taste joy. Their many hours spent sitting on hard chairs as they chanted the name of Jesus, heads bent, did not go unrewarded. Someone would be asked to give a word. The Bible would be opened and Saint Paul explained: that as all had died with Christ and been buried with him in the baptismal waters so they would share in his resurrection. As he had conquered both sin and death, so would they; their happiness now was the foretaste of everlasting ecstasy in heaven: they too would rise with the Son of Man, healing in their wings, to be seated at the right hand of the throne of grace to reign forever in a cloud of mixed metaphors.

These meetings were both terrifying and glorious to him; God knew the secrets of his heart and that which was hidden would be bawled from the rooftops. The Lord was in the habit of speaking directly to and through the people present and he was not known for being either discreet or subtle; sooner or later the truth would be outed and there would be no hiding place. Someone or other would say, 'The Lord has laid it on my heart, McGillivray, to say to you...'

God was either merciful or biding his time. Perhaps he had a wicked sense of humour for it never happened. No one spoke.

McGillivray hoped for a cure, believed that the Lord would heal him in time but this was his cross to bare, his cliché to carry and, in the mean time, he had to prove himself. The best way to keep safe would be to make sure he never strayed far from those from whom he could expect protection. Where could he be safer than with those who had resolved to serve God as clergy? Amongst those holy men prayer and miracle would surround him. Divinity was the academic study for him. Maybe he would receive the Call and be entitled to wear a dog collar, the eternal ring of confidence. There he would be safe.

CHAPTER 3

Scottish theologians maintain that a Divinity degree from one of their four ancient universities provides a superlative foundation for the Ministry of the Gospel. Others have pointed out that if all the ministers in the nation were laid end to end they would still have no point. Unkind children ask how many light bulbs it would take to turn on one cleric. Despite these critics, men, and now women have for four hundred and fifty years been manufactured who are able to expound the Word and administer the Rites and Sacraments of the Kirk with a certain facility, grace and, when all else fails, decent diction. Their sermons have excelled but had little direct impact on popular impiety; preachers have always been six feet above contradiction, their sermons over long and over the heads of their people.

The curriculum then approved by the princes of the Kirk for the edification of students covered core disciplines, some of which were to be expected: Old and New Testament Studies with Greek and Hebrew; Systematics, with its sub disciplines of Philosophy, Dogmatics and Apologetics were clearly necessary. Church History with a specific focus on Scots Factionalism taught who should be hated and why. 'Practical' Theology was perhaps more unusual and needed some explanation. This 'discipline' was intended to cover a burroch of topics from the choice of hymns to holding a baby at the font to homiletics and all others that though not included in other classifications yet seemed to be essential to the proper conduct of public worship and the life of the faithful.

The young McGillivray had no experience of the South, of the Mainland of Scotland, until he took the boat to the grey city. His choice was the university nearest the islands; Aberdeen's Faculty of Divinity was located in the quadrangle of King's

College, a fifteenth century foundation erected "through the grace of the most serene, most illustrious and most victorious King James IV" by Bishop Elphinstone in 1495. Flodden was not significant enough an event to require the inscription to be amended.

The Victorians and Edwardians decided to improve the place and thought to give their Founder a more fitting tomb. Sadly the rule of faith proved inaccurate, as the effigy they made was too wide to be carried through the chapel doors. Being practical men they left it outside where even now it dominates the lawns, testimony that a mustard seed may move a mountain but nary a Scottish cleric. A later generation added the stained glass windows. Filial devotion ensured that here, alone in all the churches of Christendom, Pope Rodrigo Borgia smiles down from the windows on to the worshipping students below. He gave the University its charter with the specific aim of creating a well-educated clergy in the North of Scotland. Famously good at accounting he deserves his place of honour; the old skellum has proven an admirable patron for generations of Presbyterians. No one today would advocate or condone some of his recreational activities but he loved his children, was an admirable administrator, a fine committeeman, and a skilled diplomat. His hypocrisy was exemplary and he was efficient with the lunatickal fringe. There were never any flies on him.

McGillivray was one of the fledglings who arrived from the hills, islands and towns throughout the nation for their first year of study. About thirty matriculated that year, only two of whom were women. Nearly all the others were older than him and had completed an honours degree in arts or sciences before moving onto these more complex studies. Most were candidates for the Ministry who had heard the Call; they were married to but one wife, a primary school teacher or a nurse who was perpetually expecting their first child. They entered the Faculty through a stone gate on which was carved in soft stone the sinister motto that would direct their training, 'Sapientiae Timor Domini Initium,' 'The Fear of the Lord is the Beginning of Wisdom.'

Being interested in religion, the students were not representative of the wider membership of the Church. The Kirk of Scotland is as broad as its bishop-ridden equivalent in

England and like it, has many rooms in its theological mansions. Much to the mirth of the ancient Celtic saints, the liturgical wing considered a few responsorial prayers in the vernacular, good quality candles and the odd trip to a derelict shrine sufficient to make itself their spiritual heirs. On Iona, in the comfort of their stolen home, they specialized in bad verse set to popular airs of the Highlands. To these innocents, fresh from the Gorbals and Govan, the island provided an unfamiliar sense of isolation that they easily confused with the spirituality of the grey dove that once came over the waters from Ireland. They are however irrelevant. Aberdeen was a faculty they avoided mostly; it was too drab for their trumpery.

On the other extremity of the broad Kirk were those who had a taste for hard stone and only drank from the careful and non-alcoholic draughts from the Calvinist waters of Lake Geneva. These 'reformed' students endured their classes dutifully but were mistrustful of speculation. As inoculation against the infections of the Higher Criticism they attended a forbidding church on Union Street. There they learned what passed as theology from a former pianist who preached arse-blistering sermons with long vowels, 'liiperaal,' to him, an insult.

McGillivray was hungry to get started on his learning although the Wise back home had warned him that his faith would be tested. They worried it would be hard for him to stay close to the Lord and prayed that he could find the strength to gird himself with both the sword of the Spirit and the armour of righteousness. He felt their well-intentioned advice was superfluous. No darkness could slocken his light. He would be safe.

Indeed, the first few weeks were spiritually unthreatening and it was not hard to follow their advice. McGillivray attended the chaste parties arranged for the welcome of new students by the Christian Union, the evangelical body that sought to protect students from the more noxious effects of Higher Education. Prayer groups were held in each of the halls of residence where he found comfort amongst the fanatics from the other islands; together they pined for the preachers of home and the sermons of their youth. On Friday nights, 'teaching' meetings were held where these careful ones would listen to sermons and sing their trite modern hymns to a God who had surely heard it all before. Afterwards, over small sips of instant coffee served in glass cups they pitied all those who were drinking their way to perdition in the Saint Machar bar across the street. Members of the highland congregations that met in the city also took special interests in the students; many families would cook extra food so that the youngsters could dine off roasted chicken and potatoes, the cabbage well done and gravy bitter with piety.

During that initial period, pragmatic concerns were to the fore of his mind. It would be inaccurate to say that McGillivray had never been to the South before; he had visited his Auntie in Arbroath when he was eleven. Furthermore, he had spent a few days in the Babylon of London just before his sixteenth birthday. Despite this rigorous preparation, he was woefully unprepared for the commercial challenges of the high street and public transport. The roads held particular terrors for him and in particular that wide thoroughfare outside the Cowdray Hall and City Art Gallery. Stinking rivers of transport flowed past without cessation. On his very first day he knew he had to cross over to the right side of the road but he had no idea how to forge the metallic waters. There was no bridge. He remembered from public education broadcasts featuring squirrels and green crucifixes that he should look to strange beasts like zebras or pelicans for help or he could ask a police man, but there were none. A narrow band of black and white stripes stretched across the road but the etiquette was unknown to him and he could not remember how it worked. There were no instructions. He stood patiently for a while waiting for the yellow lights to change but nothing happened; there were no buttons to push. In growing panic, he plucked up the courage to step off the kerb but when the cars slowed down he jumped back in terror onto the safety of the pavement. He tried again and failed. A furious motorist lost patience with him and began to gesticulate. After a few curses thrown at his head, he thought he understood what to do; he gathered his courage and ran across without looking either to the left or the right. When he got to the far side unscathed, he leant against the wall of the Gallery gulping in the polluted air and thanking the Lord for saving him.

In many other adventures he learned how to use keys to lock doors and to get to sleep at night by imagining the roar of the traffic to be the breaking of waves against the walls of his room. On the third day he went into a bookshop and marvelled.

Of course, this happy state could not last. The teaching was gentle initially; none of the staff wanted to frighten the new students too much and so nothing controversial was touched upon until the staff felt confident they could find their way to the toilets unaided to be sick. In the seventh week of his first term they were judged to be ready and the first crisis came; he succumbed to the epidemic of Intellectual Malaise that struck most of his class. The outbreak was attributed to something said by a Professor that caused the Thinking to break out. Older students who had all been through the contagion themselves regarded it as a kind of rite of passage, an intellectual mumps. Eagerly, every year they would look out for the onset of symptoms; bets would be taken on which of the Freshers would be struck down first, what form the sickness would take and how many would survive.

For some of his colleagues the infection was acute; they would shake a little and be cognitively disturbed for a matter of days or weeks. Careful application of sound dogma would carry their barque through dark waters to the sure havens of certainty. Once there, the effort to square impossibilities would have a cost; they would become dowdier and middle aged before their time. Their noses would narrow and they would start to speak like ministers.

For others the condition was more serious and could threaten salvation. Those who appeared the most certain were often at greatest risk for their faith was the brittlest. They would be least likely to forgive those who had tried to shore them up with pretty lies. The pious filth they had swallowed since childhood would be vomited up until there was nothing left but the dry boke. They would purge themselves again and again with more and more thoughts until nothing was left but bitter conclusions and an acid throat.

The inevitability of this Dark Afternoon of the Soul, this period of trial and temptations was well known. Over many years a great deal of ecclesiastical creativity had gone into clinical measures to support students so that when outbreaks occurred those infected could be quarantined for the spiritual hygiene of themselves and others until the detergent powers of the blood of the lamb took effect. Whilst cognition amongst the clergy has never, even to this day, been officially banned by the General Assembly of the Church of Scotland, care has always been taken to ensure that simple souls in the pew do not have their faith clouded by unwarranted speculation. Moderate thinking has never – and indeed must never – be a bar to the appropriate exercise of the ministry of the Logos. Yet the willy-nilly expression of novel ideas in public cannot be commended and the Church has always followed the wisest pastoral course of 'least thought, soonest mended'. The words of the justly celebrated Reverend Gordon Cleuk of Inverhavering in his speech to the Assembly of 1928 echoes through time:

We have to love the thinker and not the thought; if a young minister thinks excessively for himself or expresses thoughts in an injudicious manner he disturbs the peace and faith of the simple souls gathered in the pews below. Our youthful colleague can be cautioned gently and guided along to the middle way where, safe from the Tempest and the Earthquake he will learn to trust our collective wisdom as expressed in the still small voice of this august body. We have protected the faithful from the reckless utterance of original thoughts in the pulpits of our happy land since 1560 and in the grace of God will do so until the last Trump gathers us home and the sea gives up its dead.

McGillivray had never been troubled by thoughts before and so he was at high risk – his faith, the brightest and shiniest sort, was of least substance. Of course there had been small Doubts but never anything that threatened to undermine the foundations of Faith. Not for him the questions about the essential validity of Scripture or even the expression of surprise at the revelation of the divinity of Carpenters. On the contrary, it was self-evident and true that the world had been created in seven days and how else could a kind and merciful God respond to the sins of his children but by a Flood?

His faith, of solid rock he thought, was no more than an illusory mansion placed upon the sand. When other school pupils challenged him he would always go to handy compendia produced by the Scripture Union or Inter Varsity Press for the assistance of the Confused. He would learn the answers he found in them by heart and regurgitate them the next day to his incredulous classmates. Of course the world was created in seven days, evolution no more than a theory and the great Judge of Israel, Joshua, commanded the sun to stop in the sky until victory over the Midianites was complete. When his bemused schoolmates mocked him, he rejoiced inwardly that he was able to share in the sufferings of Christ. His trials were from the Devil who prowled like a lion, waiting for the most pious to backslide into his jaws. Those who teased him were persecutors who did not know what they were doing. Their actions fulfilled the prophecies of Dark Times foretold in the Apocalypse. Thus McGillivray was a true bigot and well defended, yet doubts filled his head like the traffic fumes and began to confuse his thinking. Even for him, the effort to reconcile himself to the implausible made his credulity stretch so far that damage was done to his immune system. His retching made his entire world shake. About time. If only he had been bullied more.

CHAPTER 4

Life for the first year McGillivray was by no means restricted to the heady delights of Greek vowels and the theological implications of one *yod* or *iota* of the law being changed. Thrilling though these disputes were and useful, for they replaced the need for central heating in the Common Room of the dear Faculty, they did not satisfy all the needs of a keen young man.

He ventured out of the intellectual fastness of the faculty into the city which was to him unto a garden wherein the flowers of earthly pleasures grew. The heady perfume of these blossoms led to the intoxication with the carnal that cost him his soul and caused lamentations amongst the faithful in the islands whose prayers over the shortbread of bitterness availed him naught.

Too late he learned that the determinants of his morality and faith had been the binoculars located on every front room window to watch the boats. That the all seeing eye of the Almighty was not sufficient to ensure his salvation.

The worst dangers were not to be found in alleyways or brothels but at the foot of respectable George Street . On the ground floor of the red fronted Workers' Educational Association a radical, where 'radical' meant dirty and disorganised rather than politically subversive, bookshop was located. McGillivray went in out of curiosity one idle Wednesday after the Practical class in Christ's College. To his horror and churning delight there was a shelf on lesbian and gay themes just below the window. His face burned with shame but prayer enabled him to resist and turn away. It was on his third visit, under the cover of a new interest in dialectical Marxism, that he dared to scan the pages of 'The Milk Man Only Comes Twice'. His breeks felt uncomfortably tight. He returned the book to the shelf and left the shop, stopping to use the public toilet on the way back.

On his next visit, he hid some free news-sheets in his shoulder bag to smuggle back to his room in the Halls of Residence. Late that night he poured over the lonely hearts advertisements and tried to guess what the abbreviations meant. He writhed and twisted on a bed hot with a hankering that burned in his head and throughout his entire body. The flames and smoke blocked out the eternal and mocked at his prayers. Desperately, he tried to shift his mind to higher things but the earthly man kept pulling him down into the mirk and the filth of his mattress. Later, in a stram of guilt he repented, throwing himself on his knees before the Mercy Seat. In the deep silence of his room, Grace touched him gently and he knew that even he, in his misery and sinfulness, was redeemed and beloved of the Lord. He gathered up the besmirched papers to take to a waste bin far from campus. There, he disposed of them, confident that no one had seen him. On the way back to his room he sang the words of Charles Wesley, who, long dead, now finally knows the truth. Perhaps it was worth it.

> Long my imprisoned spih-ir-ihit lay,
> Fast bou-ound in sin ha-and nature's night;
> Thine eye diffuse-ed a quickening ray;
> I wo-o-o-oke, the du-ungeon flamed with light;
> My chains fell orf, my ha-art wa-as freeeheee, I ro-ho-ose, went fo-o-ourth, and fo-hollow-ed Thee (repeat last two lines)

And so he was safe.

This was the year of the Miners' Strike, the great blaze that left the working classes of Scotland defenceless against That Woman and the four-headed beast with many horns. To many in Orkney, disputes between right and left were concerns for the South and so best avoided. That fine Mr. Grimond looked after the Northern Isles for the Liberals and wouldn't do them any wrong. So when McGillivray expressed a political view it was naïve. He was not sure that Christians should dirty their hands in the political waters. This vacuity so irritated one woman at the Christian Union that she decided to shock him into sense. She was wise enough about the nature of Islanders to know that argument would simply entrench him further and so she decided on shock therapy. She dragged him into a palace of sin on Union Street where for the first time he heard a singer use a guitar as a revolutionary weapon to advance the cause of the strikers. His doctrines were about a social justice that had no truck with the subtlety and beauty of grey. The lyrics accompanied by thundering acoustic guitars were a straightforward call to arms; backs were all turned to the wall, everyone was under attack and the inevitable question was repeated with unnerving force: 'Which side are you on?' This dialectic appealed to the world-view of the fundamentalist. McGillivray was convinced that any reading of the gospels would redeem the Miners and damn the Bosses. In the parable that Jesus told, the rich man called Dives would inevitably join the unrepentant managerial classes in his ever expansive version of Hell. Lazarus, the poor man who had starved at the gate of his employer, rejoiced in the knowledge of bread to come in the Hereafter. Blessed are the poor in Spirit for they shall inherit the earth. Tomorrow. Not today.

CHAPTER 5

McGillivray's people have never been known for their ability to compromise. Amongst his near relations were many ayatollahs of the Isles. Rumours about a moderate cleric from the Outer Hebrides have spread but rigorous investigations unearthed no substantiating evidence. Most scholars concluded that if such a person had ever existed he did not have a long life and no one remembers the grave-site.

Although without religiosity to defend, Orcadians are as flexible in outlook as the standing stones themselves. These least pleasant traits of the diverse island groups merged in McGillivray's psyche into a kind of unattractive Calvinist socialism that led inexorably to activism, barricades and smugness. He stood for election as a faculty representative on the student body. As no one else was interested, he was returned unopposed. Once installed, he took to the political world as a pig takes to muck and innocent as he was, had no perception of the risk of contamination presented by those whom he now considered to be good people. In contrast to the religious believers he had always known, these secular politicians seemed to have consciences and, despite the skepticism of the non-voting majority, appeared to do the right thing because they wanted to, not because of the love of dead carpenters or from fear of damnation. In long conversations in the pub over his orange juice or cola he began to see how his faith was observed from the outside; that the sanctitude of their tidy minds made believers appear ugly. The odour of holiness smelt to truly decent folk like the stench from neglected latrines. The problem of Thinking began to return. He stopped eating meat.

On one of his furtive trips to that bookshelf in that shop he purchased a copy of 'Gay Scotland,' a title that in those days was surely ironic. On the inside back cover a directory of services for lesbians and gay men listed a switchboard, a social group and one bar in Aberdeen. He tore out the page and shoved it at the back of the drawer where he kept his underwear. For several weeks he strained and resisted Temptation until one Friday evening he yielded to the Devil who led him down the broad road from College Wynd towards the docks. His prayers were not heard. Sinful imaginings drew him on drying his mouth and cavorting in his stomach. The venue's boarded up windows were covered with curvaceous and very female silhouettes and the alluring words, 'go go dancers daily.' A piece of A4 paper was pinned to the side door. Through the condensation on its plastic envelope he read, 'Upstairs, Private Function, for friends of Dorothy.'

He checked the address; although he had no idea who Dorothy was, this seemed to be the right place. The door was stiff and resisted him but he pushed in and began to climb the narrow stairs. To his surprise neither Damnation nor Lust both dressed in Scarlet were waiting for him at the top intending to drag him to hell. Instead, a man with sad eyes charged him £1.50 and gave him a ticket. He went in through the doors and saw Maggie Folster from the year above him at school sitting beside the DJ stand, her back slightly to him. He did not turn around. He walked out backwards and ran down the stairs, not having been in there for even five minutes. When after the use of an asthma inhaler he could breathe again, he realised that she could not have seen him and so yielded thanks to the God who in his Infinite Mercy had sent him both a Deliverance and a Warning. He repented his sin and asked Jesus back into his heart. Now he would listen and be thankful for Salvation had found him, the wandering lamb, and brought him back rejoicing. He was safe.

Poor McGillivray. How wrong he was for there was no eternal salvation for him. His cravings reappeared in the following weeks with even greater force and he felt like an observer in the conflict between heaven and hell, unable to influence the conflict over his own soul. It was not that many weeks before he uncrumpled the listings page torn from his precious magazine and, with the taste of sulphur hot in his mouth, rang the Switchboard from the public kiosk in the entrance to the Halls of Residence. On the fourth ring a quiet woman with a Doric accent answered the phone. She asked how she could help him but he could not answer her. There were no words left to him. Through the wall of his silence she reached out lovingly and told him to tap the phone to let her know he was still there, that he was welcome. For half an hour he pushed the coins into the hungry maw of the machine and tapped. At long last he hung up the receiver to go back to his single bed and the silent Lord.

Perhaps God did something; the non-interventionist deity turned in his slumber and caused a happening to take place. Grace is such that even in the most surprising places mercy might still be found. Oases only occur in deserts. Even the Christian Union was not entirely closed. Every so often it enabled discussion, within Biblical parameters, on issues that were considered difficult so that the perplexed be kept safe from the ever-present threat of the Vagabond. One such issue was the possibility of Christians being queer. The committee invited a representative of an 'ex-gay' ministry to speak to one of their routine Friday soirées. When McGillivray saw the advert he gave thanks to the Lord in his heart and went to the meeting in fear, hope and with great joy. Although fearful of discovery, he was thrilled that at last a gospel message might be proclaimed for people like him. Hope helped him through the door but there was no reason for fear. More than normal attended the meeting . All his familiar friends were there and there were even some new faces. These McGillivray scrutinised with interest. A young man with attractive eyebrows seemed particularly moved.

The speaker, Jonathon, was appropriately fey with wiry hair and high cheekbones. He was English and so sounded effete, yet his message was lucid and clear. It began with him giving his testimony of how as a young man he had been part of the gay 'community', the inverted commas were silent; he had even gone to bars and had sex with men. One night, walking home from what one can be assumed was either not getting laid or something less than satisfying, he was feeling rather lonely. In his self-pity, he heard the very voice of Jesus himself telling him to lay his weary head on the divine breast. At that moment, he was converted. Salvation entered his heart. Jesus showed him how he had fallen short of the image of God. Now, all his desires, all his needs were met in Christ. Jonathon was unmarried and claimed to have never taken drugs.

After the presentation there was an opportunity for questions. No one asked Jonathon who he fantasised about when he was masturbating or even if he did. Scriptures were explained. It turned out that Paul was not quite up to the mark psychologically. What Scripture meant to say was that no sin existed in suffering from same sex attraction as long as there was no follow through on desire. All are tempted, all fallen and gone astray but only in Christ is there liberation. Healing was possible. Anyone diverted by inverted, retroverted or perverted desires was advised to seek the support of other believers, to not be alone. The church was wrong to condemn anyone repentant, even if they were a murderer or a fornicator. This was no different. There was hope.

McGillivray had never heard anyone so practical or honest about sexuality and desire. Given hope by this, he decided to take the risk of seeking help from the possessor of the beautiful eyebrows. Getting introduced was no problem. They had a mutual friend in Jesus. After the study of scripture they knelt in prayer by the single student bed. McGillivray experienced the relief of shapely hands being laid on his head and the exorcism of the demons that were tempting him. He was safe.

CHAPTER 6

McGillivray should have got away whilst he was safe, but no, he did not learn. He continued with his political activism. He read Machiavelli and learned some lessons well. He became canny, only offended the people who didn't matter, crawled to those who did and smiled at everyone. He laid the foundations of hypocrisy so well that when he stood for election to a salaried post on the Students Representative Council he was victorious. Although he had stood as an independent, his considerable majority was due to getting out the Christian vote. His opponents were beaten into the ground by the power of prayer and an exasperating humility. The munificence of the Body Politic gave him his first living in an entirely secular environment. He was successful. Auld Rodrigo sitting on his stained glass throne was very proud of him.

The small stipend enabled him to rent an attic room in a street made of pink granite on which there were many roses. He had a black and white rented television and an ability to watch it alone. That summer, the adolescent Channel 4 tried to shock its elders and betters with a season of Lesbian and Gay films entitled 'In the Pink'. One of its offerings was a documentary about a then more or less unknown American politician called Harvey Milk, the first openly gay man to be elected to any public office in the United States. In 1978, an unsuccessful rival, one Dan White, gunned him down with the Mayor. The courts did not condone the murder but they understood that a real man could not tolerate the humiliation of an uppity fag and sentenced him accordingly. White was paroled by 1984. Within a year or so of release he had gassed himself in his garage. His defence attorney explained his suicide by saying that since getting out of prison, family life was less than ideal because he had not yet *come to terms with* the situation he had created. Good.

McGillivray had known of many saints. He had been reared on stories of martyrdom and suffering that would have made de Sade go pale; impalement was nothing, nor being stretched on a wheel of fire. Pious self slaughter was the evidence of redemption, Jesus demanded no less. Indeed the Vikings of Orkney had been brought into the respectability of the Kirk by their repentance after the slaughter of the holy incompetent Magnus and the subsequent pious destruction of the heirs of his murderer.

To one of this mindset, Milk's death stood witness to authenticity and forced him to think. He covered endless sheets of yellow paper with twisted blue scrawls that seemed to draw blood from the page. All his attempts at healing and cure had failed; no matter how hard he repented and experienced short-term deliverance, nothing changed. Thoughts persisted. He had no reason to suppose that anything would be different in the future; given this, the people whose faith he had loved and trusted were, at least on this score, liars or fools. For if the merciful God had made him gay without possibility of change then the sole purpose of his creation was damnation. In the past, there had been no problem in believing that other people had been condemned from before the creation of the world but now he knew that predestination was only fine when other folk were lined up for the barbecue.

Their argument that his desire to love men was evidence of his fallen nature, his cross to bear, appeared now to be the fallacious nonsense it had always been. Those holy people who claimed their love for the homosexual but their contempt for the naughty bits did more than emasculate him, they denied his humanity, both the capacity and capability of love. Sexuality is more than genitalia and reproduction. Television is indeed a bad influence.

He started to go to the University GaySoc that met in the offices above the radical bookshop on George Street. On his first attempt to go he walked down the road towards it, got nearly there and turned back. On the second, he got right up to its front door painted a brazen red, lingered, with his fist in the air to knock on it and didn't. As he got towards the huge junction he gave himself a kick. 'How can you come out McGillivray', he said to himself, 'if you cannot go in through a door?' He turned around, went back and went in. They were lovely but he was disappointed by the lack of brimstone. Walls were not scorched by lightning. Rather than the collective casts of 'The Killing of Sister George' and 'La Cage au Folles' accompanied by a camp actor, they were just students, ordinary folk.

At the back of the room was a blond man leaning his chair back on two legs, maroon Doc Martin boots shameless with polish placed on the able. His hair was like one of those beautiful 1930s poets but tangible. He wore jeans and a heavy cotton knit jumper whose sleeves were stretched over his hands. When McGillivray walked in he straightened himself up, laughed, 'It's the Holy Politician, we all had bets on how long it would take. I won.' A woman at the end of the table with scarlet hair said, 'Don't worry about Lance, he is convinced that everybody he fancies is gay.' There was even someone there from the Christian Union. McGillivray would get to him later in a more theological way. They would spend a lot of time on their knees and follow the quest for God prescribed by William Boroughs.

Everyone laughed. McGillivray took one of the chairs down from the stack and the conversation continued. Complaints had been made about their posters. Him with the blond jumper had put up pictures of Pope Paul the Whatever being carried on his fancy chair by adorable lads into the Basilica. His caption had been 'Everybody is going to GaySoc.

After the meeting they all went to a pub, normal until they walked in, thereafter a thing of wonder. McGillivray had a half pint then got up to leave. It was all still a bit public and a few of these folk were rather noticeable.

On Friday nights, they all went together to Daisy's. This second time was rather easier than the first. McGillivray paid his money to the man with sleepy eyes – later he got a lot more than small change from him – and walked in. Maggie Folster was not there. Nor was anyone from Orkney. From everywhere else though, some guys in Biker Leather, a fat man with a rubber vest, a couple from the Highlands in Fair Isle and even someone in a kilt. The place had a friendly atmosphere. Lance bought the drinks.

McGillivray began to tell his colleagues and some of his friends that he was gay. They all promised to keep the news secret and so it soon spread far and wide even as far as the Halls of Residence on the far side of the Park. Word got back to him that the Federation of Conservative Students had uncovered his news and were delighted. They were extremists who were eventually disbanded after offending the tender sensitivities of Norman Tebbitt. Pinko fags were their declared enemy and they sought his blood.

McGillivray's hand was forced. To deny his sexuality would only serve to give the rumours credence and leave him open for future blackmail. To do nothing would give his enemies the victory and imply that he was ashamed. The only other option was to tell the truth and as publicly as possible. So, he gave an interview to the student newspaper that kindly embargoed the story until he had spoken to his family. They coped. This is not their story.

On the day of publication he felt as exposed as the cockle does when the seagull lifts him high up into the air, only to drop him onto the rocks that his shell might be smashed open and his tender flesh ripped apart by that very particular beak. He had no reason to be so worried; rather than pain, exposure brought him love, some cheered him, a few avoided his eye. Two fine ministers sent letters offering particular counselling. A beautiful young pastor made a pass, which McGillivray was too self-righteous to follow through. Most, including the FCS, said little. Life went on.

CHAPTER 7

After completion of his sabbatical year and his return to study, the rules that regulated life amongst the Divines offered protection against those of his fellow students who would have tried to deal with his backsliding ways. Of these, the law of silence, the Presbyterian 'omerta,' was most important. Long experience had led theological discussion in the common room to be suppressed as a prophylactic measure against the mingling of blood amongst the packed lunches. Of course, every year, the Freshers would have to be taught the lesson anew; wanton students who made accusations of heresy against each other and would have to be cautioned against the repetition of episodes of verbal incontinence.

One morning in his sixth year, after spending an unprofitable hour trying to make some of Saint Paul's opinions palatable for decent society, McGillivray descended from the sanctum of the upper library to the common room. A group of first years, all men, were grouped around the central table in heated discussion. The seats about the edge of the room were all full, and he did not notice the sudden silence that fell upon the older students as he entered. Lost in his musings on the precise translation of the Greek word *arsenokoita* in First Corinthians chapter six verse nine of the New Testament, often rendered into English as 'homosexual,' he tried to make some redeeming coffee. Did Paul really include the mutually loving relationships that now were known to exist amongst men? Was it a specific reference to dirty old men? Do not dirty old men need loving too? What shade of pink tee-shirt would the old rogue have worn? Was he sober? Gradually McGillivray began to realise what was going on. The first year students were having 'that conversation' at the table and the old lags on the outer ring were watching his responses closely. They were anticipating a fight with playground relish and wanted blood. Lessons had to be taught.

One of the central warriors for truth, a man whose complexion merited the nickname 'Pleuk' declaimed, 'If I ever met a Christian homosexual, this is what I would say...'

A brazen band of voices broke over his head, tried to drag down the unfortunate and almost overwhelmed him. McGillivray watched and felt smug about the physical ugliness of homophobes. He wondered if their hatred was simply jealousy, as they could never get laid. Expectant eyes were on him but still he said nothing.

The fool persisted in his folly. Pleuk continued, 'The Bible is clear; in Leviticus it says: *"If a man has intercourse with a man as with a woman, they both commit an abomination. They shall by put to death; their blood shall be on their own heads."*

McGillivray noted that the New English Bible was being used, an edition of impressive size with a soft binding that enabled its pages to fall open, shamelessly displaying their gilt edges to all who could see. This, he decided, was the appropriate moment to intervene.

'And on the same page, it recommends that children should be stoned to death for cheeking their fathers; an admirable principle. Look at verse nine.'

There was quiet approval around the edge of the room. A hit. A very palpable hit.

Piteous Pleuk remonstrated, 'Don't be ridiculous, a loving Father would hardly expect that.'

Someone unsheathed a Bible, looked up the reference, scanned down the page, smirked and handed it over. 'Read it out loud', someone said. Pleuk obeyed, his voice getting a little huskier as the words burned his throat.

There was little more to be said; the conversation moved on leaving McGillivray back alone in his thoughts. Most of the other students disappeared off to lectures, some to the Public House, a very few to read. All regretted the low body count. Pleuk alone remained, yet unaware that he was in danger of contamination. McGillivray went over to him, shook his hand, and introduced himself.

'I am a happy homosexual,' he said, 'and a Christian.'

Pleuk pulled his hand away and jumped backwards sending

his chair flying.
'Oh!'

'Pride comes', as the wise woman has so often said, 'before the Fall.' McGillivray's smugness was noted by those in the higher echelons of the Kirk who record such things in their ledgers under the column headed 'Conduct Unbecoming.' A few weeks after the unfortunate encounter with Pleuk, and in no way connected, McGillivray sat with McTivock, a friend of his who enjoyed church politics, and over a cup of instant coffee discussed the implications of what had happened.

'I was at a meeting in Edinburgh,' he said. 'I was asked if I knew you. When advised that indeed I had that privilege, I was informed graciously that you have been 'noted'. This means,' he continued, 'that you will never be ordained. You will never be told why'.

And that was that. The door was closed, no matter how hard he knocked. Christians cannot be honest.

Word of the homosexual from Orkney travelled north. Phones rang. Letters were written and read out at the prayer meetings in the solemn white bungalows. Worried stalwarts stirred on sofas throughout the islands and bowed their heads over pious tea.

'Let us just remember', the farmer of Ostness said, 'young McGillivray.'

'Please, have another biscuit, John,' said Mrs. Howe, the wife of Ostness and hostess.

John Wishart nodded solemnly, 'Aye, a fine boy from a Christian family.' He worked on the Boats.

'More tea?' said Mrs Howe.

Peggy Gabb held out her cup, 'He went tae University tae study the Divinity.'

Andro Huip intoned as if each of his words was insufficient to bear testimony to the horror of backsliding and the damnation to come, 'And then he began tae doot the autheniticitie of Scripture.'

Ostness opened his Bible to the book of Romans. If such a fate could befall McGillivray, if he was prey to unnatural lusts and the worship of demons, who could count on their own salvation? All were afraid.

Ostness concluded his reading with words that summed up the feeling of the meeting there gathered.

'Aye, and let that...be a lesson to us all.'

They all said,'Amen.'

CHAPTER 8

After his disagreement with the Kirk on the theological implications of man on man fellatio, McGillivray drifted south. He went all the way to London where he persisted in the study of what is termed grandly 'Biblical Hermeneutics', the arcane science of explicating texts out of existence. The process involves first bleaching existing colour out of the words, then dying the text in a light solution of rationality and finally fixing the changes with piss water. Preferred shades are those that will not clash with the more strident hues and wear well. Magnolia is perfect. This is a convincing explanation for the appalling stench emanating from most seminaries. The text cannot mean what it says because what it says is wrong and what is written is infallible thus the text must mean what it does not. This kind of argument has driven many people into madness, not that it was a long way for many of them to go.

When resting from his more scriptural labours, McGillivray continued his research into the Five Points of Federal Calvinism amongst the gay bars near Trafalgar Square. He applied himself with a single-minded devotion that he had hardly shown whilst translating Biblical Greek. In these establishments, the name of the most famous, 'The Brief Encounter,' ringing down to this day, he devoted himself to the study of total depravity and the perseverance of the saints. When any of his acquaintances called him 'loose', and it is sad to report that some did, others even going so far as to use the word 'promiscuous', he would purse both his lips and start to talk with animation about the importance of the doctrines of unconditional election and the irresistibility of dear Grace and her wonderful parties. When he decided that the Bread of Life could no longer satisfy his hunger he dropped out, an event he celebrated by doing cartwheels along the Thames.

On Wednesdays he would go to Westminster Abbey to hear choral evensong. It was there that he first set eyes on Raphael and Grace, who was wearing a small hat with a little black lace. Although the effect was electrifying there were no thunderbolts. Their friendship, based as it was on shared piety and mutual depravity, lasted through the travails of postgraduate study and beyond. It was to them that he broached the subject of his future career.

Raphael spluttered on his gin. 'Applying for jobs, but why? You are still quite pretty!'

Grace fluttered her fan and ordered him never to mention the word 'work' in her presence again. Yet, despite their protestations he persisted looking for roles that he thought would make the world a better place, the misguided desire of youth to 'give something back.' The role of Messiah being already taken and there being no shortage of Popes, he decided to try social services.

As this was in the middle reign of John Major misery was a business that was doing well. He was not totally unqualified. Over the years he had done odds and sods of work, both paid and unpaid, skivvying for the unhappy. He had done enough to create a delusion of competence on an application form but had not enough skill to actually help anyone. The job he applied for successfully was in a county council, now abolished, and consisted of trying to work with unpleasant young people whom everyone else wanted to avoid. It had been created because 'something' had to be done. He was to be a salve or a balm to slightly disturbed consciences. Only a cynic could possibly claim that the accident of McGillivray having met his new manager before, though not in the Biblical sense, smoothed the process in any way.

He was the son of a Catholic mother whose unfortunate passion for priests led to him having been named Jerome. His earthly father being busy with the Mass, the little boy modelled himself on his heavenly protector and commemorated his festival with solemnities of his own invention. He was very fond of both books and cats. Ecclesiastical Latin excited him, especially the dirty bits. He would use it in conversation as if he knew what it meant. The suits he chose were black rather than cardinatial red but always exquisitely tailored and looked rather expensive to be in the wardrobe of a council officer. He was very thin and had exquisite hands, which he considered his best feature and tried to display constantly. On one finger he wore a gold signet ring that had been blessed by the pope. The emblem on it was a lion.

The town that would become home to McGillivray was called Grimsbrough and is located in that absent part of the country that seems equally far from Whitby, York and Durham but is no real drive from any of them. It is served by a branch line from Darlington that goes through both Middlesbrough and Stockton on Tees. It is a prosaic place that is famous for its unattractiveness. The nickname locals use for it is 'the Grims', its football team, 'the Reapers.' An unfortunate royal duke invited to the Town Hall for some kind of banquet commented on the amount of filth and smoke in the town; the host retorted with the now famous line, 'muck is brass.'

Jerome arranged for McGillivray to have accommodation in the house of a colleague called Adam in the North Malmsbury district. Its avenues of grey houses were laid out in 1970s patterns, designs that could only make sense or be pleasing to angels who sometimes flew overhead but more normally averted their eyes.

The accommodation arrangements were satisfactory but temporary. Adam was gay, which was a relief, but rather too attractive for McGillivray to stand a chance. His eyes were of proverbial beauty and he played baseball for an evangelical Christian team. Perhaps because of the aesthetic mismatch they bonded immediately with the kind of intimacy that is unique to people in their late teens and early twenties.

In any case, McGillivray's experiences of both lovers and flat mates had taught him the importance of a front door with only one key, a place that was his as long as the lease lasted, a home he could not be evicted from without due process under law. So he experienced the misery of so many in a new town, of having to trawl through enthusiastic estate agents, of accepting their invitations to tour dismal flats, to try not to blanch at the sight of orange wallpaper and teak effect furniture, to be content with endless shabby rooms with tiny windows. These eager landlords were all variations of the same; the expression worn on their collective face always a mixture of greed at the prospect of rent and shock that anyone would dare suggest that furnished flats should have equipped kitchens.

His mood approaching despair, he spread the local newspaper's classified columns on his office desk and started to work through the adverts making the calls with endless variations of the same answers, 'No, sorry, it was let an hour ago.'

Fortune, standing just behind him, pointed at a boxed advert two thirds of the way down the second column. 'House, near Town Centre, Three bedrooms, £240 per calendar month.'

He rang the number straightaways and spoke to the owner's mother who introduced herself as Mrs. Sutherland. All his questions were answered quickly.

'No,' she said, 'the house wasn't taken.'

He told her that he was new to the Town and so no, didn't really know the area at all.

He could hear her voice smiling, a welcome sign of friendliness he thought. She was sure he would be very happy there and asked if he worked. The sense of relief in her voice at all his answers, even those that would normally discourage a landlord coupled with the lowness of the rent made him feel vaguely suspicious. He asked the further questions that should have highlighted the kinds of problems that appear like damp from behind fresh paint. He heard nothing to cause anxiety; on the contrary, he was told that the house was modern, equipped to a high standard and fully furnished. As an after thought, he asked,

'What's the neighbourhood like?'

The old woman paused slightly to consider her answer and then spoke hastily, smile taut over dentures, 'A little rough, I believe, yes, a little rough, but nothing to worry about, yes, really nothing to worry about. We have never had any real problems ourselves.'

An appointment was made for him to view the place for that evening. Harriet, the owner, and her husband George came in their Volvo to pick him up from his lodging. They seemed a pleasant young couple, perhaps a little eager to do business but none the worse for that. McGillivray asked some more basic questions and got equally basic answers. 'Crime in the neighbourhood,' they acknowledged, 'is high, but isn't it everywhere?' He nodded. He knew about crime.

Harriet asked, 'Do you have a car?'

'No', he said nervously. This one question had never counted in his favour before. His past landlords had never approved of tenants who chose not to drive. Pedestrianism was to them at best a social disadvantage and at worst an eccentricity, a sign that one had not yet arrived, was not quite serious about life and probably not credit worthy. He was confused but not suspicious, not yet, that Harriet and George both smiled, their faces wrapped in teeth that were very white, as if delighted at a wonderful joke or a sermon that was shorter than anticipated.

'Well,' said Harriet, 'let's go.'

George drove the Volvo along the long artery road that still goes down past the pseudo Gothic town hall and the modern shopping centre until it ducks under the railway line and re-emerges in St. Hilda's, the district of Grimsbrough nicknamed 'The Frontier.'

The railway track was the line of demarcation between the modern town and the old, this Border that changed him forever. He did not notice, there were no guards with guns, no checkpoints. When McGillivray first took the low road down from Scotland he was disappointed that the only evidence of crossing below was a sign that said 'Welco e t Engla d.' His depression developed as the train went farther South and the shabby warmth of red brick began to replace honest stone.

This railway line here, this line that ducked underneath but did not go over or along, was by far the most dangerous kind of frontier; the type that never enters discussion because it can never be mentioned. To talk about it is to acknowledge its reality and this no one can bear. To common sense, it is self evident that these liminal places, the hearth and threshold, have to be warded with iron and rowan against the Perils that wait in the cold outside for the cracks to open wide enough to let them scramble into the warmth of humanity. These borders only reveal their existence to the fly after the trap has closed and she has slithered down the slope into a delicious honey pool of death. Those ensnared are blamed after the event. 'Surely you knew. Didn't they tell you?' And then after a pause, 'I didn't like to get involved, to interfere.'

McGillivray didn't know. He soon learned though.

CHAPTER 9

The car skirted the long playing field with its broken goal post, 'the site of the old church,' and turned into what appeared to be a pleasant square. Three sides were lined with houses in the mid-Thatcher style built from a terracotta coloured brick, the fourth taken up by a large and rather Italianate building with a clock tower. Its door was heavily bolted. Huge black shutters hung over its arched windows. Tattered posters hung from a notice board. Above the boarded up doors were the indecipherable tags of graffiti artists, 'Twocka woz ere'.

McGillivray was fascinated. 'That place looks rather interesting. What is it?'

'It's the old Town Hall, Lowry painted it,' replied George breathlessly. 'If you do not mind, I will stay with the car as Harriet shows you around. It is her house after all.'

They got out and walked up the short path to the front door of number 37. She had some difficulty turning the three keys and muttered under her breath about getting it sorted. Eventually each of the locks clicked and she pushed the door open. McGillivray was hit by the smell of paint. 'Very nice,' he said. 'It feels very fresh.'

'All new builds around here, the council has been trying to improve the neighbourhood.'

Her last words were swallowed quickly and she added, 'Well, everything needs a spruce up now and then.'

She pushed the door open and stood to one side as he entered. Straightaway, he loved the house. Whilst nothing was quite to his taste there was nothing in it so bad as to offend his more delicate sensitivities. Nothing was embarrassing. He was standing in a large entrance area with a greyish carpet. Insects seemed to be buzzing around what looked like a red wine stain that seemed to have resisted persistent attempts to clean it. Apart from that it was fine. The walls were light and free of the normal landlord beige. Everything felt fresh and newly cleaned. He went through the far door and found himself in a long and narrow living room with patio doors that opened out onto a small lawn. Flypaper curtains hung from the rail. The furniture was appropriate for his station in life, a grey three-piece suite dominated that looked comfortable and cheap. An empty bookcase with a glass front was in the hall. Some shelves. A yucca plant. McGillivray looked around, impressed.

'This all feels very new. It's lovely. I'm surprised you don't want to live here.'

The landlady repeated the explanation he had heard the previous day, 'Oh, my mother is needing some care and it does,' slight emphasis, 'make more financial sense, you know.'

He asked her about the terms and was surprised by how easy she was about the formalities that would have been so important in London or careful Aberdeen.

'No, no need for references, yes a deposit would be good, of course you can move in straight away.'

Everything seemed perfect. Without any hesitation, he wrote a cheque for a month's rent in advance and another in hand as his deposit. Harriet handed over the keys there and then. She seemed very keen to get away. George was waiting for her, she said, then something about dinner on the stove. He accepted her excuses, held the door open and watched as she walked down to the end of the garden path and got into the waiting car. The house was his.

McGillivray moved in the next day, excited that for the first time in many years he could live entirely alone and in such a large space. The taxi driver looked at him strangely when he heard the address, Tower Green, then shrugged as if absolving himself of responsibility. He parked and hovered nervously as McGillivray unpacked his bags from the boot. The engine was kept running. McGillivray went to pay him with a tenner. The driver looked around them as if to check no one was watching. He said quietly, 'Don't flash your money about around here, Mate.'

There was not a lot to unpack; more packages were due to arrive up from London in the next few days with his little essentials so all he really had to do was choose which of the two decent sized bedrooms to sleep in and where to lay his Calvin Kleins. These simple tasks completed, he went into the kitchenette to boil his hired kettle to make some instant, in the absence of the cafetière, coffee. He opened the fridge out of habit and was surprised to see a carton of milk there. On sniffing, it turned out to be fresh. He poured some in, stirred it, staring out of his window at the ersatz piazza as he sipped. Finished, he left the mug in the sink, opened his brand new front door to look better at his garden and take in the air. He breathed in deeply and immediately coughed on the pervasive stink of rotten fish. Blinking his burning eyes, he left the house, turned the key in the three locks, and pulled the gate behind him.

He crossed the square diagonally, and took the route around the back of the Hall. Posters advertising long cancelled events were pasted onto its boarded up windows. McGillivray could just make out the shape of three women playing what appeared to be Celtic instruments. There had been life here once and it may have been good.

To his right extended a long unenclosed area of mud and trampled grass that led down towards a horizon sculpted from tall chimneys of what he later learned were paint factories. Their poison seeped down into the once good earth made barren so that the walls of the prosperous elsewhere could be decorated with bright colours. The palette here, in the lea of the lowering building, was limited to shades of black; only the red and blue plastic of broken play equipment, beer cans and other trash relieved the grey of the grass. Crows and a club footed pigeon brucked about in the bright litter scattered under the climbing frame. There were no flowers. He walked along a street consisting of what architects mockingly call 'town houses'. Most were fortified in some way by railings or a portcullis arrangement over the front door. A few had CCTV cameras in place. Those that were empty had their windows blinded with metal. At the crossroads was a pub, The Queen's Head. Under its painted sign a group of kids loitered, all of them about stone throwing height; the dogs ranging about them were not on leashes. Big dogs. With teeth. He walked past on the other side certain that it would be safer not to attract their attention.

The only grocer's he could find was one of a small parade consisting of a chippie, a boarded up launderette and a betting shop. Outside, an old man with the appearance of a tramp was making a phone call to his bookie on a Newkie Brown bottle.

McGillivray managed to open the heavy door. He had expected to see shelves but any browsing was impeded because all the goods, even the baked beans and the packet soup, were displayed behind heavy metal grids that had to be unlocked and relocked by the merchant for each item. He asked for a few things, more out of politeness than need, and immediately regretted his purchases when told the price. He paid up with a smile, left the shop and began to walk home. The talkative tramp made a follow on call to his mother. She was doing very well now that she was out of the hospital and was positively sure that she needed no messages.

Opposite the shops a large church of deep red brick held sway over a vast expanse of car park. Its door was filled with a large glass window engraved with a dedication to 'Our Lady of Perpetual Succour.' McGillivray, always fascinated by Victorian churches and the Catholic re-establishment, thought he would have a lookie inside but the door was locked; the service times were recorded on the information board. Beside it, the primary school had barbed wire over its windows.

The next day in the office a colleague, Maria, asked him if he had found somewhere to live; she looked rather surprised when he told her he had and where it was. He did not think about it that first time but the same thing happened again later that day. Whenever he gave anyone his address he got the sense he was being looked at oddly. They would always ask if he had experienced any problems and he would laugh. 'Oh come on,' he'd say, 'it's not that bad. You get by.'

He was wrong. No one new arrived in St Hilda's by accident. Grimsbrough is off the mainline, a branch line that leads nowhere. To stand on the platform and see the train departing is to understand the feelings of a beached whale watching safety ebbing out of reach. McGillivray was now amongst the wrack and flotsam of the unsafest town in England and he did not have the wit to know it.

CHAPTER 10

The absence of secondary characters in the story so far illustrates how little interest McGillivray had in anyone else. It would be wrong to take from this the idea that he was alone, or had need to be. Despite the unpleasant insularity in his character that gave him the ability to do empathy rather than to feel it there were many people around who had been good to him and to whom in response he tried to show appreciation, not with a great deal of success. Adam we have met already, but now his best friend, a straight girl who had tried to make her way as a model in London flounced into his life. Her lipstick was amazing. Economics or a man had lead to her rapid departure back north and now, after the abortion, she lived in a village about 10 miles north of the Grims. There, bored quietly to death despite her mother's attempts to get her to volunteer at the WRVS, she considered becoming a nun. They had more sex.

Maeve escaped down to see him most weekends. Her mother was rather worried about yet another unsuitable man but relaxed when reassured that the sole purpose of the frequent visits was to help a poor friend who, after his retirement as a teacher, was finding it hard to adjust to his new life in the North. Adam was always ready for some kind of mischief and so, with their help, McGillivray was able to start orientating himself to living on the wrong side of the Frontier. Adam told them both about the kind of law or Law that existed in St. Hilda's, that it was a place outside the normal rules of decency. The writ of the Police was tenuous, they came in numbers and with care when called, if at all. Maeve was thrilled. Her experience of community had been the Edinburgh suburbs and so she was fascinated by how this place worked, how its standards existed and were passed on down through generations to be enforced by the current fistful of wasted young men who gathered at the corner of the road. These bonny boys were the legislators, the parliament, and the chattering classes that mattered who kicked beer cans around and looked out for, after and against each other.

There were decent folk around. Martha, who lived nearby, befriended him and helped him not be alarmed by the rhythms of life; that cars were burned out every Sunday night exactly one hour after the pubs closed, that mornings were safer as the twockers, those who took the cars without their owners consent, were in bed; that when they behaved responsibly no one was at risk. They only drove the cars around for an hour or so and then fired them on the huge area of waste ground known as the Fankle so that no houses would be damaged and their wreckage became useful as climbing frames and practice grounds for the juvenilely delinquent.

McGillivray's people, as we have mentioned, were from the island of Lewis and had a love of interfering, which explains in part their need to evangelise the heathen. The whole island had once been owned by a certain gentleman, a Mr. Matheson who had made his money from opium and tea whilst always having a King James Bible in his jacket pocket. Disraeli found him disreputable. Even Ian Smith of Rhodesia was said to be related. So McGillivray was predisposed to join, at Martha's suggestion, the Residents Association chaired by a useful Priest, and attend its meetings. A housing official came to address them at a meeting in the Old Town Hall on the other side of the square from his house. A nice young man, good taste in shirts, very committed, an evening meeting so he gave up his own time. He introduced himself as 'Cawmejim' and then declared that the house for the disabled at Tapper's Corner had been repaired and new tenants were expected momentarily. That the last ones were so terrorised that they fled in the night was not mentioned. Nor that as soon as they left, the house had been given the full treatment, windows smashed, central heating systems carried away in the night by watchful men.

Dear, dear Cawmejim told his audience that a huge proportion of the devolved neighbourhood-housing budget had to be utilised to repair the damage and now the decree was out that the community had the responsibility to ensure that the same thing wouldn't happen again. The re-repair money would have to be found from the routine maintenance budget.

McGillivray asked the pleasant young man what responsibility for the house meant. 'Should I challenge the young men dismantling the property to put the radiators back?'

The official looked bemused at the question, 'No, of course not, people should not put themselves at risk.'

'Then should I phone the police? By the time they arrived, if they arrived, the work would be done. Wouldn't it? Wouldn't it? And they would know who made the phone call. And then I would be a witness. And they know where I live. My windows would be broken.'

Sweet Cawmejim looked away from him and said nothing more; an argument would be unwise for him in front of that audience and besides, he took no pleasure in the ingratitude of the People whom he had so wanted to empower.

CHAPTER 11

A few weeks after McGillivray moved in to Tower Green, Adam turned up at the front door and said, 'Enough of this quiet life, we are going out for a drink.' 'Where are we going?' McGillivray asked. 'You'll be thrilled.' McGillivray looked suspicious. 'But be prepared, you are not going to believe this.'

The treat that Adam had in mind was a visit to a club night in the upstairs bar known locally as 'the Pig's Arse,' a pub down the civilised end of Linthorpe Road. Clearly it was all planned, as Jerome was there with his boyfriend who was looking away from them towards something happening in the far corner. 'This is McGillivray,' Adam said. Lance turned around. 'I know. We were students together.'

McGillivray choked on his pint. It was not so much that Lance had aged, more that he had improved, become more himself. Everything about him was memorable; he had taken to swimming and his body seemed taut under his jersey. His face, so beautiful, had now been made startling by his habit of dying one eyebrow bright pink. That he could carry this off in the Grims showed that he was no wimp.

'How the hell did you get lost down here?'

'It was love', Jerome said. 'I fell in love with him and so darling Lance moved down here.'

'Yes', said Lance, 'I had nothing but the novel on at the time. Here I can write it in peace.'

Jerome smiled indulgently, 'And you take care of me so well! You must let Lance cook you dinner sometime.'

The DJ was a tall thin rather camp man who put on a yellow wig just before he played some Madonna number. His jokes were awful but the capacity crowd greeted each with a cheer as an all too familiar friend. During the last number the staff all got up on top of the bar. 'What are they doing?' McGillivray asked. 'Just watch,' Adam said, and held his finger to his lips. Lance moved ever so closely to McGillivray. As the music began to speed up the staff began to dance with tambourines irrespective of their shapes. Adam whispered, 'They do this every week.' Lance laughed to see the shock on McGillivray's face. 'You're not in London now.' McGillivray sipped his half pint of bitter; he could never bring himself to drink a full pint of the noxious brew, and grimaced. It was true; he was a long way from any home. Lance laughed and patted him on the arm in mock consolation.

The bar they went to more often, partly because it was Maeve's favourite, was called 'the Alabama'. It had recently been refurbished and large amounts of money had been spent on Southern States flags and other memorabilia. That racist symbols could be used in such a way had at first grated on McGillivray and Maeve's consciousness but now they did not even notice. Sexual and racial politics was not something that many people did those days outside the big cities and the cheery red flags with their pretty blue stripes seemed almost innocent, reassuring. The staff had been welcoming and helped him a lot with the outreach work he did for the Council. He had ensured that trays of flavoured prophylactics and sachets of lube were placed on the bar so that anyone who was caught short could get lucky.

Barbarella held court behind the bar. On the nights when drag acts were imported he transformed himself into a Russian dowager whose tiara and diamonds frequently outshone the unamused visitors. Some of these acts were indeed spectacular. Grace O'Malley once cartwheeled around that very stage singing, not miming mind on, but singing, 'The Hills are Alive to the Sound of Music' without her wig falling off. She was acclaimed as 'fresh from New York'. The response of the local crowd did not thrill her. The only admiration she received was from Adam who loved her wonderful eyes. He doted and danced about but the only rewards he received were trinkets and a put down. 'He got mah ear rings, he got ma lashes and that is awl he is gonna get.' Lance, on the other hand, seemed very attentive. Grace looked at McGillivray and smirked, 'I was wondering what you were going to do for men?'

Drag is freedom. McGillivray in his previous pelvic affiliations had become political in that dreary way championed by the Marxist feminists who devastated families through their trumped up allegations and spurious good practice. They had despised 'camp' and drag as in some way mocking women and trading in cheap stereotypes. Lord have mercy. Those stereotypes were hard won and wear well. Drag gives permission to be appalling, to be crude and to laugh when under Conservative rule little was funny, and the left seemed to think jollity some kind of denial. Barbarella put up with none of that crap. On one memorable occasion she persuaded McGillivray to wig and frock up to raise money for the charity that the Manager was organising. Dazzled by lights all he achieved was three days off work with a sprained ankle when he feel off a heel. To add insult to injury, his normal clothes were stolen and he had to buy them back at auction. He was not amused.

McGillivray still wanted to go to church, the Church. Some kind of personal faith still kept him shackled. That other Christians – most Christians – regarded people like him with fear and contempt, he felt, was more to do with their lack of education than anything wrong with the paradigm itself.

He felt the need to try something new and so began to attend at the sacrifice of the Mass at the Old Cathedral, the church he had tried to enter on that first day. The structure was about 150 years old, built from an industrialist's desire to keep the immigrant Irish population civilised. The bishop had long since packed up his throne, his pyx and his hymnbook to move out to a modern structure known to all as the 'Cheese block'. He abandoned the faith to a small and stubborn congregation who were harassed by an administration more concerned with the finance of the witness than the message itself. There were plans to turn the building into flats. Demolition had been considered.

McGillivray and Adam went to a service there together on what was perhaps his second Sunday in the new country. They tried the main door but it was shut fast and so they entered through the side door of a small porch. Nothing on the outside prepared them for the vastness of the unlit space they encountered. Down the long nave from the high altar a gloom seemed to eddy tide-like towards them that left them looking at each other confused, saturated by the cold and draught. Their skin told them that they should be outside; only the senses of sight and awe confirmed that they were indeed inside, in a true sanctuary, an illusion of distant gold. Craning their necks, they could see where the water pouring through the ceiling made huge white stains on the tiling. Damp stippled the building causing the paint to peel from the plaster and from the underlying brick; the saints were blinded. Black mould continued the grain of the marble high up into the eaves. Adam tapped McGillivray's arm and pointed above the high altar. In the perpetual twilight they could make out the shapes of icons, but at the centre, at the highest point, the most holy of places gaped. There was no image of the Christ, no crucifixion but instead a vacuum, a missing front tooth.

They moved further in slowly. This decay, this rotting broken place felt fitting to them both. There seemed no reason that God should live better than the people clustered around her house like chicks around a hen. Their homes were also often terrible places. Mice, cockroaches and black fungus scarred them. Neglect hung its own tapestries of damp upon their walls. They heard that week a rat had bitten a bairn sleeping in a makeshift cot. Outside the older children had been watching and waiting.

This house of the abandoned faithful was not empty though. The walls of the Blessed Sacrament chapel were full of angels glistening in mosaic tiles. They stood very still and listened out for the slightest sounds of feathers moving as the six guarded the small red light that showed something alive amongst the shadows.

The worshippers used a chapel on the other side of the Lady Chapel for services; it had been screened off from the nave by a glass wall that enabled a bit of heating and so held in a little warmth. There, a single priest went each day to elevate the bread and wine, the forgotten heartbeat of a community ground exceedingly small by mighty wheels.

He was the man who greeted them both. He looked Adam and McGillivray up and down twice each and took their precise measure. His broad smile made his dogma very clear; they were both emphatically welcome. The service was delightful, gentle and informal. McGillivray had had no real experience of Catholicism before and was utterly charmed. The support of the liturgy led him gently towards the appropriate adoration of the Lamb. A sermon was preached from a liberation theology that never condescended and felt appropriate to both the place and the people. They clearly loved him.

After that, they both went most Sundays and had lunch together afterwards. Whenever Maeve was down, she would join them. Whilst they could feel the congregation's speculations behind their back at the state of their relationships, no one seemed that bothered. McGillivray took particular delight at the thought of his Free Kirk cousins in the Western Isles turning in their whited sepulchres as he participated in the idolatrous sacraments committing the twin sins of being both papistical and high. Sometimes in the evenings, Jerome and Lance invited Maeve, Adam and McGillivray to their delightful home in the suburban deserts outside the Town. Jerome was a remarkable cook who took great pleasure in the elaborate presentation of food and wine.

McGillivray learned to appreciate what was around him; gorged as a child with the island beauty the urban decay was not unwelcome. Ugliness refreshed the eye. Poetry and prophecy were written on the broken walls of the estate with spray cans. A different music from one he had ever heard before filled the air. Strange art. One morning a ghetto blaster woke him up blaring out women's voices. He looked out of his front window onto the square to see it festooned with videotape. Black streamers hung in huge swags between the branches of the stripling trees and lampposts turning the whole area into a carnival of mourning. Children danced.

CHAPTER 12

McGillivray committed a poem.

> If I had a magical coat
> I would muffle my face in it
> and hide from the eyes of the guards
>
> If I had seven league boots
> I would pull them onto my feet and run
> all the way to America
>
> If I had a belt studded with stars
> I would put it around my waist
> and rip out the bars with incredible
> strength
>
> But I have no coat
> and I have no shoes
> They have taken my belt
> so that my trousers are falling down
> and I am very cold.

The next morning, Joan Baez sang over the radio to Maeve and McGillivray about New York. For her, it was four in the morning, the enemy slept with one eye open and had it fixed fully on them.

For them it was Saturday; McGillivray and Maeve had both slept late in their separate beds. Outside, the sun shone down on the square; no traces of the car's cadaver remained there, no evidence that anything had ever happened in the shadows of the stripling birch trees with their black streamers fluttering in the wind.

Adam drove down to join them. The three of them sat long over coffee and croissants in fervent debate about how to squander the day. They were sick of the Grimsbrough shops, had been in them all and were craving novelty. After some indecision they decided on a day trip to Whitby. Adam drove there fast before they could have time to change their minds again.

The scenery Adam was taking them through confused McGillivray. He had had no idea that just beyond industrial Grimsbrough with its swathe of factories and chemicals there were farms and a multitude of small independently minded villages and market towns, many of them ancient. They tended to look shabby now. Grimsbrough growing from nothing like a wart on the region had eclipsed their wealth and importance. Then, of course, there are the great moors of North Yorkshire. McGillivray had only seen the soft and bland south, he thought England was always green and pleasant. This landscape he understood, far closer to home than the delicate South and its priorities. This was a place of infinite browns, bog cotton, a kestrel pursuing something small and tasty. In the summer distance he was sure he could see a man who looked familiar flaying the earth with a long knife so that peat could be dug and then laid out, all moist and damp. McGillivray grew maudlin. Maeve gave him an apple.

Whitby lifted his mood. The town had been constructed from a vocabulary of flagstones and herring that he understood. His father's mother, he told Maeve proudly, had been one of the island women who came this far South chasing the silver; hauped up against the cold in scarves and shawls, their Gaelic laughter gutted the bold men as efficiently as their sharp steel did the herring. She looked as if she was interested.

The three friends caleeried over junk shops and into the souvenir stalls where they enthused over seashells turned into frogs and bought each other rings made from Whitby jet, that fine fragile stone much admired by Victorian dowagers.

Across from one of the junk shops, there was an old evangelical chapel with a big shop front, purveyors of the gospel by special appointment to God. A service was taking place.

Adam wanted to open the door and go in. He was very ecumenical but the others persuaded him not too. Instead, they climbed the hill to the abbey where St. Hilda herself had mediated between kings and popes and stood by the stone cross of her protégé, Caedmon the Shepherd, father of poets. They leant against it, lightsome with laughter and looked down over the steep kirk yard of St. Mary's. It was a marvellous day.

They returned to their own St. Hilda's at about seven sated with familiar stories and singing. Waitrose had been rifled and McGillivray arranged their booty on some brand new plates, his very first matching crockery, plain white and nothing fancy. They opened some Sancerre, another treat, and let Joni Mitchell's music soothe their spirits. Rather than making them stupid or ugly, the fragrance of the wine made them sharper, more lucid; harmony, life, flowed from both sides now bringing to mind illusions of love until the ringing of the phone splintered the mood.

They all swore under their collective breath. McGillivray let the bell continue to ring for some moments before answering with reluctance. His sense of horror grew stronger when he recognised the distorted voice of the beautiful Raphael. The receiver crackled out crisis at him. Grace had been telling him to reconcile with his parents who lived just outside the Grims. He had not wanted to but Grace believed in time, healing and honesty. She was sure that love would win through and the clouds would part. She had been in a lot of musicals. So the wee angel had come up from London to give his parents news they could never have wanted to hear and he had fled from their violent reaction. He was sitting in 'The Alabama' and having a drink; he needed somewhere to spend the night. Could he stay? Of course he could. He needed to be fetched. He would never get over The Frontier alive.

Raphael was already well ensconced in drink when McGillivray arrived; he took the stool opposite and ticked through a risk assessment form in his mind. No sophisticated analysis was needed. They were in the shit; a high-risk situation, where something major was likely to happen with serious consequences for self or others. Raphael was never understated and now that he had something to be dramatic about, there was no holding him back. His ram-stam moods were as inconstant as the November weather and as varied; aggression, argumentativeness, and acute grief chased each other through him without warning of change. One moment he clutched at the red velour walls for only they could hear him and understand his pain; the next an offensive light fitting sparked screaming hysterics at the vile aesthetics of the North. McGillivray realised quickly that he was happy enough in his misery and didn't want to leave; it was going to be a long night.

Now Raphael was an undoubted beauty; his apparent youth coupled with the effects of dissipation gave him an ethereal look of sullied innocence that was irresistible to the more attractive type of predators. A few of them began to circle around now; their welcome attention caused him to blossom. He fed from the lust light in their eyes and greedy for more wanted to go on somewhere else to continue drinking. McGillivray should have left him there, he knew that, but he felt too responsible to be sensible.

It was so late that nearly everywhere, both gay and straight, would be closing and so only one option was available: 'The Paradise.' 'The Paradise' provided the only gay venue that was open in the normal course of events after 11pm. The building consisted of two terraced houses knocked together into one. The phrase Dante saw over the gates of the Inferno would have done nicely, 'Lasciate ogne speranza, voi ch'intrate.' In formal English – 'Abandon hope all ye who enter here,' or in Scots, translated as 'Yer Fucked.' Everyone came sooner or later to the Paradise. All have been there, do so now or will eventually. Everyone hated it or at least pretended to. Its habitués, the drag queens, butch dykes, lipstick lesbians, even respectability queens and they should have all known better, were made fabulous because they danced there, those whom the world was beating with its hardest hand, danced. During the day they mingle and pass as normal through the application of jacket and tie but at night they are transfigured, lifted up in glory to sit at the right hand side of She who will come at the end of days to judge the quick and the dead. In their own dark kirk with its strange and glorious lights, their own music, their own drummers they are transformed by the dance. And that is why they call us gay.

McGillivray loved the place. He found it easier to relax in the half-light and sometimes got lucky but it was about the last place to let someone in that condition loose. So despite his better judgement, they went through the new bus station and out onto the shady part of Linthorpe Road. They arrived at the middle of a long terrace and stood at a door that could have withstood a siege. Above it the name was inscribed in neon letters. Dante would have been in stitches. They rang the bell, the slot was pulled back and after their suitability was assessed, they were admitted by the woman who sold amyl nitrate and baps filled with cheese and raw onion. Not in the mood for either, they crossed the carpeted floor and went up the narrow stairs to the main floor. McGillivray wanted to piss but the men's toilet was out of order; the sink had not been repaired since being broken for weapons in a fight the previous week.

Raphael started to dance to some Gloria Gaynor with a moderately attractive young man McGillivray knew from before with an improbable name like 'Buba.' McGillivray settled back to watch them from the sidelines. He leant back on one of the red velvet stools against the black faux brick walls and got into deep conversation with an acquaintance for whom he felt a slight frisson. It was just possible that something would yet come of the night. So he stayed; hope makes fools of both the old and the young.

A night at the Paradise always ended to Whitney Houston's 'I will always love you;' the final failure was to have no one to snog as it came on and then having to head home to a lonely bed. Panic broke out when the DJ began to play it an hour earlier than expected allowing insufficient time to form the necessary arrangements. Mutters and shouts filled the room. Maestro lifted the needle off the record mid warble and bawled out an angry announcement that the club was closing an hour early as the clocks were being put forward. Raphael and the few others who had not yet copped off remained on the floor. They clapped their hands to set up a beat that set them dancing under the silver globe.

Buba leapt on top of a chair, and to the accompaniment of his own slow clapping began to agitate for everyone else to continue the party. 'This was the moment,' he declared, 'when

Moses would lead them all, lesbians, gay men and others in the acronym to the Promised Land of good drugs and decent soft furnishings'. The subversive dancers cheered him on and some began to sing. In a sudden flurry of movement he who would be activist was on the floor flattened by a flying leap from the DJ. Screams, lights all on, blood pouring from Buba's marred nose and lip. Running. Various dancers pulled them apart and jostled the lad out.

Raphael panicked and lost what little control he had left to him. This kind of thing didn't happen in the London bars he was used to and as he began to scream, a cordon of policemen came up the stairs and forced their way through the crowd in tight single file. They started ordering people to disperse and go home quietly whilst their presence in the exit made departure impossible. McGillivray knew he had to get Raphael out and home as quickly and as quietly as possible but he was brimming over with romantic stories of the Stonewall riot. The hour and the man had come. Once long ago, the police raided in far, far away New York an illegal establishment. It was nothing new. They would pay it a visit when some politician made some demands on them to increase arrests, improve the neighbourhood or just fancied giving a queer a good kicking. It was for them a team building experience. Many of the regulars in the Stonewall wore frocks and heels and these men could accessorise with purpose. On the day the guardians of law and public morality came to close them down they fought back, armed with heels and handbags. Transsexuals, transvestites, and drag queens threw the first stiletto in the name of freedom even to the extent of breaking nails and smudging mascara. The riot lasted for days. The militia were drafted in. They were fabulous. None of us have ever been the same since, except the drag queens; they are still despised.

Raphael, although intoxicated by fairy tales, was somehow persuaded to leave the club by McGillivray's increasing desperation but hated himself for what felt like selling out. As soon as he was outside the door he turned on his heel and began to try to force his way back into the building screaming abuse at the police all the time. The two nearest policemen started to get visibly angry and fingered their batons. McGillivray tried to explain by promising he would get Raphael away and they they would be quiet queers, good queers. There was no need for anyone to get excited.

McGillivray took him by the hand and began to lead him on the long walk along the brightly lit road but adrenaline was flowing through Raphael like good whisky, further exciting and inciting him to action. Suddenly, just before the crucial turning, he stopped. 'No', he bawled, 'this is the moment; we cannot leave! We must go back! They cannot do this! We have rights; we must not let them win; if we don't do something, who will?'

McGillivray sighed and got himself between the would-be revolutionary and the pub in an attempt to shepherd Raphael down the road. He kept his voice quiet and holding his arms out wide like an open cradle walked forward slowly, Raphael's fists and emotions breaking against his torso in a constant dandering. A red car slowed. McGillivray could just make out the two men in it, vaguely recognising them from the bar. The door opened; a voice: 'If he carries on like that he'll be arrested.'

McGillivray thanked him for their concern and tried to refuse their offer of help with politeness. 'Don't worry, I'm only trying to get him home, we'll be alright,' and then pleading to Raphael, 'See? Come on please.'

CHAPTER 13

Strong men were all around McGillivray, but not in a nice way; his back was held to the car and he was immobilized, but not in the way he so often dreamed. Brightness in his eyes made it impossible to focus, his arm held in a way that was on the edge of pain. He could only look ahead. He could not see Raphael. A voice in his ear said with studied calm, 'You're nicked' – and meant it.

McGillivray's world slowed down slightly around them as he stood totally still, paralysed with anger and affront. He felt steel on his wrists. They took away his hands.

Later, from his own room, from his own safety, he could not recollect how they came to be in the police van, a fortified minibus reminiscent of school jaunts with its hard wooden seats and vague scent of disinfectant. He did not know how they had come to be there but there they were, and there were the officers between them. Raphael craved a tearful absolution from McGillivray in one breath and with the next prophesied a doom that would be visited upon the police by his powerful friends. They laughed. McGillivray's face became hard and cold, his anger suffocating him as work and complications flooded his brain. He could see the words 'conduct unbecoming' before him, felt the threat of dismissal, the return to the dole and bad references. He refused to shrive Raphael; he was no priest.

The van pulled into the back of the police station. Doors opened, they were told to get out. Raphael stumbled but was not allowed to fall.

They entered a long room with slatted benches around the walls. At the narrow end was a window through which they could be watched but could not see. Like the good dogs they were, they sat on command and waited, the arresting officers beside them.

The door opened. The Voice summoned Raphael through the narrow door into a bright space. He got up quickly, looked at McGillivray through his long lashes for a brief desperate moment and was taken away. McGillivray was left alone with his personal officer, a man with no face, who could not bestow the blessing of silence but instead persisted in giving weary advice that seemed simply immoral.

'You should have had the sense to stay safe, left him to his own devices. Any sane person would have left him to look after himself.'

McGillivray tried to ask how he could abandon his friend, that overgrown child, to the pain and the blood but his magical helmet made the policeman deaf. It was very tight and fitted close over the ears.

He was spared further judgement by the electric illumination that flowed with the Voice's commands to pick up his things and walk. He obeyed and crossed the well-warded threshold into the custody suite. He was ordered to the right and to stand precisely in front of the counter where the Voice was enthroned with a typewriter. Writing was to be done. He was to be reported on and observations made.

The Voice took on human form. He was not a tall man and had a remarkable nose, one that testified to many years of solemn drinking. He did not introduce himself but instead required McGillivray's full name, age, date of birth. They pretended not to understand his accent and forced him to spell it all out then repeated it back to him; capital M, not an N an M; small c; capital G. They didn't ask for his address. They knew that already. There was a significant pause as details were removed from him and entered in the ledger.

The Voice flashed his rights before him on clashing sheets of green and pink paper. He was made to sign a receipt so they could prove he had seen them before they were taken away unread and returned under the desk. All the bad television dramas he had ever seen flashed through his head. He knew that he should request a solicitor.

The Voice made a considered decision, clicked his teeth and then informed McGillivray that he would be allowed to speak to a duty solicitor over the telephone. An important person like that would only condescend to come down to the cells for a case that appeared to be a priority. McGillivray was left with no illusions that his case mattered to no one but himself. It did not cross his mind to ask, why, if no one cared about him, they would not let him go.

In the same bored tone, the Voice told him that they could notify a person of his choice of his arrest. McGillivray ran through the short list of the people he could rouse at that time of night. Adam and Maeve were sound asleep in his house and would not hear the quiet phone and the only other number he could remember by heart was that of Jerome. The Sergeant typed it into the form. McGillivray could not see what was being typed. He did not know what was happening. No one told him.

The Voice emptied his wallet onto the desk, noted the plastic cards and counted out his coins. There were no notes. Along with his keys and an asthma inhaler, its contents were all filed together in a transparent bag and sealed with a strip of green plastic. They told him to remove his belt, his shoes and his suede jacket and then they took him away. A junior officer, Pirrick, told him to walk before him down a long corridor, controlling him through bored orders that caused confusion. Bewildered, he bumped into a long metallic strip that ran the length of the wall. It set off a shirramuir of bells all around that caught him up in their noise and spun him stumbling back against itself and started up again. The Voice stuck its turtlehead around the corner and left McGillivray in no doubt about his family or his intelligence. They placed him outside a steel door of his very own. He was told to lay his belt, boots and coat down on the floor to his right. Pirrick unlocked the door. He crossed over. He became a prisoner.

CHAPTER 14

The door swings back on its oiled hinges and closes with a sigh. On the wall facing him is a large round window. A lightsome breeze billows out its muslin curtains. Through it, in the middle distance, the shapes of poplar trees are arranged in some vast formal garden. A table groans loudly under the weight of the food, drink and crockery upon it. Pasties, pies and other delightful pastries are arranged on platters. The meat, he thinks, is Parma ham served peppered with slices of melon. He hopes they managed to get hold of Bresaola. A huge basket is filled with peaches, plums, apricots and bananas. Small dishes have strawberries and sugar although there is no cream. To drink, flagons of claret and large jugs of mineral water have been provided. No bottles will be allowed in a prison cell of course. He makes a selection from the salads and decides to leave the meat for later. He settles down into the armchair, spreading a white napkin over his lap and begins to eat. A white horse is neighing somewhere nearby. Bells ring.

A slab of wood without softness, neither blankets nor pillow, had been fastened to the wall. There was nothing else there, nothing, save for graffiti and a window made out of small glass bricks arranged in four rows of six. Night glimmered through them but no air was admitted; there was no way of looking out. Bars were outmoded.

There was nothing to do but sit on the bench. He crawled to its far edge, leant against the stained wall and cuddled himself. There was a draught on his back. The ventilation came from underneath the seat allowing no possibility of escape, no prospect of ever being warm. He wasn't that worried; soon everything would be rectified, order would be restored. He would be free.

In detective programmes after the cell door closes on a prisoner the camera shifts to the action, normally to the conversation back in the CID room. The Guv'nor comes down and asks questions designed by the scriptwriter to contrast his stupidity with that of the hero. The prisoner is forgotten until the last bit of evidence is revealed that exonerates him and leads to the car chase that lets the poor blond woman be rescued from the villain just as he raises the knife to slash her throat. That only happens in stories. In the cells, nothing discernible happens. He sat still for a time. There was nothing else to do but ring the bell.

He rang it.

A shattle of keys sounded outside. The door opened. Pirrick looked in and grunted.

McGillivray spoke urgently, 'I need to see the Doctor, my friend is ill, I have to tell him what happened.'

Pirrick looked at him and grunted. The door closed. Nothing happened.

A shattle of keys sounded outside. The door opened.

Pirrick said, 'You wanted to see the Doctor.'

He was walked down the same corridor. This time he knew enough to avoid the ringing of the bells. They entered him into the consulting room where a police surgeon was seated at what looked like a very normal medical table. The man smiled at McGillivray in a way that emphasized the oddness of his face. It looked like the drawing of child who had not yet realised that eyes had whites and thought skin could be pink. He wore a stethoscope and was very fat.

McGillivray hovered by the chair designated for the use of prisoners until he was commanded to sit down. The doctor smiled and used a voice at him that contained an illusion of professional kindness that aimed to be both therapeutic and to invite confidences. Before proceeding, he assured McGillivray of his ethical boundaries; nothing he was told would be passed on to the authorities. McGillivray trusted him but not quite enough to tell him most of his fears for Raphael. The doctor seemed concerned, but not sufficiently. McGillivray tried not to think how doctors are normally employed in torture scenarios, 'this far you can go, and no further.'

The doctor was silent for a moment and then delivered his considered opinion. 'Your friend will obviously need support after recent traumas but seems well placed to be able to access services. As to your unfortunate circumstances,' a tactful pause, 'they will be quickly resolved. You will certainly be let go in the morning and then with a good solicitor, the magistrate will surely see sense.' Gratitude flooded McGillivray's heart that someone had spoken a little sense to him. His eyes stung. He asked the merciful Lord to forgive his unkind thoughts about the doctor's appearance. This man knew the system and said that he would be free. McGillivray had no reason yet not to believe him. 'Oh sweet angel, oh blessed light,' he gave thanks that he would be home in time to let in the central heating repairman. That the doctor had failed to promise to do anything escaped his notice.

He was returned to the cell. The door clanged.

Every time the keys rattled past outside he assumed that they were coming for him; that the door would open. That he would be released. There would be an explanation offered, an apology. He decided on the best strategy to adopt; forgiveness and grace would be the most appropriate tone, he would understand that mistakes happened in the Grimsbrough cells and of course there would be no hard feelings.

The keys rattled. He sat up on the edge of the plank, alert. Someone else's door opened.

Nothing happened and again nothing happened and nothing happening stretched into a long nothing not happening. He waited amongst walls covered with text and cartoons drawn in body fluids; huge spurting cocks; names and dates; league tables of successes drawn up by car thieves. Some of them were very successful. He read the inscriptions.

'Bazza ov Grangeside'

'Kevin'

'I woz ere, now I'm not, you are'

'Mark'

'Grangetown twockers rule'

The keys rattled. He sat up on the edge of the plank, alert. Someone else's door opened.

A vast cartoon of an animal called 'Twocia the cat'

'Don't worry, happy'

Words, words, words, and himself. He would add his name but he had nothing to write with. He had nothing.

The keys rattled. He sat up on the edge of the plank, alert. Someone else's door opened.

The keys rattled. He sat up on the edge of the plank, alert. Someone else's door opened.

The keys rattled. He sat up on the edge of the plank, alert. Someone else's door opened.

The keys rattled. He sat up on the edge of the plank, alert. Someone else's door opened.

The keys rattled. He sat up on the edge of the plank, alert. His door opened.

Pirrick spoke,

'You can speak to the duty solicitor now.'

He was taken to a telephone that was fixed to the wall at shoulder height, its receiver dangling like a hanged man on the end of a long chord. The policeman picked it up, checked that there was someone there, handed it over and moved to the edge of earshot. McGillivray cuddled the handset. An educated voice spoke through it to him, not posh, but someone who although English was rather like himself. In the morning, he was told, he would either be charged or cautioned and then set free. He would be ordered to appear before a magistrate's court and be bound over to keep the peace for a bond of either £100 or £200. No money would change hands and there would be no fine.

'But I didn't do anything.'

'That is an irrelevancy. Look, the whole business is unfortunate,' that word again, 'this kind of case simply doesn't matter, and you won't even get a record. Don't make any trouble for yourself. Just keep quiet, wait and when you're out...'

Pirrick shouted down the length of the corridor, 'Hurry up, someone needs to speak to him, more than you do.'

They were done.

He was returned to the cell and given a tablet that made him sleepy. The door clanged behind him.

He tried to settle down on the plank but there was no way of avoiding the draught; however he turned it seemed to reach his bare skin. He was very cold. Eventually simple exhaustion dragged him almost to sleep and freedom for a space but always the keys would rattle and he would sit up on the edge of the plank, alert. Someone else's door would open and he would lie down again shielding his eyes from the eternal brightness of the damnable bulb.

Nothing happened. Hope was his enemy, the tormentor that made the present cruel and forbade adjustment to the unbearable.

The keys rattled. He sat up on the edge of the plank, alert. Someone else's door opened.

There was screaming outside. He could hear walls being kicked. A solicitor was not coming. More angry voices.

Silence. Nothing happened. The keys rattled. He sat up on the edge of the plank, alert. Someone else's door opened.

He needed to piss.

CHAPTER 15

The colour behind the false window changed from black to grey as early morning replaced the deep night. They had taken time from him with his watch and he had no idea whether dawn came at four or at five. Outside, where he used to be, dawn happened to the sleeping, an unnoticed transition; here in his new world without time, the ending of night mattered far more for it was the first sign of the morning that would let him out. He shrank from it into his own world. The window mocked at him as it grew new shadows in the contrasts of the empty room, its sad light mingling with that from the electric bulb. He shrank in terror from the fear that inhabited the corners and took on forms in his waking dreams.

Near the steps of the red cathedral, faggots are heaped around a wooden post by a small group of town labourers. The work has been hard and so now they are glad to rest. They were having their breakfast. Ale and bannocks had been brought out to them from an old woman in the pub. Their laughter pierces the red stone walls and is heard by the prisoner who is waiting through one more day.

In the early evening, Pirrick comes to McGillivray, the man with the black mask, except that he is not wearing a mask yet but a professional face painted with kindness and a half smile. He is embarrassed. McGillivray has wondered who they would use and was surprised to not recognise his executioner. No local will do the blood work. They all know too much of what has happened. She has brothers. They had been seen often in recent days in the alehouse and the gathering places talking heatedly. There has been a fight: a bishop's man received a bloody nose and a broken tooth. The authorities are so concerned about the vengeance of the ignorant and uneducated that they have consulted in committee to decide on security precautions. Health and safety for their staff is always a foremost consideration. Pirrick has been brought up from Caithness especially to perform the death work.

Pirrick has already been paid half his wage and received expenses. Board and lodging are both provided in the Earl's great house across from where they are now in the cathedral cell. Although they have not been mean with the food and have given him a place by the fire, he has refused ale that the guard had tried to force upon him. He knows now his mistake; it would have been better for him if he had been drunk, if he too had made himself insensitive. He hasn't. And he stands there in her cell with the pincers in his hand. Tradition decrees that the nails on her hands and feet be pulled out to prevent her scratching her guards and spreading the witch contagion; no one means to be unkind; it doesn't form part of her sentence but is simply a matter of pragmatics. Public Health.

McGillivray screams. No one that matters hears. A sharp knife causes torn hair to fall around them in little pools of blood.

His need to piss pulled him round. He rang the bell. He waited. No one came. He waited. No one came. He counted to fifty, and then fifty again, pain increasing. He waited but no one came. The pain dreadful, he rang the bell again. Counting to fifty slowly and ringing the bell again. Thirty and the bell. Twenty and the bell. The pain in his bladder grew all the time and no one was coming.

Within him a division occurred. His two minds separated as he stroked his cold arm slowly examining the blue of the veins. One mind, a feeling mind, a dispassionate mind scrutinised the flow of the blood and the texture of the pale skin. His other mind was somewhere above. It observed the action of the hand and saw the other mind's speculations. It comprehended what was happening and saw his own weakness; it knew they had him broken now and he would sign anything that would unlock that door that would lead into the good air. It was relieved too that the police had the sense to remove his sharp things for his own safety. He was no hero. Hand wondered what red would look like on the white skin. No one came. A nail made a mark, a slight sensation of pain. He pressed harder. He hurt.

No one came. He wanted to bleed to see if he still existed. If he screamed he would know that he existed, that the window was lying, that he had a voice; even in this concrete vault he would have a voice despite the bell being unanswered, the cruel bell, the silent bell. He waited. No one came. He waited. No one came. No. He had no voice. He drifted and was not.

The Lady in the Tower places her hands around a slender neck. 'What will they call me in history?' she asks. 'La reine sans tete', she decides. 'I have but a little neck.' Her most immodest laugh fills the apartment. Outside, the note taker by the door writes, 'At four o'clock, the Queen laughed.'

The door opened.

'You were ringing the bell.'

'I need the toilet.'

'Get up.'

The toilet was in a small cubicle with no lock. It stank. He forced himself to sit down on the stained metal ring but the stinging piss would not come. Pirrick commanded him to get up. He rinsed his hands with the pink gel provided and he was walked back.

Outside the cell door were the shoes and coat he had been wearing.

'Can I take the jacket in with me?'

'No.'

'When are you going to let me go?'

'I'll ask. It might not be until the first available court, Monday.'

McGillivray laughed. Pirrick was obviously winding him up. He would not be fooled and the Solicitor and Doctor both knew what they were talking about. The cell door clanged behind him. He lay down on the board. Again exhaustion dragged him down into a shallow sleep.

CHAPTER 16

Nothing good lasts long in the cells. McGillivray was forced back to the world by the sudden clang of the shutter falling open. He uncurled on his board and walked up to receive a tray that was being held by two hands through the feeding hole in the door.

'Breakfast for you.'

He took it and went back over to the bench. He sat down and put the brown plastic tray on his lap. He prodded the food with his finger; it consisted of economy sausages, the type labelled 'meat' rather than pork or beef, with a dollop of garish beans over a kind of watery reconstituted potato. It was all placed on a paper platter with a brown check pattern on its rim. He thought that the presentation could have been improved.

He was given plastic cutlery, a fork, and a spoon to eat with. There was no knife. He could have cut himself with a plastic knife. The sausage skipped out from under the spoon and fell on the floor. He ate it.

A thin polystyrene cup contained strong tea made sweet and scummy with milk. He hated tea with sugar and milk. He drank it and felt more vile and thirstier than ever. Yet even those contemptuous victuals had a healing effect; he began to feel alert and his eye focused on a benediction written in brown on the wall: 'Don't worry, be happy.' He laughed. He gulped in the air and he laughed. He decided to obey. He stopped worrying and was happy.

He begins to build himself a home out on the moor near the cliff edge. He constructs the walls and roof from a rite that some women had taught him to make holy an unholy place. He summons up from the dark air that which is needed, the salt, and the lavender oil.

Three times three he describes the circumference of a circle by scattering the salt with his hand so that it lies in a thick ring all around him. He places the sprigs of lavender in a stone jar full of water in its heart. He marks each of the cardinal points with large stones taken up from the beach one hard winter; sweat breaks on his brow with the effort of shifting them into each place. They balance well. In front of each he stands for a piece, his arms raised and invokes the come-all-ye. He recites the words slowly:

> Power of the East, sea gives birth to the
> light; the morning rises and is filled with
> the glory.
> Power of the North, high is the sun in
> the sky. Hot is the day. Hard is the work.
> Power of the West, fire in the water, red
> spreads in the sky, laughter and good
> wine.
> Power of the South, the sun travels
> under the earth, the night is cold, the
> pain of the exile, children leave the good
> land for the distant country.

Light and shadows gather at the boundary of the salt, those welcome and unwelcome alike. Hooves clatter; a woman with black hair holds his gaze. He continues to pray.

> Come, be thou the light in this mirk, that
> we should see;
> Be thou the voice that speaks in the
> night, that we should be heard;
> Be thou the arm that cradles his head
> that we should be loving.

There is a memory of silver bells borne on a distant wind. He kneels on the floor, hears nothing, feels nothing. For time without measure he kneels on the floor, hears nothing and feels nothing.

CHAPTER 17

The circles were broken by the opening of the door. Pirrick commanded him to get up, to leave the cell obediently, to bend down to pick up his shoes and coat, and carry them before him. Pirrick walked behind him but had no need to shout. McGillivray knew the drill.

When they got to the reception area, the Voice ordered him to stand in front of his desk and informed him that he would be charged with breaking the peace the previous night on Newport Road. They would keep him there until the next available court on the Monday morning.

The Voice continued, 'Your friend has been let go because of his bad health.'

'Bollocks,' McGillivray thought indignantly, 'you were afraid; you couldn't control him and didn't know what to do.' It was only then he realised that they were not going to let him go. They were going to keep him for twenty-four more hours. He felt sick.

'His things are in your house; we need your permission so that he can get your keys and fetch his bag. We are requiring him to leave the town immediately.'

McGillivray looked puzzled. He started to tell the Voice that Raphael did not have anything with him, there was some kind of mistake, but he took breath just in time and stopped, lips tight. Raphael was smarter than he was, perhaps had been in that kind of place before, and was trying to tell him that he was alive, well. He would get news out and summon help from Adam and Maeve. They would get him out. Hope sprang up and gave him the courage to challenge, 'Why won't you let me go?'

The Voice explained it all slowly again; he had better things to do that needed his attention. 'You have been charged with a common law offence, we haven't got the power to let you go. We have to hold you over until we can produce you before the next available court, tomorrow morning.'

'Can I have a copy of my rights? You didn't give me a chance to read them properly last night.'

The Voice maintained the effort to be professional, just, clicked his teeth twice and reached beneath the desk to produce two pieces of pink and green paper. McGillivray took them up carefully and put them in his jeans pocket.

'You can make a call to the duty solicitor.'

McGillivray thanked him politely. He got to the phone and was disgusted to hear the same blatherskite as the previous night on the phone and as wifferty-wafferty as before. Perhaps he was tired.

'Unfortunately', he said, 'they're right. There's nothing that we can do just now. Just wait the night. They can't do anything else to you. They will have to let you go in the morning after you've been to the magistrate.'

McGillivray wished later that the numptie had said something real. A useful advocate would have pointed out that as he was in as much shite as he could be, bar the bruises, he could use the time to enjoy himself and let off a little steam. 'Look, fuckhead,' he could have been told, 'they're bastards. Don't stand for it. Throw your head back Girl and howl, howl, howl as only you can. Show them what a Queen can do. Don't be good. Keep some dignity intact and go down fighting and, let's face it, dignity is as close to virginity as you are going to get these days.'

However, McGillivray was not told this truth by the Duty Solicitor and, in any case had no dignity left: he collaborated. All of his training had taught him to not make a fuss. He wanted to be a good boy, a good queer and then, just perhaps, they wouldn't be horrible to him anymore. Poor dear.

Maybe, just maybe he was right. Certainly, his immediate circumstances improved. Collaboration brought him the immeasurable comforts of an adult cell. The one he had been in, they told him, was for juveniles. In the shadow world that was now his, 'juvenile' meant harsher treatment, a room without any facilities.

'Give them a mattress and they'll only piss on it.'

'So your trousers are falling down because we've taken your

belt; be grateful that at least you won't be throttling yourself with it.'

A stainless steel toilet stood shamelessly in the corner with a little pile of relatively dry and clean toilet paper on the floor beside it. A man is advantaged if he gets a toilet in his cell and only loses his soul. In his excitement he tried to sit on it but there was no seat and the cold rim disgusted him.

Whilst squatting in mid-shit, the door opened, and Pirrick handed in two blankets. He apologized that they couldn't give him a mattress as they had run out. McGillivray thanked him profusely. His gratitude was charming. He appreciated that they were not being deliberately cruel, simply pragmatic.

Time passed, nothing happened.

The door opened and a plastic bag was shoved through containing gifts from Maeve and Adam. He took out from it an Observer newspaper, a large bottle of diet coke and a bar of dark chocolate. There were also some new black socks and a striped shirt but nothing warm. He put on the new clothes quickly. He had things. He was safe.

Adam and Maeve had written in the margins of the newsprint small words in tiny black letters that surrounded him with love. He hugged them both and thanked them. He then unwrapped the chocolate carefully, broke it up and divided it into little heaps to be eaten throughout the night.

With his bodily needs taken care of, the time had come to think on higher things. The gold wrapping foil from the chocolate was transformed into the shape of a Celtic cross. He laid it in the centre of a spread out double news page. Beside it he placed a square of chocolate and a thin plastic cup with a little cola in it. He cast the circles again and then bowed his head to give thanks.

The carvings of the virtuous queens on the stone screen seem animated in the half-light. Before it a plain prison altar is set up and has been provided with all things necessary for the Mass. There has been no skimping. The rich embroidered cloth covers and the candlesticks are of old gold. The light burns clearly here that has never been overwhelmed. The cup and plate are made of simple silver in the old Scots style. Beautiful.

Simple. Ageless. Bread fresh baked and the fragrance of wine. The woman with the grey eyes has put away her silver circlet and vested herself as a Priest. She speaks the ancient words of invitation in a steady voice in which he can hear the ringing of silver bells.

> 'Little children, draw near to this, the
> Table of Festival. Know there is nothing
> beyond and nothing to fear.'

The people's voices soar in the psalm to the heavens. A fulmar rises from the cliff and falls in a moment to kiss the waves before hanging, feather taut in the wind. McGillivray lifts his eyes to the purple hills and knows that his aid will come from the Creator who gave birth to heaven and earth.

The priest invites the saints of the people to join her in prayer.

> 'St. Tredwell of the Loch, when the King
> demanded your maidenhead, you sent
> him your eyes: let the truth be seen for
> us.
> St. Cormac of Hoy, mad man who came
> from the waves, dweller in stones of the
> dead: plead for us.
> St. Hilda of Whitby, who scolded both
> King and Pope: fear naught for us.
> St. Columba, liar, stealer of books,
> disturber of peace and spiller of blood:
> fight for us.
> St Brendan the Voyager, seer of islands,
> follow the wild goose over the waters: be
> free for us.'

Feet and fabrics rustled as the congregation stood to listen as the three women in the choir sung the words of the creed.

> 'We believe in the Mother of all things; a
> child ever comes to birth, all things are
> whole.

We believe in the Great Clown; the
Juggler balances earth, sun and stars in a
tumble of laughter.

We believe in the deep womb of the
Earth. Sap rises from mountain roots to
greet the wide sky.
We believe in the door, the last long bed.
On the shore is a house with four dark
walls and a bonny green roof studded
with daisies.

We believe in the fire, Gallowsha', the
ash in the wind. Grey snow is scattered
on Wideford Hill.
We believe in the absence beneath and
beyond, the longing for presence, the
journey, the dance.

We remember the flames, the bishop's
candle, the tearing at the stake, the smell
of our own flesh, the choking.
We believe, help thou our unbelief.'

The Priest invites the congregation to kneel and confess their sins. All do so, McGillivray within the rings of salt along with those unnamed ones who gather in the furthest and darkest corners of the cell.

'We have sinned in thought, word and
deed.
Shrive us the unshriven, the done and
the done for; they will not.
Grant us quiet of heart and peace in the
darkness; they will not.
Forgive, if you will, the lawmaker thief
of our children; the beater, the hater.
We will not.'

McGillivray knows he is not worthy. He asks the word to be said that will heal him; that will pronounce him whole and enable him to approach the holy table.

He heard a man's voice from the cell next door. He looked up and saw a cigarette pushed through the ventilation grill and two matches. He wept and felt Peace. Blessed is he who comes in the name of the Lord.

The priest stands and faces the altar, her long hair falling down over shadow robes formed from green and silver. The Light that shines in the eyes of those on the wrong side of the circle of salt, the heretic and unelect alike consecrate her with a savage grace. All who have ever sung the Trisagion sing it then in a language that only some of them can understand:

'Holy God,
Holiness in strength,
Holiness without death,
Have mercy upon us.'

The congregation prays again to ask for bread and protection from the evil time. In the dread hour, they take divinity upon themselves; they forgive their enemies and know forgiveness themselves. Mercy, peace, gifts, are a grace bestowed freely. The Woman raises that which in that place is represented by bread. Her hands break its moon in two. A tear rends the tapestry that divides humanity from the shrine. No protection is left to them from the all seeing eye of God.

A man screams. Beneath his feet a small group of soldiers throw dice to win his stained garment. The corporal rattles them in his hands, blows on his fingers to invoke his lady. A tension. The dice tumbles over each other. Four sixes. He laughs in a fashion that is hardly unpleasant. The cloak was not worth anything so nobody bears him a grudge.

In the same way, after supper, she raises that which represents the cup of the new covenant and blesses it.

'Blessed the God of the Vine.

Blessed the Laughter.
Blessed the Drunk.'

The routine miracle takes place. The elder takes the beaker-cup out from the sanctuary to the people.

'The blood of Christ shed for you.'

McGillivray takes hold of the cup firmly with both hands and lifts it to his lips. He tilts it steeply that he should be better able to drain the blood of his God. He was sated. He has tasted and seen that the Lord is good. The Shekinah, the living glory of the Lord, surrounds them.

'Amen.'

She who is Priest in that place gives out the final words:

'The Mass is ended, go now in peace.'

She walks out, the congregation beyond the salt disperses whence they had come, but McGillivray is unable to follow them on account of the locked door.

CHAPTER 18

Cramp woke him up. 'Maybe,' he thought, 'I will make myself very tiny and grow legs. I will become a spider and crawl out through the feeding hatch. Or perhaps I will make a nail file out of thin air and pick at the mortar between the bricks until I can loosen a couple. Then I will be able to squeeze myself out through the gap.'

He began to scratch at the wall. Nothing happened.

Pirrick opened the door and said, 'You are allowed to use the exercise yard for twenty minutes.'

He was marched through to the end of the corridor and outside into the kind of place where people die without ceremony or dignity, just an unfinished sentence, a shock and then darkness. All prisons touch each other; all are symptoms of the same madness.

There was no colour there. Little children learn their world through colours; grass is green; sky blue; clouds white; sun yellow; as they grow, complexities are learned. The blue sea becomes green, aquamarine, and brown, from certain angles black. The sky moves from heavy grey through slates to sapphire tinged with red in a single afternoon. Even the wet sand left by the pull of the wave reflects a mauve sunset.

McGillivray could not conceive of a world without colour. This world where the wall and the ground were all the same chalk white was a world inconceivable. Without colour, it became invisible and those within it disappeared. This was the empty place.

'Ye'll not try any funny stuff.'

An eye shone from the wall, an eye with a cataract lid that clicked up and down to ensure he did no damage to the yard or himself. For a few moments he stood stock-still. His unfettered limbs were stiff and in need of stretching but he was unable to move. The camera held him tight stealing his image, to be kept confined on the tape forever. One day, after his death, and certainly without his consent, it would be exhibited in a paper on Queer Studies: 'A Prisoner. Grimsbrough 1993.'

They were watching him and he could not see them. There was a man whose job it was to watch the prisoners in the yard doing what prisoners do. Perhaps they were not looking. Perhaps they could not see him. Perhaps they were not watching, perhaps they were laughing but not at him. In the room with the eyes on the wall the men gathered around the table. The magazine on it was spread as wide open as the woman over whom they salivated, her genitals salt red-rubbed and raw.

The King stirs in his sleep. Even in this house where she has never been there is no safety. Out of the shadows she comes into the room and examines the images of the Biblical Queen in the tapestry, Esther with Ahaseuras. After all these years he could still recognise the gesture of the translucent hand, feel its touch. A dead man comes through the opening his mind has made as well. They clasp, embrace. The shades entwine like candle smoke or rope before becoming a single strand before him. He is not able to take his eyes from them; he does not want to shift his gaze and wakes screaming, cursing his clemency that he hadn't insisted they put her goggled eyes out before the axe kissed her neck that morning in May on the small green within the Tower. Ah hindsight, such a sweet teacher.

McGillivray started to do what prisoners do, to measure, to define the space that he was locked into. He had seen the woodcuts, the heavy, Teutonic images from the 1930s of the men going around in endless circles. Perhaps they were singing but probably not. Communication would not normally have been allowed.

In his turn now, he measured things. The area was six cells wide by one deep. Two square concrete pillars supported the grid above his head. A gull looked down at him, shat, and flew off with a croaking cry.

He saw himself through the gull's eyes. He would not

complete this circle and be like the others. No, he would do what he wanted to do, try some funny stuff. He started to juggle three multi-coloured absences high into the air in a simple pattern then switched into under arm cascades throwing them to the left and then the right. He burst out into frenetic activity and hurled them high into the air to set them free as wild geese that flew into the sun. *A child in the crowd laughs.* He ran the whole length of the yard, the length of the six cells, as fast as he could, stretching his stiff muscles, his hard muscles, his pain. Then the cold embraced him again. The cheap yellow shirt was too thin for a bitter evening and still he had no coat to put on.

He had had enough. He waited.

No one came. He waited. No one came. He curled up in the corner of the yard and became invisible. He waited. No one came.

The door opened. He was returned to the cell.

CHAPTER 19

The little bit of warmth that could be salvaged from the blankets let McGillivray sleep through that night until Pirrick woke him with yet another platter of slop. After he finished the food and placed the paper plate delicately on the floor, he lay back down and settled comfortably back into the boredom. The door opened again and he was commanded into a cold and un-private place at the end of the cellblock; they issued him with a regulation sliver of soap and ordered him under a naked showerhead. He tried to get wet under the pitiful drizzle of water but the soap hardly lathered and with all the shouting he was unable to get properly clean. The official towel left him feeling so itchy that he needed to scrub up again.

They kept him for a short space in his cell before summoning him out for the final time. They allowed him to bend down to put on his shoes and pick up his jacket. He was marched down to the duty desk where the other prisoners were assembled. The Voice checked all their property and told them that they were to be taken to court. They filed around a glass brick screen behind the desk and through a hidden door that led deep down into the earth and an underground corridor, its concrete walls wet with condensation running down them like sweat.

They emerged from it into the bright custody of the court; names checked off another list, confirmation that none had escaped and then more cells, cleaner than before. The police herded them all in together, their harvest from a fruitful weekend. The benches were so crowded that McGillivray had to squat on the floor. There was nervous banter; lots of them knew each other, everyone was curious, jokes were made and advice given.

He was the first to be called up. An unfamiliar guard escorted him up some narrow steps into a small three-sided room. He found himself gaping and blinking through an open window into a larger space where he could just make out an old man in a blue suit seated on what appeared to be something like a throne. Above him the royal arms were carved in wood. McGillivray realised that he was already in the dock. There was no more time to think.

He lifted his eyes up and was delighted to see Maeve, peelie-wally and unkempt though she was, seated in the Public Gallery. Her lipstick was the only colour around. Martha was sitting beside her and looked rather grim. This place and process held no surprises for her.

The charge was read out and he was asked if he would agree to being bound over to keep the peace. He refused.

He tried to keep his voice level and failed. 'I don't know why I'm here; I haven't seen a solicitor yet.' Fear leaped out from his voice that no one was going to give him a chance to say what had happened, to tell his story, to give him his day in court. There was going to be no apology.

The magistrate looked angry, and not with the prisoner.

'You have the right to a solicitor, nothing will happen until you have seen a solicitor,' he said in very measured tones that implied he was not unused to petty injustice.

He was taken back downstairs to the holding cell. The others greeted him cheerfully and were keen to know what had happened. When he had got it all out they laughed at him. He was clearly not fit for their world. After a bit and another, an officer called him out to see the Duty Solicitor in what passed as an interview room. Although it couldn't possibly be the same man he had already had dealings with, he looked as pathetic as that voice had sounded that long ago night. Perhaps, like the doctors they use, cheap solicitors in police stations form a distinct species or anti-type. Interchangeable.

He was plainly annoyed to be bothered by a simple binding over. There were far more urgent and interesting cases to deal with than this purely routine Friday night brawl amongst the gay middle-classes.

'I don't know what you're worried about,' the Duty Solicitor started impatiently.

'Look,' McGillivray managed his anger with difficulty. 'It may cost me my job; I work for Social Services and I didn't do anything, nothing at all.'

The Duty Solicitor began again using his I'm-explaining-this-carefully-to-an-insolent-child voice. 'As you well know, that you didn't do anything doesn't matter. You won't even get a criminal record. Just do what they say and get it over with.'

He replied in the same tone, 'But it's not justice.'

The Duty Solicitor retorted angrily, 'That has nothing to do with anything.'

Trying to keep calm, McGillivray asked, 'What happens if I refuse to accept this binding-over?'

'It will go to trial. It's not worth it. Binding-over incidents never go to trial.'

McGillivray squared his jaw in a futile effort to look butch. 'This one will.'

'You'll only give yourself a lot more grief over something that is simply not important.'

The Duty Solicitor collected his papers and stood up. McGillivray did not mind; there was nothing else useful he could get from this man with no purpose. He now knew he was on his own. Of course, the police didn't care about what they had done to him, that they had stolen his peace and filed his laughter in plastic envelopes. He was no more to them than a statistic, a performance indicator who would now be processed according to standard procedure. The role of the Duty Solicitor was not to maintain the rights of the accused but to facilitate the whole mean process of clearing out dross from the cells so that the court could get on with its more important work. If the police had made a mistake, this would be a convenient way of rounding the whole thing off quietly and in accordance with due process.

McGillivray was not amused. He didn't feel like dross and was not going to be treated like it. As a Lewis man and an Orcadian, he had both principles and cussedness. They all knew that they would have to let him go now and he was not going to give in out of desperation to get out a few minutes earlier. He decided to refuse, to not comply, and to become an Inconvenience.

What was left of his rationality was sufficiently powerful to keep him quiet. Even McGillivray could realise that this was not the appropriate time for gesture politics, so rather than making a fuss, he bowed his head slightly and thanked the Duty Solicitor for his time demurely. This seemed to cheer the poor man up a bit and he looked decidedly happier as he bustled out to his time sheet and expenses form, both of which were rather overdue.

McGillivray was left alone for a few minutes until the officer arrived to take him back up to the dock. The magistrate this time was a woman whom he had never seen before. He felt calm and knew what he was going to do. She asked him if he agreed to the binding over and to her evident irritation, he refused. A trial date was set for the end of July. The magistrate said he could go. He exhaled.

CHAPTER 20

The court officials were gracious enough to let Maeve down to the prisoners' area to witness the exquisite humiliations of McGillivray's release; how they removed his handcuffs with a 'sir' or two and returned his possessions item by item. He signed the receipt for his cards and money to certify that he had not been robbed.

At long, long last, they left. They escaped the Court through modern front doors that opened automatically on their approach with a gentle sigh. They stood on the marble steps. McGillivray gulped in the stale air blown over from the ICI chemical plant; its fragrance bore him up on the wings of an eagle. He soared up and around the Town Hall clock and looked down on the miniature Cathedral far below, the vast emptiness of the Sussex Street Car Park and the dereliction of the Wreck stretching down towards the Tees. He flew on, fascinated by the two kids emerging from a kitchen window and doing the 250 metre dash towards the safety of their own homes and was astonished by their speed. They seemed to be hardly burdened by the weight of audiovisual equipment in their arms.

St. Hilda's had become his; its laws his laws; his whole land, small and shabby though it seemed, was all together excellent to him. He felt the draw of the river out towards the sea, but Maeve's clear voiced summonsed him back down to earth. He landed heavily, stumbled and fell. She helped him back to his feet and slapped his shoulder in mock irritation. He winced.

'For God's sake,' she worried, 'they'll have you back in there again in a flash.'

'Ach,' he shrugged, 'it happens all the time here, no-one will have seen.'

The two of them walked down to the Frontier. At the entrance to the underpass beneath the railway line three women were busking. Maeve said, 'Strange place to be hanging around, who has any spare money around here?' McGillivray nodded in agreement but put his hand in his pocket; the coins returned by the police felt warm to his touch. He stooped down to put them all in the hat. The money felt dirty and he wanted rid of it. The oldest woman, the one with the drum smiled thinly at him. They entered the tunnel with its dirty tiles and familiar smell of piss. The overhead light flickered madly against attempts of the gloom to extinguish it forever.

They crossed Tower Green. When McGillivray got to the house, he turned the stiff key in his own house door, pushed it open and walked around to make things his home. Every thing had to be touched, all the corners marked. His territory marked, Maeve brewed a cup of real coffee and ran him a bath with lavender scented bubbles.

He went upstairs and undressed quickly in urgent need to get rid of his soiled clothes and to get clean. He scrubbed both his skin and scalp to get rid of the smell of his custody. For the first time since Friday, he shaved using a sharp razor.

Although the next few days were as vacant and dreich as even Grimsbrough could produce, there was no opportunity for him to cease functioning or have a rest. The next day, apprehension drove with him into the office for a formal meeting with his employer to discuss the Situation.

That he was taken into the small counselling room marked the severity of his offence. Two padded chairs without arms faced each other over a waste paper basket and a box of tissues, just in case. The sole window looked over towards the factories. McGillivray was certain that he was waiting to be sacked. He did sums over and over in his head, trying to work out how long it would take him to get back to Scotland and if he would have his fare.

He wasted his worries. Jerome viewed the whole affair as an affront to his managerial dignity and assured McGillivray that although the Bureaucracy did not see the situation as disciplinary, it would be appropriate to seek support from his trade union; the Department viewed the incident as harassment and a formal complaint would be sent to the police in due course. The Manager exhaled, pleased at the effect of his own eloquence and then in a slightly more confidential manner continued to both caution and comfort, 'Gossip being what it was,' he smiled, 'it would be best for everyone,' an emphatic nod, 'if the whole matter was kept as quiet as possible.'

Jerome as Manager leant forward over his magnanimity and peered into McGillivray's eyes closely as if looking for a mote to remove. He finished with a flourish. 'We,' deep breath, 'pride ourselves on taking care of the psychological,' exhalation, 'well-being of our staff. We will arrange for you to see a specialist in post-traumatic stress disorder.' Another pause, longer. 'We will pay.'

The Manager in Jerome pursed his lips and examined his immaculate nails. After McGillivray bowed his head slightly he pronounced the dismissal with a gracious wave of his hand.

McGillivray maintained his pretence of being calm until he was out of the door. He ran to his desk and dialled Maeve's work number on his phone. She was waiting for his call. Both breathed a sigh of relief. After leaving a message for Adam he rang the specialist. To his relief and in breach of all protocols she agreed to see him in his own home.

Her manner seemed competent and invited such confidence that he felt no need to use the normal ploys of the Islander in peril, the casting of glamour over the English and the Southron Scot. They were always too easily entangled in a yarn spun from Celtic or Norse mythology. Adding in a dark colour of John Calvin and a little scarlet of queer-dom and a counsellor could be entranced for an hour and left with a comfortable sense of their own skills and a general fulfilment. But this time he really did have some work to do and thought it best not to fall back on textual duplicity. Maeve suggested an idea to him from some self-help book that seemed useful: that he weave a tapestry of his life, a working made from fabrics that would represent where he had been and who he had become. The counsellor agreed to support him in the making. Together they gave it form from the rags and rat tails of fabric ferreted out from around the house.

A bobbin of yarn that his cousin, a weaver of Harris Tweed, gave him long before became a warp and weft on a loom made from broomsticks. He weighted them down with wooden branches, sea-blanched, harvested from the shore beneath the British Steel plant in Redcar.

Glad to help, his anxious mother sent down a parcel of oddments she had reserved for patchwork. He tipped out on to the floor a scrag bag of memories: a fragment of a floral blouse that had belonged to his grandmother and still had the smell of her perfume, a duvet cover, all that was left of a pair of jeans with orange piping, his father's pyjama trousers, the detritus of many lives.

He had nothing to represent where he was now. So, on the first available Saturday, he went with Maeve around the fabric, junk, and charity shops of Grimsbrough. The haberdasher opposite the bus station was particularly fruitful. From there, he garnered coloured beads, gaudy feathers and edging fabric. There was even some heavy brocade, green, gold, and gorgeous.

He built up the work in layers, each representing some event or mood. He used grey and white wools intertwined with sea gulls' feathers bound with strips of herringbone tweed to represent the islands. Coming out was all scarlet, crimson, and pink. He added in gauze and cotton from some cheap scarves. More recent times were black, grey and a little beige. In a fit of giddiness he added in tinsel bought in a fifty pence shop.

Newer materials pressed down on earlier ones until they began to take on the compressed nature of the sedimentary rocks that run along from Hamnavoe, through Breckness and Billyacroo until they become gigantic at the Black Craig. Their meaning changed as the weight of fresh interpretation forced them in strange directions. Shadows appeared where there had been none before under strange over-hangings of significance. He wanted the work to be harmonious and integrated but it wasn't. Only he could have found it beautiful. The counsellor was polite, smiled, her head to one side as she encouraged him to clarify, to reflect and explain.

'Tell me more tell me why and what then where who?'

Her questions unlocked in him a frenzy for icon making that transmuted everything associated with his imprisonment. The cigarette pushed into his cell became a symbol of ultimate charity and was placed reverently in a little plastic box on the mantle above the fireplace. The golden cross and the 'Rights of the Detained' were mounted on card and hung on the wall. He bore witness to a truth known to all truly gay men, that anything can be made pretty with a little effort and some glue. On the far side of despair is hope.

CHAPTER 21

The house became more and more his as he continued the making, St. Hilda's too. Martha told people what had happened and so some of his neighbours began to smile at him more. Wrongful or rightful arrest was a common experience. He began to nest and to buy things, new bed linen, towels, a clock made out of debris from an old car. Some rather horny safe sex posters got stuck on to his bedroom wall to help him sleep. He had more sense though than to feel too easy.

Perhaps this need for comfort was due to the fear that grew gradually within him until it became like the wind back home, the distinctive element of his life. It developed within him as a wild flower, as lovely as a dandelion, a thistle, beautiful yet always unwanted and hard to remove. He had no idea when it began; perhaps its spores had always been around him but here in the fertile ground of Saint Hilda's it found all it needed to germinate, to sprout and develop leaves and buds.

He became a connoisseur of terror, able to appreciate its subtleties and distinguish between its different flavours and aromas. In the Old Cathedral or on the island shore, he knew the awe that arises, the numinous that gave birth to the sense of the holy. He had felt unbearable loss as a child when losing sight of his mother and knowing that she was gone forever he had screamed in the shops and would not be consoled, even when she found him. There was the pleasant fear, the adrenaline rush that draws some up cliffs and others to fairground machines. He remembered the certainty of damnation, the abyss that was always waiting to devour him.

He knew all too well the delicate anguish of waiting for a loved one, the fear that they will not phone, that something has happened or someone has told them the truth. He had seen in others the horrors, the delirium tremens, as undiluted emotions returned after years in the bottle.

There was fear, and there are fears, and McGillivray walked amongst them all and became sloppy with their love. In his arrogance and stupidity he grew almost to despise those who were unafraid and lived their pretty lives in an unreal world. He had become a wanker.

At first, he was more afraid of the dogs than the young men, the big dogs that roamed across the estate, their behaviour never predictable nor the edges of their territories evident. Their shifting dynamics made walking risky. A new head dog could render a whole street unsafe. The loners, the Tysons and Daisies, bred for their charm and their way with visitors were problematic enough yet they were nothing like as frightening as the packs running together. Not just one or two animals that temporarily escaped from the settee and Pedigree Chum for a wee jaunt with their mates but mobs of street dogs used to the exhilaration of the wild hunt, the pursuit. They were not untamed as such but semi-feral; they might respond to 'good boy, nice boy, let me past, please,' or they might not. One learned the rules on how to handle them.

Don't look them in the eye.

Don't act scared but be humble.

Respect.

The discomfort manifested itself in the unease he felt every evening as he came home from work. His routine was consistent. First, he would feel his chest tighten as he approached the border and have to make the decision about heading up past the young men assembled at Tapper's corner or take the long way round and brave the dogs. Then, when either peril was safely behind him, he would exhale and reach for his keys. He would feel relieved to find them but then there would be the new tension of what he would find in his home. His teeth would be clenched again until he got up to the corner of the Old Town Hall and saw that his front door was intact: a moment's relief.

Next, he would walk up the path, turn the stiff key in the lock, push open his door and enter. Each room would have to be checked in order to ensure that the computer, the telephone and the video recorder were all still in place and that no unclean spirits had entered the house uninvited. Only then would he put down his workbag beside the grey sofa and go back into the kitchen, switch the kettle on and make some proper coffee in a plunge pot. The dregs of the previous day would be scattered out over the back lawn as a libation to the new evening.

But nothing happened and he began to assume he was immune. Of course he was Deluded but he was not alone. Many others were also surprised at his ongoing good fortune. Various well meaners gave assurances that they later forgot. It seemed to them all that as nothing bad had happened so far, he would probably survive. He might even be seen as useful.

So, his unfortunate decision to stay in St. Hilda's was not reckless nor lightly made but based on the sound advice he received from decent people. He adopted the strategies they suggested to help him fit in and they seemed to work. Some of the local kids befriended him at an after school club where he volunteered; his hamfistedness caused them much mirth. He listened to their grandparents' stories in the Cathedral and attended their funerals, some with more pleasure than others.

CHAPTER 22

McGillivray was not alone on the night things changed; Maeve had travelled up from London for the weekend. They had spent the morning idling over newspapers, croissant and coffee that naturally proceeded into bread, cheese and home-made soup. Washing the dishes and looking out of the kitchen window he noticed that a red car parked under the stripling trees had become the centre of some children's attention. They danced, sang, and clambered over it crawling through the windows onto the back and the driver's seats to play real racers turning the wheel all the way to the left then all the way to the right. Screaming, screeching, swooping noises filled the air. The youngest was blond and adorable in a bunny jacket, maybe four or five, the oldest no more than eleven. Somehow or other, they puzzled out how to lift the bonnet and revved up the engine. A couple of older teenagers came up and had a poke about, offered a little advice then wandered off.

McGillivray lost interest in watching or more truthfully, did not want to be seen watching. He had learned that when he wanted to observe it was necessary to look from the corner of the eye. To see without being seen seeing means one cannot be called as a witness, the paramount rule of estate life. He got back to his own business and tried not to listen to the game going on outside. A short afternoon pleasantly spent cooking and gossiping, setting the table, a day of normal things. McGillivray got a bottle of aspiring white wine from the fridge and poured two large glasses. Maeve served up the food from the wok; pesto and pasta mixed with a little cream and some mushrooms fried in olive oil. They put on some Cowboy Junkies. Maeve asked him what he thought would happen outside. He was matter of fact about it, pragmatic:

'They'll torch the car; they have to, to get rid of the fingerprints.'

She laughed at him, 'Don't be silly, they're far too young.'

She had almost stopped chuckling when a huge explosion outside, the petrol tank erupting, caused them to choke on their drinks.

They leapt out of their seats and ran to the window squealing with excitement. Noses jammed to the window, they watched the dirt red flames consume the car. Common sense hit McGillivray hard, he ran around shutting the windows to stop the acrid petrol and rubber smoke filling the house. He had learned the hard way that the stench of burning could linger for days. He phoned the fire brigade who arrived within minutes all lights ablaze. The sirens scattered the kids at first but only as far as the nearest wall. Squatting behind it they watched the men in their yellow helmets and facemasks spray gallons of water that were turned to steam by the burning hulk. When the fire began to be under control, they showed themselves again and began to skip around the firemen, jumping up and down, their fingers twitching with excitement. No one chased them away. As the flames from the bonnet were extinguished they clambered up onto it and began to dance. Maeve and McGillivray watched their cavorting and pirouetting through the smoke and the steam whilst the fire fighters turned their attention to the rest of the blaze. It was a great game.

He put his arm around her and together they enjoyed the show. To the sound of lesbians singing to the accompaniment of acoustic guitars they talked excitedly for hours about how interesting the place was, about the creativity shown in poverty. They forgot about the conditions of the children playing outside or the pace of decay eating through the pavements.

A juggling group was set up at work. Learning to throw coloured balls in the air was meant to help social workers manage stress. They performed with a group at a multicultural festival designed by the council to promote harmony and diversity. Lost in unfamiliar scents, he allowed an Asian woman to paint his hand with an elaborate henna design. Some of St. Hilda's younger kids did too, but because they fidgeted and lost patience she only drew an initial letter surrounded by a heart for each of them. They were charmed that a grown-up wanted to play the same game as them and laughed around him and with him. The artist giggled for the whole half hour she spent working on a magnificent design. Only later did he appreciate what was so funny, that this was something that only women did just before they got married; he was cross-dressing by accident.

People were surprised that he was getting on so well over there. When Marie, a very pleasant social worker who was based in the next office, asked him if he had any difficulties, he became angry, and demonstrated the same defensiveness as the real locals at outsiders who tarred them all with the same brush or provoked trouble by asking too many awkward questions.

He told Adam about the conversation the next time he saw him and he explained to him that the narrowing of eyes that happened whenever he gave his address was basic risk assessment normal in the Boro; his new home was in an enclave where even the police accepted they had no jurisdiction. If he lived over there and liked it, if he was unmolested it meant that he was well connected, more dangerous than he seemed and therefore a threat. The listener would have to work out which pack he belonged to, what it was they didn't know about him, whether it would be safe to continue the conversation. He experienced guilt by accommodation. He stayed on because wildness exhilarated him and was energizing. He felt acclimatized, became complacent, and began to enjoy himself. He was an Idiot.

Perhaps the portents were obvious to everyone else but not to him. They are easily determined in hindsight but McGillivray did not notice; he had no crystal ball and could not tell the future. There were no clear omens; he did not hear the cuckoo call his name and no clock struck thirteen. Even black cats had more sense than to come to Tower Green.

CHAPTER 23

After integrating so well, or so he thought, he was more disappointed than angry when the thieves came for the first time to his house. It was a Saturday evening. He was driving back from a club with Adam when he took a call from the Police to tell him that 'Addicts no doubt' had flipped open the patio doors in his living room and helped themselves to what was there. They were not sure what was missing.

McGillivray's initial mistake was to ignore the state of the garden. His own patch of grass had begun to resemble a field with his pride and joy in its centre, a thistle that grew to the splendid height of five feet. Rumours spread that it featured on the latest ordinance survey maps; however, his immediate neighbours saw it not as an achievement but a threat to property values. A delegation was sent to his door to inform him of the collective will and suggest the appointment of a gardener who would bring order out of chaos for a decent rate. That he was able to pay someone meant that he had some disposable income. This was noticed.

The thieves had been efficient and considerate; no damage had been done apart from the destruction of the French doors. The Police told him not to take it personally; they had taken their time to get round to him and it was something that was always going to happen. If they had disliked him, there would have been shit on the walls and the sofa would have been slashed. McGillivray was hugely relieved that nothing worse had happened and went through to the kitchen to make tea for Adam and himself but the kettle was gone.

He rang Harriet, the landlady, on the phone that the thieves had left him. She made immediate arrangements for the house to be made secure. Some rather attractive men came round that evening to wall up the broken windows with huge sheets of plywood that Maeve covered in collage and poems copied out with garish marker pens. They were rather proud of the effect.

On the Monday following, the temperature began to change. He was on the way home from work as usual and had just got past Tapper's corner when one of the youths muttered something about fucking queers and idly threw a stone at his feet. McGillivray was not too concerned, blew him a kiss and called him observant. He waved, walked on, and didn't look around. Perhaps he wiggled his hips.

On the next day, a broad faced young man with a distinctive Adam's apple leant on a low wall outside one of the terraced houses near the shop. It was a hot day and his shirt was around his lean waist. His torso was beautiful and the prison tattoo seemed to enhance rather than detract from his beauty. He had been chatting to a neighbour but as he saw McGillivray pass on his way to the Border, he looked around him and swore. He asked a mate for the loan of a brick and complained loudly that one was never to hand when needed.

McGillivray thought it a great line and laughed when he told his colleagues about it. No, homophobic insults were not in themselves enough to provoke anxiety. Then, they were all around. Everyone hated queers. A gay man could be sacked if his breathing offended his colleagues or clients. No redress to the courts was possible; 'A Commonly Held Prejudice' was sufficient grounds to take away someone's livelihood. Bishops debated the humanity of homosexuals on Radio Four in loud debates about their ability to access the unconditional love of God. Murderers claimed to their Judges that the existence of the gay men they had swept away was so threatening it should be considered mitigation; the defence worked. Even in nice neighbourhoods the poofs got hurt. They probably deserved it. If only they didn't mince or kiss, or get so militant.

CHAPTER 24

McGillivray wrote a little poem about fear.

> It is fear that has built the stonewalls
>   and placed the bars at the window
> It is fear that has hung chains on my
> wrists
>   and set a watch at the door.
> It is fear alone
>   and I am very afraid.

The next Wednesday was his last normal day in that house. He had got up, gone out, locked the door, been picked up for work, worked and come home. He had made an uninteresting meal from some pasta and a jar of pesto and eaten it without joy. The insurance money had not come through yet so he had not been able to replace the stolen kettle or TV. Adam had leant him a radio and so he could at least console himself with the six thirty comedy. As it ended he realised that the prospect of the Archers was far more than he could stand. He decided to go out to Church.

A Mass for Peace was held each week in the Old Cathedral; chanting congregants served each other from a common cup and shared the sign of peace. Never more than half a dozen attended, the atmosphere amongst them always gentle and heavy with absent frankincense. He loved the service but their prayers went unanswered. There were never enough of them there; maybe six or seven more would have done the trick.

McGillivray left the house and crossed the plaza; the chemical breeze still fluttered the remnants of its video streamers from their lampposts and trees as he took the turning by the side of the Town Hall. The sun hung low over the Wreck, that long patch of wasteland that dropped gently down to the distant chimneys and factories, purple in the light. It was a fine evening; the weather had been good all that summer so far, the dandelions were doing well as were the nettles and the docken. He exhaled with relief as he went past Tapper's Corner, for once empty. The name callers and throwers of stones were elsewhere; Eastenders or Corrie were keeping the peace. Just past the pub, almost at the church door some kids from the play scheme shouted to him to stop, to show them the henna on his hand.

As they chatted, a beautiful child, the sun in his blond hair gleaming, cycled over and circled around them, proud of his new birthday bike, squirming with glee at his own speed and the excitement of his mission; some grown-ups nearby had sent him over to warn the other children of their imminent danger. With all the energy of his five precious years he screamed out his lesson again and again:

'Get away from him, he's a child molester.'

There was no malice on his face. He liked the sound of the words and was trying them out; they felt nice in his mouth and had an exciting effect. Anyway, he was just doing what they told him. McGillivray was sure he didn't understand their meaning. Then again, maybe he did know what they meant. Maybe he knew all too well.

The two McGillivray was talking to did understand; they turned around, their small faces white with fear and confusion and gaped at the cyclist. McGillivray was about to bawl back but he was just a kid on a shiny bike. What harm could small blond boys do? For a long time afterwards McGillivray would see that face and hear those words with their simplicity and clarity. Thoughts came as hard and fast as his breathing. If out of the mouths of the babes and the infants these accusations were allowed to come, if their foul names, untrue names were allowed to go unchecked, trouble would accelerate until there would never be peace again. Rumours would become facts and then he would be at the mercy of Tapper's Court.

He remembered his learning on how to handle dangerous dogs, good guidance for what to do now but he didn't want to just slink away with his tail between his legs. Sometimes danger has to be faced. If he acted scared then all would be lost and rumours would spread.

A young woman he knew offered flowers to the policemen before the battle of Trafalgar as a gesture of non-violent resistance. They were probably trampled in the first charge. McGillivray had no flowers; he chose to shout and, anyway, shelter and safety were not too far away. A risk could be afforded.

'What the hell do you mean by calling me that?'

Angry adults who do no worse than shout fail to intimidate Hilda's children. They had all seen far worse than that. The child continued to stare. His clear blue eyes fixed on him waiting for him to be dissected like a dead frog, curious to see if his dead legs would twitch when the electric charge was applied.

The court assembled behind him; the crowd poured out of the houses. Windows opened. Some men in the pub even left their yellow pints undrunk and cigarettes burning in the ashtray. It wouldn't take long. The jury was sworn in and prepared to deliver its verdict. McGillivray could not see them all. Later events swallowed some of their faces; of his neighbours, those he could see, some were curious, a happening here; others excited. The children in the playground were yammering 'Fight, Fight, Fight.' Others showed a certain kind of passing interest in what would happen but not sufficient to get involved until the outcome was finally decided. None of them showed any compassion or warmth for him. He had it coming.

McGillivray knew he needed sanctuary and was thankful it was close. He climbed the steps to the cathedral and took the large black handle shaped like a lion's face in his two hands. It would not turn. The door was locked. He had forgotten that the Priest was away on holiday. The door of the church was locked against him and there were stones in the air and falling at his feet. In the slowing of time he saw himself from above and it was like watching a film, not a high quality drama, nothing literary but a cheap morality tale from the 1950s from Hammer, the villagers come out with the pitchforks and torches to the vampire's castle demanding revenge. This was no film: it was happening to him; he wanted it over and with a better ending.

He knocked on the door of the priest's house but of course it was shut. He tried to regulate his breathing and keep calm. If he turned his back on the mob and took the long route home there was the risk of the unseen response, the knife or the brick behind him. They knew where he lived and would be able to cut him off. His other option was to walk through the crowd and try to face down his tormentors, not through some sort of courage but through a need to get back quickly in one piece.

The mob had now swelled until it filled the whole breadth of Sussex Street. He plunged into the swarm and they divided before him as the waters of the Red Sea did before the Israelites, and he forced his way through the tumult of shouted obscenities.

'Cocksucker! Child molester! Bastard! You had blue movies in your house. Pervert! You had filth in your house. Get out of here!'

The realisation hit him harder than stones that these people knew more than they should about him. They were not accusing, they were not taunting as children do. No, they knew he was gay and the only way they could know was because they had been in his house and gathered the evidence. They had his Apple Mac. They had read not only his diary but his private correspondence and business letters too. He had been opened to them and they were able to access as much of him as they wanted. They had seen that poster, the one on his bedroom wall. They knew.

The mob reformed around him. Some of the faces of the crowd were unfamiliar but he knew most of them. One, from the second or third house from the end, his sharp face contorted by hate, was screaming at him to get out, to get to fuck. Above all others this man was desperate to be heard. McGillivray's type, the queer type were not needed over there, in the Frontier lands. His friend beside him was taking his line from him. He had bad spots.

McGillivray knew that to falter now would mean his death. He kept his eye fixed on the goal of the corner by the Town Hall and kept walking steadily on. He was not silent but pleading. 'I live here too, I only ask for your respect. I am no different to you.' And them shouting in his face and him repeating himself. The stones.

CHAPTER 25

'My table thou hast furnishéd
in presence of my foes.
My head, thou dost with oil anoint
and my cup overflows.'

That verse from the Psalm, the 23rd, the one they sing at funerals was strong in his mind and it was for his funeral, but no he was not dead yet. The ordeal lasted for only seven moments. By the time he was through Death's Darks Vale and at the end of Sussex Street the shouting had ceased; they did not pursue him and so he allowed himself to breathe more easily. Still, when he got through his green door he slid home the two additional security bolts. The air in the house had changed, felt different, unsafe and unwelcoming. He tried the invocation that had worked in the cells. He cast a circle and lit some lavender oil but unable to risk salt in the landlady's carpet, the incomplete charm couldn't take effect. The lavender filled the room with the stink of decomposition, of all that air fresheners are used to mask. He picked up the telephone and dialled the emergency number of the police. Twenty minutes later, a small blue woman knocked at the door quietly. Her manner was rushed and breathy. She sat down on the edge of her seat declining a cup of coffee, nodding sympathetically as he told her the story and then offered advice. She genuinely did want to be helpful. She knew she wasn't going to be able to arrest anyone but still felt the need to be useful. She had got a community job because she was known as a good listener and so was very happy to tell others what to do.

'How did they know you were gay?'

'Because they broke into my house last week. They took some videos and they must have seen the poster on the bathroom and the bedroom wall.'

'Well', she said, 'Perhaps you should be more careful about

the things you have in your house.'

He wanted to scream at her. 'I am not allowed to have the things I want in my own living room in case I upset the burglars? A poster in my bedroom is hardly mincing down the main street in pink heels.'

She changed tack; bit her lip. Next time, she wouldn't make that mistake. 'Do you own the house?'

'No. I rent it.'

'That's good. Get out then. As soon as you can. We've seen it time after time in these houses. They take spite against someone for no reason and then they make their life hell until they have to get out. They shouldn't do this to you just because you're gay. It makes me sick.'

He wanted to say, 'If it makes you sick, if you feel a bit queasy just hearing about it, live my life for just one moment.' He asked rather faintly: 'Can you do anything to protect me?'

She seemed surprised to be asked the question.

'Not really. We could pursue some of them down there for public order offences but that would only make things worse for you. I will have a word with the local community officer. I think he'll be supportive.' She added reflectively, 'They wouldn't all be, down at the station. You know what I mean?'

He thought he did. He thought he knew very well what the police could be like.

A voice on her shoulder radio summoned her away. She went. McGillivray was left alone in the house in Saint Hilda's. He looked around for an activity that would focus his mind on something else.

He flitted through a book and thought wistfully about turning on the absent television or making a diary entry on the missing computer. The telephone, they had left him that, so he rang a friend in London who had endured serious harassment on her estate. Dog shit through the door, threats, but no actual physical violence. She stayed on in her home and survived. They chatted for a few minutes. 'Keep on going,' she said. 'There is nothing else you can do. That you've got a job doesn't help. You get resented if you have money, money that you get legally anyways.'

He looked out of the front door, the coast was clear and he scuttled around the corner to knock on Martha's door. They were not all rioters there. He was no Fag Friday surviving in a desert semi. She was horrified about what had happened, but hardly surprised. She made him coffee and broke open some chocolate Hob Nobs. She bestowed a couple on him and thought for a long moment before saying quickly, 'It can be like this, really bad. It will probably get worse before it gets better, but do not worry too much; their attention will soon get diverted on to something else. Don't let the bastards grind you down.' She offered him another biscuit. 'You know the Girls' – a lesbian couple who had one of the larger houses – 'they've never had any trouble. I'll get Margo to have a word with them. We'll see if that will sort them out.'

McGillivray drank his coffee.

'If you have any more trouble, it doesn't matter when, for God's sake come and get me. Yes, come and get me,' she repeated.

He went up to see the landlady. He was shown into the large kitchen of the rather fine house she shared with her husband and assorted members of her family. Over mugs of coffee they chatted about the situation. McGillivray laughed and began to tell jokes about what had happened. Fear lingered yes, but terror was too intense, too real an emotion for him to carry it for long. The unacceptable gets dismissed, it could not have happened to him and so it had not. Nor did the couple want to believe in the reality of danger. If they did, they would have to refund the deposit. Harassment, yes, they suffered harassment but physical violence did not happen there. Limits existed. She learned never to walk past Tapper's corner because of the comments and appreciation of the youths. Perhaps she even felt sorry for him, but he seemed determined enough and they were keen for him to stay on. The situation would be held in review but, of course, they would not stand in his way if he chose to move. Besides, no one should give in to intimidation.

As he left and started on the way home he invoked the Orkney Saints, a rune to protect him from his enemy.

Magnus be with us.
Ora pro nobis.
Rognavald defend us.

That night in his sleep, he strings the diamonds from the gutter on a golden wire and makes a necklace for himself. Lady Luck is with him for there are sufficient left over to make some dangly earrings too. He designs them to be suitable for all kinds of occasions, with a business suit for work or with sweater and jeans for Saturday pottering. They will even do for grand occasions too. Weddings. And Funerals.

CHAPTER 26

The old moon reclined in the arms of the new above Linthorpe Road, the long straight artery of the Town that ran from St Hilda's to the Suburbs. The pavement was clogged with couples thrown out of the long lines of fluorescent pubs. McGillivray tried to avoid their arms flailing for taxis and clutching at pizza and Parmesan as he pushed his way through with his eyes fixed on the pavement. He felt invisible, they were not his folk and this was not his time.

He was on his way to the Paradise. He had been sitting in the house with some poetry, listening to the Cowboy Junkies. Their music emphasised his sense of being alone, of it being night and so he became horny.

People who go to places like the Paradise have no need to justify themselves. Yet McGillivray felt the need to do so, to make something political out of it. When pushed by his own conscience or a third party he would say that he liked to 'people watch' or 'sleaze was part of the struggle'. All claptrap. His pretending to be an observer was, of course, a cheap sham. His pretending to be a wall flower was no more than an emotional camouflage to mask continual rejection, the same feeling he had as a small child, the little boy who longs to be picked for the team but is only accepted reluctantly, the clever boy who will never score. His queer politics was an attempt to justify his bad behaviour.

No one looking in from outside would have told him apart from the others. He fitted in with the pimps and the faggots and the whores. He went because he was desperate and needed to fuck. No reasonable offer refused, so he was far lower than the men and women who sold sex. He got paid less and was nothing like as picky, not even able it give it away.

He went up to the bar and had his first drink. Before he could order his second, the barman put another down in front of him. 'It's the guy over there,' he said, 'on the other side.' McGillivray smiled, thinking that not only was his luck in but that he was wearing his posh underwear. He gestured his gratitude by raising the glass. The man grinned back in reply and came over.

With clichéd blue eyes he looked hungrily at McGillivray and asked, 'Are you the dealer?'

'No', trying not to sound bitter, 'I am the drugs worker. The dealer is the other guy with long hair.'

The guy wandered off leaving McGillivray to contemplate the walls with their black, fake brick tiles. The glitter stuck to them sparkled in the solitary disco light. He sipped his beer. Who the hell comes to a place likes this? People like me.

And then Lance walked in.

No less than over the Frontier, in places like the Paradise rules are different. On a previous night, after a huge crashing noise, Adam pulled McGillivray into a corner. 'All hell is going to break loose. That was the porcelain in the women's toilets being broken up. The Lesbians will use it for ammunition.' McGillivray assumed that it was a sexist wind-up but a couple of minutes later he watched as a woman ran past with blood streaming down her head. Sanitation related injuries were not uncommon.

Yet, even in the Paradise, certain universals apply – even amongst the antinomians gathered in that upper room to dance, drink and copulate. 'Do not fuck the boyfriend of your Boss,' is one such. Not something that normally needs to be said. Indeed, to even mention it is sufficient to set the story into motion. Everyone should know what happens next. Yet the detail has to be spelled out. Inexorable justice follows upon folly as so often does the Clap Clinic and Rehab. Only a fool would think they are exempt. McGillivray thought himself exempt. He was a fool.

So they fucked. Together. McGillivray fucked Lance and Lance fucked McGillivray. At least they had the sense to go back over The Frontier and not do it in the soon to be sullied nuptial bed. They had a lovely time. They must have said to themselves that they did not mean for any one else to get hurt. Of course, Lance promised not to tell. Of course, he did. He must have done. Jerome was sufficiently professional not to show that he did and either conflicted or clever enough to wait. When one does the unjustifiable it is comfortable to blame intangibles. It was God's will. Inshallah. 'It wisnae me it wiz the drink.' It was McGillivray's fault. He should have known better. Should. What a fine word. Would. Could. Did.

CHAPTER 27

The Northern Scots have long perfected the combination of smugness and self-righteousness; McGillivray, on account of both heritage and training had evolved into a fine exponent of both arts. He was thrilled to be given a chance to demonstrate his skill by delivering a conference presentation on the kinds of outreach work he carried out in gay and lesbian bars in Grimsbrough for the County Council; his distribution of condoms to other gay men and the lesbian safer sex packs were always well received. The event he was to preach at was a regional conference on the 'Economic Impact of HIV'; a very proper and rather thin Tory Baroness was coming up to hold court and give the keynote speech. It was going to be a big shindig; scurrilous and nameless people spread false, though credible rumours that the Minister had not been north of Camden before.

McGillivray felt it important to look the part for that kind of gig. This was the time, he thought, to finally get shorn of the long, radical locks he had worn as a student and appear in public for the first time as a respectable grown up. Life, he felt, was finally going his way; the court case had just been resolved in his favour. The Police had caved in at the very last moment and the Magistrate had awarded costs against them. A solicitor friend who had given him advice took him out for a lavish afternoon tea in a department store on the proceeds where they sat in state to dine on crumpets and cake. Revenge is best served with lashings of real butter and Earl Gray tea.

So to further the celebrations, he made an appointment at the hairdresser nearest the New Town Hall. Throughout the long day of his scheduled transformation he felt nervous and fiddled with his doomed tresses. When work finally finished he crossed the Town Square to the hairdresser through the grey evening;

it was the kind of light that showed Grimsbrough at its best, the cracks and details blurred out of sight and out of mind.

The salon was an intimate place. Although it claimed to be unisex it was clearly unused by normal men. The sharp smells of hair lacquer, bleach and nicotine emasculated him as soon as he entered. Two or three other chairs were occupied. Someone was getting the special done, a blue rinse, and a close wet shave, cheapest component free.

The hairdresser he was allocated was the auntie he should have had, a middle-aged woman with long auburn hair, probably dyed and a green housecoat worn over formerly elegant clothes. She sat him down in front of a merciless mirror made even less charitable by the light bulbs that ringed its frame. He gripped the arms tightly as he was wrapped in nylon. When she heard what he wanted her eyes rolled with concern. She advocated caution.

'Sonny, are you sure? Your hair is very long – it's a big change you're making.'

'Yeah, that's why I want to make it,' he affirmed.

She shook her head slowly and advocated a compromise. This was the kind of situation she positively enjoyed. Whilst it presented challenges, it was well within her professional ken and she handled him competently and well.

'Look, I'll cut off a little bit first, three inches or so – we'll see how it goes from there.'

She took the scissors out of a lovely little silver cup that stood by the mirror. Some long dead artisan had fashioned it in the shape of a horse and there was something vaguely familiar about it to him.

'Where did you get that from?' he asked.

'Oh,' she laughed, 'I got that from my mother. It's been in the family for years. Pretty old thing, isn't it?'

She started to snicker snack with the shears, all the time mithering at how dry and brittle his hair was. 'There is no excuse for poor conditioning these days,' she said.

As the small piles of trimmings around him mounted, he closed his eyes and clung tighter to the protective arms of the chair. Three years of his life lay on the floor. He felt sick.

'Does your girlfriend know you are having this done? She'll

get a surprise.'

He looked at her closely, rather surprised that she hadn't cottoned on to him and shook his head. He felt far too tired for anything but the easy lies.

'I haven't got one.'

'Is it for something special happening?'

'No, no, I just thought it was time for a change.'

'Well, look in the mirror now and tell me what you think.'

He unscrewed his eyes, put his spectacles on and stared. The glass man surrounded by lights was at least five years younger, with a clean, bright face and laughing eyes. He began to smile.

'For goodness sake, take the rest off as well. In for a penny...'

She laughed and got back to work. The atmosphere between them changed completely into something playful and intimate, confessional even. In only another twenty minutes or so he was lightheaded and free.

That evening, before going to the Alabama, he dressed himself with especial care. He turned up about an hour after opening time, went straight up to the bar and ordered his usual. No one recognised him.

Barbarella was serving, took his order, pulled the pint of bitter and served it before meeting his eye. She pouted at him, pursed her cherry red lips and blinked twice, all at the same time, as she lifted the beer on to the counter.

'Good God man, is that you? I would never have believed it! You're almost cute.'

The news spread through the bar and beyond faster than the clap in an old time molly house. Someone applauded; another guy, someone he had fancied for ages but never dared speak to, bought him a drink. Thrilled by the unaccustomed attention, he hung around till closing time and then wandered home. It was a fine night, the clouds earlier had all cleared and so he – well, they – took the long way round avoiding Tapper's Corner. Better safe than sorry.

CHAPTER 28

The next morning he rose early for the conference, his speech, the recognition of his work well done. He took more than usual care over his appearance. The Manager had white polo shirts made as a fundraiser; white ones with the red AIDS ribbon printed on them above the left nipple. He put one on with smart jeans, shoes polished for once and a short cut black jacket of military style from Camden Lock. It was very calm, the early sun still low in the sky colouring the smog with blues and pinks. There were no dogs about and as it was far too early for the thugs to have recovered from their thievery of the previous night it was safe for him to go the short way past the Town Hall, across The Frontier and into the heart of the Town. He noticed that some of the lead was missing from the cathedral roof.

The conference was well attended by those who needed to be there. The Conservative Baroness read with appropriate conviction the speech that her researchers had prepared for her; in it, she acknowledged the sterling work done by his team and then sat primly in her chair of estate whilst polite obeisance was made around her. It was a shame for her piece of mind that no senior official had the wit to vet McGillivray's speech as a prophylactic measure.

He said what he thought. He thanked the Minister for her kind words and explicit endorsement of the free condom distributions, the lesbian and gay youth group, and the workshop, 'Hot, Safe and Horny'. No one had told him she was a Catholic.

Government Ministers, especially the Tories, were normally well protected from the views of the likes of him. She did not enjoy him saying how foolish it was to expect health responsibility from gay men in a society that denied them their civil rights, that equality in law was not just a human right but a matter of disease prevention. Without it they were wasting their time.

Adam had wangled a ticket to the event and found himself a seat at the back of the hall. Throughout the speech he had sat grinning and bounced up to him the moment it was over, all smiles and bear hugs. It was good, he said, to see the Minister squirm. Indeed, he thought her make-up would crack. McGillivray felt small eruptions in his stomach; he had not learned how to be politic and had no idea that he had been brave. He realised that he was going to be in trouble and felt the urgent need for something restorative. Some of his colleagues agreed to go over to the Alabama with him to 'celebrate'. They had a few and, it being a Wednesday, he went on afterwards by himself to the Paradise. The glorious moment had passed. He only had a half or two and left long before the ritual 'I will always love you' was played out christening the brand new couples who were swearing an undying love that was sure to last until morning.

He left. It was night.

CHAPTER 29

The night was heavy over Linthorpe Road. McGillivray was alone again; he faced the inevitability of the solitary walk home, the short walk to the empty house through the quiet streets, the dark streets. In cities, it was the night that McGillivray loved, the silent night when the cars and the shoppers were gone and only the others, those without good reason, were out. He had always loved the night, a time to think and to remember.

His encounter with the raw power of the Conservative party brought to his mind a night not that long before, his favourite night, better than his first kiss, his first sex, the night three years before when Thatcher fell. He went to Downing Street with a straight friend, another postgrad, to listen and wait at what were once her gates. They hoped for tangible evidence of change, to see her furniture pulling away in an unmarked van, or Denis drunk. Perhaps she would be taken to the Tower, never to emerge again until her head was removed on Tower Hill. A small crowd of her children gathered there until the police moved them all on. Everywhere that night, the police glowered from riot vans and on foot keeping crowds moving, desperate to contain the joy that wanted to dance down to the Square. On the other side of Whitehall, not far from the Ministry of Defence, a group of about thirty young people were harried down the road in the vague direction of Parliament; a black anarchist flag fluttered above them like a hoodie crow.

McGillivray shouted, 'Where are the others? Where is the party?'

'Telling stories of how we've survived her. Use your eyes Mate, look around you.'

He was right. Trafalgar Square was gloating. It had emptied itself of unnecessary tourists and only the ghosts of protesters made any noise: the nurses, students, miners, lesbians and the gay men, all who had suffered during her terrible years. McGillivray's own ghost was there cavorting. He could see himself in the crowds at many times with many faces.

In the eye of his mind, he saw himself on the steps of Saint Martin's in the Fields with the old Quaker women angry with the Gulf War allies destroying the children and then the scene shifted into a Pride march. He was dancing with a drag queen who wore an amazing wig studded with stars. She ran her hand down McGillivray's back, felt his left breast. McGillivray laughed and peeled away into the crowd. His friend was angry.

The pavement outside the South African embassy remembered the long picket and smiled at the anger of youth. Even the paving stones were singing.

It was night. McGillivray had always loved the night.

He could hear the voice of the Southern Baptist preacher with his long vowels, 'Jaiiiisus sayyess: *here comes the test, that light has come into the world, but men preferred darkness to light, because their deeds were evil.*'

Only those who are righteous in their own eyes dare to be in love with the love of the light. Those who are not so blessed prefer the complicity of the dark. For then they are safer from those at ease with themselves and the world. Besides, it is harder to be caught.

So conspirators gather.

Heretics look earnest in their conventicles.

Under the lamp a whore shivers. A car pulls up.

For a time, McGillivray had made his own cathedral on the famous walk in Holland Park. Devotion drew him again and again: even amongst the midnight snow, the sound and the rhythm of quiet feet walking, the pause, the look over the shoulder. On his knees he would look to the stars, glad that his tribe had the lovely, lonely places where the careful ones refused to go.

On this night, only his shadow kept him company under the steady falling of the rain. As he made the almost fatal turning from Newport into Linthorpe Rd, alone and lonely, he remembered where he had been and fell into self-pity. He crossed the Border by the walkway under the railway bridge into St. Hilda's.

The vast expanse of the Sussex Street car park opened before him, its chippie already blind in the distance. The rain was still falling, so heavy, so silent, that no one stood around idly; no one would taunt stone throw gathering hate. Ahead of him, there would be nothing but the empty night; he could take the short route past Tapper's corner.

The Glass Barrel was dark but it was not empty; from its wall three young men were watching.

The door opened silently and shut itself up again suddenly like a clam.

Turned fully three men.

Turned fully slowly.

Turned slow towards him.

The stick, a stick or a baton hitting the hand.

The Leader, their Lord, the Lord of the Flies, the Beelzebub, the man with the stick, with the broad face, the character from the bad film, the inept actor, looked at McGillivray and said, 'You are the Queer who lives on the Green.'

That was all and it was enough. McGillivray knew now the role he would play, his part in the play, the worst one, the part that ends in the first five minutes. His would be the case the clever detective solves just before the News at Ten. There would be a car chase and the life of an innocent party saved as kettles across the country are switched on gladly.

The three men, the three faces, the stick, they falling, beating him down to the ground. Feet. Fists. The stick on his head, on his ribs, on his back. A litany, an invocation of beating and blows. Their mouths and their feet merged into a single clerical Voice:

> Cock sucker, child molester, bastard,
> 	Cross The Frontier,
> We don't want your kind here,
> Why didn't you go back when we
> 	gave you a chance you bastard you
> queer?

And their fists, and their feet and their voices and their feet.

McGillivray curled up on the tarmac, clung to himself as the drowning man to the weed covered rock under their drenchings of blows and of curses. There was his body sore; the evil swirling against and around yet the fear in him gone. He attained a moment of clarity as he lay on the ground under their feet. He became calm. He was no longer afraid; indeed he felt nothing, not even the pain. They were together at last; he had met his queer bashers and they knew their prey. An old enmity was being enacted; he knew that the hen doesn't curse the fox and the trout has no feelings for the seal. No one cares. It is of no matter.

The men stopped. As soon as the attack had begun, it was finished and themselves walking away in the night towards the old red cathedral. They went away but they did not leave him alone, though over the next days and the years they would all try to be free. The violent sacrament they consummated that night created a bond between them all. As lovers, they entered his life and were in him and of him as sure as it was his own ribs that were hurt, as sure as the scar that burned on his forehead.

He watched their trainers and their long, baggy legs walking away. Under the stillness, the endlessly falling rain, he lay quiet for a long moment until he could no longer hear the sound of their footfall and knew himself to be both alone and alive. He uncurled, stretched out on the ground and then got to his feet. He brushed the dirt away from his new jacket and looked around. Grey light dappled the wet tarmac around him and covered his stains. He decided to take the longer road home through the arcs of safe light. As he walked with the infinite care of the drunken man who believes he is sober, he examined himself and made a careful inventory of his injuries. His lower lip had begun to swell; his tongue found the stump of his broken front tooth; his head hurt but he could walk, breathe. He was glad, for he knew he had got off lightly.

CHAPTER 30

McGillivray skulked through the shadows of Richmond Street and around by the back of the old Town Hall to his gate, his garden, and his house with its green door and the numbers three and seven in black plastic. He sought out his keys and found them eventually in the depth of his jeans. He put the key in the lock and tried as their voices assaulted him – 'There he is!' – to turn it but there was no turning and the lock did not open.

Terror was calling him with its clear voice and a smile on his wide face. McGillivray knew him fine; in the eye of his mind he could see himself on the other side of this Door, the safe side, using his strength to hold shut the door as he drove home the first bolt, the second.

Would they then try and force entry?

Would they smash the glass and reach their hands through the window?

Would fear be enough to hold the door of his life tight against them as he turned the key that would not turn?

Then they were there, the three, the four of them all together in his little garden. Close to him and his door looking over his shoulder. They were talking to him and civil, all neighbours together. McGillivray did not understand, did not know what they wanted, could not keep up with their intentions all changing like sun on the water.

They knew what they wanted. Their brief absence had been used to develop a strategy to regenerate the neighbourhood. In order to accomplish their objectives, they needed his help and so took on a reassuring manner, one man to another.

'We're not going to hurt you anymore,' the Leader said kindly. 'Just let us in, it's not you that we're wanting.'

The key betrayed him and turned gently. And there they were

standing in his lobby, in his own front room and he was there and there they were all in his house, Thirty Seven Tower Green.

CHAPTER 31

The light is on. They stand in their brightness, these three apostles and so behold him; he could see their faces. If he sees their faces again he will know them. And they know that he will know them and the horror of that knowledge is heavy upon all of them. For they all know that McGillivray could, McGillivray will, describe their faces if given a chance. If they let him live, he will find their pictures in the big book held by the policeman. It will be their fault if he did, their lack of attention to detail. They know and they know that he knows and they all know what they will have to do. Everyone who lives over the Frontier knows what they will do.

But McGillivray does not yet know everything, he is not acquainted with their names; no introductions are thought necessary, but he knows where one of them, the Leader, Beelzebub with the large Adam's apple, lives. That will suffice. This man has his friends now and no longer has any need of a brick.

His two companions are very afraid. The one who is the most beautiful is the most afraid because he knows his face is the kind of which dreams are made. He pointlessly tries to hide his face and reclaim the sanctuary of the dark in the solace of his coat and sweaters. To no avail, it is too late, McGillivray will remember. The Leader hits him hard in the face, no longer kind and accuses him of trying to plant evidence on him by bleeding all over his clothes, spraying his taint. McGillivray promises, fervently, faithfully, begs them to trust him for he is a Good Faggot, he will not bleed, will not tell, tell, tell, begging them to cease with their hitting and stop all the blows.

But he is lying. When the time comes he will go gladly with a song in his heart to the Police Station to make plain that which was hidden. There, once cautioned properly, amongst the twelve pictures in the plastic wallet laid like playing cards down on the table he will see two of them, the Leader and Prettiest staring out at him but unable to see. He will identify them and they will be caught. They will each stand in a long line in the Police Station while safe on the other side of the glass he will walk along the line unseen and he will say Number One, Number Three. He will learn the names of all three, Dan, the leader; beautiful Scott and the ugly one, the Gargoyle, who could not get laid and is forgettable.

This, Gargoyle, this thing thrusts a cushion into McGillivray's face to cover his eyes and commands him to lie face down on the sofa.

Gargoyle lopes into the kitchen, his back is turned so McGillivray could not see him selecting the appropriate knife from the convenient block by the sink, testing their blades on his thumb and smiling when he was satisfied and, so did not scream yet but he will. Scott rips the telephone from the socket and hurls it against the far wall but it is made of strong stuff and does not break. This is a mistake, he is either inexperienced or a fool. It does not dawn on him that all McGillivray will need to do is plug it back in. When they finally leave – they will leave – he will push it back in and telephone the police. The landlady's mother when she comes to clean the house will see blood on the receiver. She will wipe it off with an old rag and a little disinfectant. A bit more blood, a little more mess.

They are screaming at him, determined, 'Where is the other one...where is your mate...where is the other one...the one with the long hair?' All the time blows to his head and his body. He is confused, perhaps it is the shock or the hurt, but he has no idea who they mean.

'There is no one else here. It's just me.'

They don't believe him. Dan runs upstairs and peers into the bedrooms, the bathroom but finds them empty. He sees, he must see, the safer sex pictures on the bedroom and the bathroom wall. These mind him on why he is there. He charges back down stairs with new purpose and fury.

'Where is he? We know he is here we have seen him.'

'I live alone who do you mean? There is no one else here. Who, who do you mean? Please, please tell me.'

'So there is more than one then, you filthy bastard, you cocksucker.' Blows.

McGillivray has made a mistake and begged their forgiveness. 'I'm sorry, I'm sorry, I'm bad, I'm sorry.'

He has fallen onto the sofa beneath the gift from a lover, the quiet voiced boy with his beautiful hair, the print of the lame girl in the cornfield who clutches the earth with her twisted hands. She tries on her broken limbs to crawl to her house, her distant house and it seemed to McGillivray then that it was forever shut to her.

His hands were raised against their hitting and he no longer knew why they were hitting him, enraged, angrier screaming and howling that they'll rearrange his face, the cunt, 'I'm a bastard, yes cocksucker. I'll be who you want me to be.'

Voices merge again.

'So why are you lying? You bastard, why are you lying? You bastard. You bastard, we'll kill you.'

Gargoyle took the melody, his voice above the combined voices of the Leader and the Prettiest:

'Where are the notes where is your money the notes?' and he was trying to persuade him that he had none; he didn't have any.

'You've been to the bank, bastard, we saw you, why are you lying?'

But Dan butts in, 'Don't give him your money, we don't want it.'

He is no fool; his actions are pure. As he is in no hurry, he takes the time to explain to McGillivray why they are doing this to him. This is no mere robbery. The Leader is well aware that if they take money and are caught the offence is aggravated. Queers can be beaten up but not robbed. Property values must be respected.

They are defending that which they love from terrible danger. He is only thinking about the children, their holy innocence; an innocence that death could preserve. Indeed, he is explicit about this and stops hitting for a moment to make sure McGillivray understood. He articulates it clearly and is almost as beautiful as Scott when he says it, despite the size of his Adam's apple.

'If my children, I have three, came near you, I would kill them.'

McGillivray sees that the Leader is no artisan. No, this is a holy man whose act of denial gives him the right to make Judgement. He is not the kind of hypocrite he detested most, the kind who would tirade against ills elsewhere and then try to ignore them in his own family.

However, nothing on earth is unalloyed; the Leader changes his mind and decides he does want McGillivray's money and wants it badly. He joins in with the thin descant: 'Where are the notes where is your money, the notes?'

McGillivray found in the depths of his pocket the black leather money pouch that has all of his cash in it. Dan counts out its contents, at least three pounds fifty. This is hardly enough. Cleverer than his acolytes, he knows that McGillivray is no longer lying. No one is daft enough to lie over money when Terror comes over the threshold. He changes tack; plastic cards are worth more to him than twenty or thirty pounds and he demands them now.

McGillivray never knew where anything was especially in a crisis. He can not remember for his life where they are and makes his best guess that they are in the Filofax at the bottom of the black shoulder bag in the living room. Scott runs through but returns without it, empty handed, red-faced with fury. They are outraged, they have so tried to be kind, to give him a chance but despite that he has dared to lie to them, must think they are stupid. So now he has to be punished properly and they are hitting him again with the stick and their feet and the fists and their mouths and him swearing he's not lying beg them to let him go through to find the cards, any other cards and anything else if only they'll stop, if only the tempest of blows will abate.

They paused, stood back; he gasping in air, filling his lungs. They let him get up and go before them into the front room, his desecrated room they had emptied of peace. The black shoulder bag had to be where he always left it in the corner between the grey sofa and the bookcase. He reached out for it but it was not there. The black bag was not there. He could not find it. He was very sorry.

Scott acted; the blow when it came, the single blow breaks against McGillivray's head as is right, salt in his mouth and his eyes and the white foam and him falling forwards into the infinite blandness of the grey cushions. He sees gold, the lightning in the corner of his right eye and also the Face. Clearly before him, filling the white page now. Impassive, immutable as a Soviet hero in stone, this man of the people, disfigured by no impure emotion neither anger nor rage twisted his beauty. His blow, the swing and its impact are measured with a simple grace that causes McGillivray to fall again from the rock into the marbled waters and he is losing his foothold, the wave pulling him into its lovely embrace. He falls into the ocean and under but struggles up to the surface breaking the waters that want now to close over his head; consciousness is not torn from him but something is, the last of his faith.

McGillivray's world was one where discourse on miracle was common place; in Hamnavoe the seals shed their skins and walked into town on their own two feet to head for the dance in the Town Hall; there, even carpenters did not have the grace to stay dead for long. Older children learned about faith in cheap paperbacks that told stories about heroes and martyrs in simple language indistinguishable from folktale that showed what God could do, would do, if allowed by the faithless. There was a book with a damaged spine and yellowed pages he had possessed in his early teens about a woman and her family who hid Jews in a secret room. Because of her simple kindness to those in the apple of the eye of God, her entire family was lost in the camps. None of them had to die. They could all have had their very own graves. In the inferno of Ravensbrück, God was with her. She never doubted, not even when her sister died. On the night that they were betrayed, when Terror and the Gestapo came to their little shop, the commanding officer raised his hand to hit the sister, not a young woman, in her face. She cried out to Jesus for help. The tormentor replied, 'If you say that name again, I'll kill you'. But he did not hit her again. Not then.

As McGillivray falls, he sees the woman as in a Seeing, hears the voice of the officer and the prayer that brings a monster almost to humanity. He knows what to do. As did the heroine, so now McGillivray calls to Jesus for salvation.

Only Dan heard him and he was not pleased, he was no Nazi.

He pulled McGillivray up to his feet; holding him up by the

shirt, face to his face, his teeth and his eyes fierce and screaming at him his liturgy, his choir joining in with the appropriate refrain for the rite of Sacrificing the Queer.

> The Priest says to the victim: 'How dare you say *help*?'
> Refrain, the people, they sing. Cock sucker, child molester, bastard,
> The Priest says: 'You ask me for help.'
> Refrain, 'Cock sucker, child molester, bastard,
> 'I'll kill you; I'll smash you.'
> Refrain: Cock sucker, child molester, bastard.

McGillivray knows now he will die, that now he knows the end of his own story, a moment of perspective denied to the normally living. Nothing now is to be wasted. Every blow scars in his memory. Broken, each fragment of every moment precious.

'Cock sucker, child molester, Bastard.'

How many blows can he count? At what point do they cease to matter? Whilst he can count he is still alive.

He knows that his blood, his good blood is on his head and his neck like a garland of roses. Flowers blossom on the grey ground of the carpet. He is trampling it in, running, now desperate to find the cards, to be a Good Fag, a Nice Queer who will give what the nice men want so they will leave go. But they don't. Dan hits him then Scott and the Gargoyle too. His thoughts collapse. Grammar falls into the pain, and they are all hitting kicking him and they will not stop and he did does know how they will stop or if they are able to stop and the front room the blows on his back fallen running the blow and the bag is behind the door where it always was and where they could not have seen it.

McGillivray laughs.

His Filofax is open in his hand and the cash cards are there in their place. He takes them out and holds them out before him, his head bowed.

The stick falls on his hand. A single blow. A bone breaks. He hears it. McGillivray screams.

They say 'Quiet,' they say, 'Shut up, be quiet you cocksucker, bastard be quiet.'

They demand, 'What is the number? Where is the bank?'

He tells them.

NINE

TWO

TWO

FIVE

'Go', he says, 'help yourself, the money is there take it. Albert Road is the bank it's not far.'

They lust to know how much they can get and he does not hold back. He had just been paid, tells them the truth; it does not cross his mind to lie. Later, his wise friends and the bank manager will say to him, 'What, you told them the real numbers?' In their comfortable rooms, they would have handled it differently. What would a man be advantaged if he kept hold of his savings yet was left with only his own blood as a shroud to cover his face?

Besides, they know where he lives. They will always come back.

Greed and excitement confuse their thinking, they stand at the front door talking quietly and quickly deciding what to do. Scott and the Gargoyle defer to Dan who with his greater experience has clearer ideas on how to proceed. He orders the others to go to the bank and get as much money as they can whilst he remains to guard McGillivray to ensure that he has not lied, bad fairy, and played them false, just to be rid of them, because he no longer wanted their company. They hesitate but Dan pushes both of his minions firmly out of the door. His back turns against McGillivray who is lying unseen on the floor. His mind is now occupied with money, greed and working out how much his friends can be trusted. Will they be faithless? Will they come back? Will they be afraid of him enough to do what they're told? In that moment he loses his vocation as 'queer basher' and becomes a mere robber. He lost his focus, so his skill, and was damned.

McGillivray has a chance now, just one and he has to decide how to use it. He has three options; the first and easiest action is to lie where he is. If he does that he will die. The Gargoyle and Scott will return to the house. They will have no need to leave and will continue their work until the longhaired lover returns; they will have time to enjoy themselves. The Police will say in the morning that it was a one-night stand that had gone wrong.

The second option is to scream, to attract help from the neighbours. He knows this will fail; all who live within St. Hilda's learn to be blind and deaf when confronted with evil. Their mouths are bound shut by the need to not be a witness, to not have to tell, to avoid the bricks through their own windows and the knife in the dark. No one will hear him, no matter how much they have heard.

His final choice is to attack the leader with his bare hands. He does not have the skills or the knowledge of the human anatomy to hurt him, let alone kill him.

He is clear that whatever he does it will not save him. He is going to die. He remembers the lessons he had learned in the Police Station. Nothing he can do will make his situation worse so he may as well resist. If he does not he will be another gay man who does not outlive his own tale. They will remember him as the passive queen left on the floor who took what they, the kind gentlemen, the nice straights, doled out to him. That outcome bores him.

Desperation and folly pull him to his feet and throw him at Dan's back to shove him out of the door and out of his life. He does not see the bread knife in Dan's right hand as it turns and splits open his scalp. If he had seen it he would not have moved. He screams out for help to summon the angels and neighbours, murder, help, death comes, help please help, brushes him off like thistledown help murder minded calling help lashes the queen fist blood toppling help snarling cock sucked the bastard the cunt summons cannot see to help him, to help to come to him, to help him the bonny brave boy who is being attacked by a vicious queen, who staining clothes blood, the poor honey, his mother, the police, the poor honey poor dear did the nasty poof hurt you did his tooth hurt your fist O, my hinny, my buddo, my lovely, my darling.

The noise, the screaming, the skrekking, the helling and ballyhooing of the Wicked Queen scares the others, they are afraid of the nasty loud queen who will not be silent and die and they are calling to him, brave Scott and brave Gargoyle call to their Leader, the good Lord Dan now, to come with them, now, to the bank, for the money.

He went. He is gone. McGillivray lives.

CHAPTER 32

The room was empty. McGillivray was alone with his blood and the fear; the door was wide open spewing its light down the path. He pushed the two good bolts home. They slid true and fastened the door. The rain had stopped.

He was safe.

He plugged the phone in and it was still working. He dialled the three nines.

A woman's voice answered 'Which emergency service do you require?'

His broken mouth said 'Police.'

He gave the phone number on prompt and the address at Tower Green blood but he was hardly able to speak, to be understood.

'And I'm bleeding they are outside help they'll kill me the bank my card.'

'Can you wipe yourself?'

'Don't leave me don't go I'll hold onto the phone breathe slowly calm down but I'm bleeding.'

'Calm down. Breathe. Can you still walk? Go and get a towel an old one, are you there is your face hurting breathe, breathe slowly in out in out in out. In. Out.'

Her voice, the voice of the breathed made him calm, as she, this woman cared and she loved him.

There were people at the door. They were banging.

He was convinced they were back and he screamed, 'They've come for me, My God, they have come for me', but the woman was calm, she said, 'It's the police'. McGillivray asked her again if she was sure they were not back. Her voice uncoiled him and he slid back the bolts, the first and the second. He opened the door.

It was the Police. And he opened his green door with the black numbers.

And they came into the lobby.

And they were there for him.

And they took him to the ambulance.

And they helped him up the steps and he was bleeding, his blood on the door and a trail in the garden and he was sat down and he was driven away and over The Frontier, safe from St. Hilda.

My friend's Hilda.
She's from Whitby.
We went dancing at the Paradise last
night.

Techno.
Techno.
Techno.

CHAPTER 33

McGillivray was in the ambulance. Although he was glad that no one was hitting him, there was no safety, not from the blue and white towel he held to his face or from the good Lord who refused to ward him from the young paramedic; the pixie in green embroidered with his badge of office continued the assault with barbed questions. McGillivray could not answer, he did not know where he was, could not think.

Leaning forward, voyeuristic and judging, the young man persisted, his need to know pushing him on.

'Why did they do this to you?'

'But why did you live here if you are one of those?'

'Don't you know what this area is like?'

'Didn't you realise what they may do to you?'

Deeper he fell, impossible, close. He chose not to, was unable to answer; answers need words and there were none left to him. But the imperatives continued their beating as the lights of the town, the why, why, why, and the uncomprehending town flashed past the window and brought him into the compassion of the hospital.

They put him in a wheelchair and left him alone, his emergency, his crisis to them now a matter of routine. Someone else was waiting, someone more deserving who was Straight, who did not live in St Hilda's. They left him there, in his wheelchair and the long corridor, the long passage that leads into the heart of the hard mound raised over the dead stones.

A nurse passed him, and another. They became like the figures of time on a Swiss clock and he learned their ins and their outs. No one who mattered knew where he was; he needed help and there was none. He had to make a telephone call but there was no phone. He attracted the attention of the third nurse who passed on her fourteenth round and persuaded her to listen. She muttered into her chin something about his impatience that he could not hear and bustled off. Time passed, yet she must have done something, or perhaps it was coincidence, but a porter appeared who wheeled him down the long corridor to the phone mounted at shoulder height on the wall. He still had some coins left to him but the keypad was out of his reach, untenable, whispering silent hatred. He sat.

Another long wait, the sands of his time sinking, and a passing nurse who could no longer avoid his distress asked if she could help. She handed him the receiver, dialled a number for him.

The phone at the other end rang; it rang again, three tones, five tones, seven tones. She pumped in his precious coins as a voice, a weary and a tired Adam asked who was there.

'It's me, McGillivray. I'm in hospital.'

'No, I'll be all right.'

'I have been queerbashed.'

'Yes, I am hurt.'

'Could you come down please?'

He had to repeat himself several times, the coins running out, so that Adam could absorb what was being said to him.

McGillivray let the phone hang where it was and hunched in his chair. Time slipped and when he looked up next Adam was there with him, leaning over and looking. Somehow he did not scream. Simple questions, kind questions, much heavy breathing, a gentle hand that cared. Touched. For the first time, the story was told.

Eventually, at long last, the doctor, the very young doctor examined him with more questions:

'Why did they do this to you?'

'But why did you live there if you are one of those?'

'Don't you know what this area is like?'

'Didn't you realise what they may do to you?'

He told the story again. He would tell it again and again in the next days. Already a formula was beginning to develop; the walk home, the approach by the young men, the first attack, the walk home and then, the second attack.

Treatment without care continued. They took him on the x-ray and listed the harm. They had broken his ribs and fractured his right arm; three teeth were snapped off, several wounds to his head. His left side, he had curled on his right, a long and sinuous bruise and, as for his face, he could not be recognised. He was in shock.

A nurse began the process of cleaning up his head. She wore rubber gloves and provided treatment of the kind a child would suggest. She glued the worst of his wounds together with the kind of adhesive one buys in a hardware store. Then she stapled its edges together with staples, from a staple gun. The only tools missing were vinegar and brown paper. When eventually she spoke, it was to forbid him to wash his hair for two weeks.

As his head and his hair were still coated in dried blood, he panicked and pleaded for her to clean him up properly. She refused. She said 'No.' Again and again he implored until at last she was annoyed into care with her bad grace and unkind hands. She had sharp nails.

CHAPTER 34

They laid him out on a bed in the vast dormitory they kept for observatory purposes. Perhaps he slept, the deep kindness of sleep allowing release from his crisis, the little death. If so, it didn't last. Despite himself, he woke into the glare and bells of the clinical morning. The whole of that day he lay still under the white sheet immobilised by the difficult pain of being alive. The huge weight on his chest stopped his breathing and his head screamed pain in his ears. He drifted off through drugs to the sleep where an angel came to him. To prove his identity he showed him the wings he carried wrapped up in a convenient box strapped over his left shoulder.

He woke to see that an unrecognisable woman had come up to his bed. She wore a blue clipboard that had all of her interest. Without lifting her eyes, without saying her name, she demanded one thing from him through her officious lipstick. Her teeth were stained red.

'Why did the police tell us that you were HIV positive?'

It was visiting time; the ward was full of the weary and the distraught. A bored man looked at him straight from his bed, his family gathered around him went silent. McGillivray stuttered, 'I don't know, I didn't know I was. I am not. They made it up.' Gay meant positive in their eyes, faggotry was infectious. That was why the woman refused to wash his hair, she had not known enough to know she would be safe.

She left him alone. The people opposite went back to their conversation, but still the bored man stared.

He was visited; he did not invite them but still they came, and more, and more as the word of what had happened spread through official and informal channels. His colleagues grieved around him, a chorus of complaint that they could not believe, did not understand how anyone could do this, behave like this to anyone they knew.

He knew though, and so did all the other people who had their living across The Frontier.

CHAPTER 35

Whilst McGillivray was lying in the hospital bed, things were being done Over There. Jerome showed his mettle and was even heroic. He rounded up some of the brawnier bureaucrats, those who looked as if they pushed more than paper around and drove them in a borrowed minibus to Tower Green. They parcelled the contents of the broken house into boxes that were distributed amongst their spare rooms and attics. They worked in a hurry; they didn't know what to take and had to differentiate his taste from that of the landlady. In this way he lost a vase bought in Whitby and acquired some lace doilies.

As they were working, Jerome, not a small man amongst the nomenclatura, stood guard clutching a hammer to serve as a club. A crowd gathered outside the house, maybe 30 to 40 people, shouting insults at them and threatening, calling them queer lovers, faggots. As the van drew away, the mob dispersed with its honour satisfied. The estate was now germ-free, cleansed.

The poor house was not allowed to rest yet. The forensics moved in to photograph and catalogue McGillivray's very own crime scene with their space boots and scattered finger print powder. They took pictures of the chaos in the kitchen.

One of them asked Maeve, 'Did the thieves do this?'

'No,' she laughed, 'he was never very good at washing up.'

That night and the next, the brother of the landlord stayed in the house by himself with a crowbar rather than a hammer for company. They were well aware of what happened to houses left unoccupied on the estate. He saved the building from cremation and ensured that the central heating system was not stolen. He risked his life to save a house worth less that £20,000. The poor lamb, he must have been very afraid.

On the third day, they painted the front door red. The carpets must have been professionally cleaned. An advert appeared in the paper. Someone who did not know the area rang the Landlord's mother and not long afterwards moved in. Perhaps they stayed longer.

McGillivray knew none of this until later. Adam and Maeve didn't tell him how they had found the house. He was unaware of the ransacking; of the torn clothes thrown on the floors in the quest for hidden valuables, the juggling balls gutted, the grey sofa shredded with knives. Worst of all, they said, was the blood; his blood was everywhere, on the carpets, on the walls and over the phone. Everything he had touched was tainted. The men must have been covered. No wonder that they were afraid. The ground is holy where the blood of the martyrs is shed.

The Police, two men from the CID came to his bedside, both middle aged and in suits. McGillivray shrank into his pillows the better to be hidden from their investigations, with no hope of gentle treatment. He was wrong. The men veiled the bed with blue curtains and drew up two hospital chairs. Adam and Maeve, fresh from his flitting, stayed with him. The men smiled at him, asked how he was and introduced themselves to him with their ranks and names. The older one, Middleton, leant forward, his manner solicitous, the jacket of his Marks and Spencer's suit straining.

'We know what happened to you and why. We want you to know that we are horrified and will treat this as a serious crime.'

The other, Clark agreed. He had the build of a man who enjoyed his football on a Saturday. 'This is obviously not a safe place for you to give us a statement. Where can we contact you later?'

Adam and Maeve looked at each other; they had nowhere for him to go. McGillivray had been propelled over The Frontier as a refugee with nothing at all, without a toothbrush or shoes, not even a shirt. Everything was lost to him apart from their love, the love of good people. The two of them conferred over his bed and made the decision on his behalf. That evening, when he was released from hospital they took him to a house they knew in a small village abandoned by the coal board. Maeve would go with him to keep him safe for the next few days. Her work was understanding. Then they would reconsider the situation. He went. The nurses changed the linen on his bed. They probably didn't burn the sheets.

That night then, he began the long journey home, just the first stage; they only took him twenty miles but it was twenty miles nearer the North. The village itself was a desolate place. The friend's house was dusty and empty but there was no need to look out of the window. They ate fish and chips out of paper. Afterwards, he had no memory of there being much warmth or anything else but the pain and constipation. He didn't have a bowel movement for four days.

The first night of his new life was marked by the visit of Middleton and Clark who drove up from Grimsbrough and arrived just as the fishy papers were being put in the rubbish. Maeve made instant coffee and found milk that was just about on the right side of turning. When all were sat down in the borrowed front room clinging to mugs, the officers asked to speak to him alone. With an indignant Maeve in the other room twisting, Middleton asked if Maeve was his girlfriend and so was unaware of the reasons for the attack. They didn't want either or both to be embarrassed. What fine men.

McGillivray called Maeve back in and all four of them laughed, cathartic laughter, healing but agonising. The pain in his ribs crushed down on him and there were moans mingled in with the laughing that turned into tears. She held his hand. 'I promise you,' McGillivray said, 'I'm not her type.'

Middleton and Clark looked at each other and nodded. Clark took control, 'Very well,' he said with well-developed level tones, 'now start at the very beginning.'

McGillivray got his voice back. He told them it all. His attackers had been right, he was a Bad Queer who would not keep his word. They should have killed him when they had the chance because he betrayed them to the Police and told the whole story of their encounter with a song in his heart. He described them fully, held nothing back about how they had first met, what they thought of him and him them. No, he didn't know their names; they hadn't been introduced even though it looked like becoming a long-term relationship. However, he was certain he knew where one lived, the Leader, he who had thrown the first stone lived in one of the houses near Norfolk Street; he could finger him. The officers wrote it all down, slowly repeating each word back and transmuting the text into evidential gold. When they had finished, all those hours later, when the official note-books were closed, his words were taken away from him to be processed with assurances that they would do what they could, the men would be caught and would do no more harm. They were sincere.

Maeve and Adam nursed him for as long as they could; their gentle love made a castle around him that only a very few were allowed to penetrate. They took him a parcel of his clothes that had been salvaged from the wreckage and laundered for him. Those he had been wearing were left stained and bloody, his white shirt with its red ribbon embroidered and his new black jacket. They were wrapped up in tissue paper and put in a brown paper bag from Ikea and laid to rest in a cupboard with other relics of the time spent with Hilda.

CHAPTER 36

A couple of weeks later he was half carried by Adam into his camper van and laid out on its back seat. They drove north as far as Alnwick, where he was handed over into the care of Rüthe, an Orkney friend who lived her life in translation. She had driven his parents' old red car all the way down the long roads from Stromness at their urgent request. On the long road back, on the A9, her earnest driving did little to ease him; each bump and jolt seemed to inscribe the miles in his ribs. They stopped in the bare minimum of places, him aware of the unhealed bruises and the grime in his hair, she watching the faces with their judging eyes. Her dominant presence formed a shield against the questions unspoken and answers refused. Accommodation was booked, no the 'full' sign was not up but there was no room in the house, try the bed and breakfast up the road. No one met their eyes. Better that way.

At long, agonising last, the little red car shook off Thurso and took the last couple of coastal miles down to Scrabster, a village that deserves its name. Some love it, but if any poet has sung of its charms, her work is no part of surviving Scottish literature. It is a ferry terminal, a pier and a place for fishing boats. That is all. To the islander heading home, it is a place of impatience that combines charmlessness with the prospect of island air, a foretaste of home. They drove the car off the tarmac of the Scottish road and onto the pier. He was off the mainland. He rejoiced. The gull on the bollard watched him and made no comment.

The day was blue; sky and sea mirrored each other under a clean sun. The ferry took the westward, good weather route past the small island of Stroma, its lighthouse pure and white on the cliff and then attained the lea of Hoy, the desert of basalt crowned with sandstone and heather, its scarred sandstone cliffs falling many hundreds of perpendicular yards to a slate sea. He had lived there a little and knew all its names, Rackwick, Skar, Rora Head, the Geo of the Light.

The Purser used the loud speakers to draw the attention of the tourists to The Old Man. They all turned their cameras to the right and clicked obediently. Their awe caused them to miss the other wonders, the Leaden Geo, the Geo of the Sow, the Head of Saint John. An eighteenth century moralist despaired of Hoy, calling it an island much given to superstition, belief in witchery and drink. Presumably, he had a point. On another kind of day, when the fog holds down the hills, its extreme and forbidding quality sets the fancy loose and easily leads into bleakness of spirit. Many ghosts are there: Nuckelavee; the cursed warriors who fight in the valley each night; the small child who still runs up from Greenhill to his grave in desperation to avoid the wreckers and placers of false lights. The Devil had chased a man along the length of the Stoney Watter but been outrun.

Then they were rounding the Kame and the Mainland stretched itself out before them. He was home. And there were the cliffs from the Black Craig to Marwick, a little more on and then the island of Graemsay with the Hoy Low light and the heavy fortifications, the gun towers and lookouts where the memory of soldiers would ward him for a space.

In the Sound there were many seals. The curve of a porpoise broke through a single wave and then was gone. The promise of Stromness, the prosaic reality of Hamnavoe filled his mind and desires. There was no more need of poetry. With Rüthe, he leant on the rail and studied the moving lines of the West Shore as the boat drew in ever closer, past Breckness and the kirk yard at Whaurbeth, the last home, where we all go when the earth, the fire, and the flame are ready to receive us.

The boat turned round the Point of Ness with its single beacon to keep vessels off the rocks. Stromness was where it always is, a dozen small piers and slipways, many closes and lanes running up the granite hill. McGillivray studied each intently, recognising them, loving them all. Rüthe put her hand on his arm but said nothing. He understood. They were back.

His mother and father, both then alive, stood together at the door of the house to welcome him; something that wouldn't spoil if the boat was late waited on the stove. They gave him frightened smiles this time and tender hugs but these did not last long, no; they could not sustain his gaze anymore than he could theirs. In front of him they tried to manage their shock but they had never seen a man injured like this before.

He was changed but the house was just the same, the coffee in its jar marked sugar beside the sink. They wept and prayed in private. Nothing had prepared them for this, no Book to guide them.

He heard their lamentations through the thin walls of the council house and felt responsible for their grief and hated them for their inability to cope. It was their misfortune to be nearer than his enemies and so they became the focus of the hatred and mistrust he had learned to feel for all heterosexuals. The three men with their sticks and their fists looked at him through the eyes of all straight people. He could not return their gaze.

Wherever he went in the house, the three men followed him just out of his vision. When he was out in the garden they would send the little boy on his bike to give him a message; he knew he was always in their minds. Sometimes, he forgot he had been attacked and only remembered when he saw his face in the mirror or laughed and felt the pain in his ribs or caught his tongue on his broken and stained front tooth.

Then his heart would beat faster. Breathing would become shallow, nausea would rise in his stomach. Hands, armpits and back would become sweaty. Pain would develop in his chest and upper back. Horror would double him up wherever he was, make him cling to his knees and keen for himself.

CHAPTER 37

McGillivray's family was well aware that he was not very well and so unable to work. To be given respite from employment, he needed papers to be signed and medication allocated by the local doctor. He would have to leave the house and go to the other end of the Town to get to their fine new premises built on the site of the old garage. They had done the place well, a good example of health authority architecture with local art hung on the walls as a humanitarian touch.

To get there he would have to walk along the Street, the theatre on whose stage all our island dramas are acted out. The high rituals of birth and death, the tragedies of the good man gone to drink, the drowning, the harvest; they all take place there in the ever watchful presence of the Town.

He would have to turn left from his house and then go down the Manse Lane and turn left again on to the Street. He would have to head past the open door of the front bar at the Royal Hotel with its small crowd of drinkers at the door; opposite it there would be sick people going into the Pharmacist for relief. He would pass the hub of conversation in the Bakers, pass the kids outside the café. The Town would see his bruises and his scarfed head. They would know and the whispered conversations would follow as a wake breaking against the piers and doors of the town, waves of meaning that cover lives in interpretation and determine their meanings over the long years.

On his first attempt to leave the house he got as far as the bottom of the Manse Lane but then a small child, a well dressed boy, maybe 5 years old, came ploughing towards him along the cobbled street on his chopper bike. McGillivray felt the beginnings of the fear in him, his shoulders tensing, the nausea rising in his guts. He ran into the support of the narrow lane and stood very still until the child had passed. When he could draw the good air back into his lungs, he turned round and scuttled up the back street home, not relaxing until he reached the safety of his front door, the door always unlocked. Anxious eyes tried to meet his but nothing was said. He cancelled the appointment and made another. The receptionist had no need to ask why. Everyone who mattered knew everything that mattered.

They learned from their mistakes. On the next attempt, his father ran him there in the small red car. The receptionist glanced at him as he gave his name and then took his seat under the eyes of the uncomfortable waiting room. No one met his eye. After an age, he was called through.

The doctor was an incomer too and a believer. With his head kindly to one side, he heard McGillivray's story, the already familiar story, and prescribed his therapy, then leaned forward and said, 'With our shared faith you know that healing comes with forgiveness – you must learn to forgive.'

Everything in McGillivray wanted to smash things, to break the head of the doctor and scream 'Shut up you fucking bastard and sign the forms. Give me the prescription and the sick note. Give me release.' He smiled slightly and said nothing.

The pad was signed, the prescription collected from the austere pharmacist but the gentle sleep guaranteed by strong chemicals took time to arrive. In the meantime, he had dreams that were so bitter and intense that sleep was as bad as waking. Some of them were no more than side effects described in the leaflets, others were the mind working through trauma in vain attempts to purge the symptoms. He had no mechanism for differentiating between the products of the pharmaceuticals and his misery; he began to lose touch with his own symptoms, even his distress betrayed him. He was going mad, knew it and was desperate for help.

There was hope though. Apart from the sickness form and the prescription for Gilead's balm McGillivray got something tangible from the Doctor that had the potential to be useful, a referral to see a Community Psychiatric Nurse at the island's mental health services.

CHAPTER 38

McGillivray was not able to get on the bus the day of the appointment so his father took him in the red car through empty chat to the named nurse at her clinic behind the Kirkwall hospital. She led him through to an interview room and invited him to sit down in the chair marked out for patients by the box of tissues placed on a small round table. There was no ashtray. He didn't want to cry but he felt the longing to inhale the comfort of smoke. He felt the tension of withdrawal.

She seemed fine to him, this CPN, this Community Psychiatric Nurse when he first saw her, a comfortable person, neither unpleasant nor uncaring; indeed she was fairly middle – middle aged, middle height, middle dressed but rather thin.

She did all the right things; she asked him what had been happening and gave him the fine gift of silence. She waited. It was not her fault that he was tired, that he had run out of words, was sick of his own story and had resorted to the Selkie cliché. She must have sighed. Of all the stories in Orkney that are used up, wrung out and best left, it is the myth of the Seals who become human and leave descendants. Gay love stories have been written about them, performance artists have turned them into foam sculptures. The only humiliation left is the inexorable descent into animation by the spiritual heirs of Walt Disney.

'The seals', he said, leaning into himself, 'had been reckless enough to leave their skins above the high water mark as they played in human form in the shallows. Obsessed with their games they had been unaware of the man who, hidden amongst the dunes, had been watching them from his loneliness and lust, how he had found the pelt and taken it away with him to his low croft on the hill where he found for it a dark and secret place.'

His eyes fixed themselves on a box of big words and bright colours to her left. He gulped in some breath.

'She couldn't find her skin; the seal woman couldn't find her skin. She couldn't get back. They had to leave her alone. She was afraid, naked and afraid. There was nothing she could do. Then that bastard went back down to where he knew she was. He pretended to be kind, to be surprised and offered her help. She thought he was her friend and that he was kind but he wasn't. She thought it was love that they were making but it was rape, he owned her, possessed her and used her for years. She did not know she was a prisoner.'

He stared at the white bookshelves which were empty of anything apart from unread reports that no one was brave enough to discard, good work wasted, poor practice unchanged.

'She lived with him for years; they had children, five I think. Some of their descendants are in Stromness now. Anyways one day the bastard and the oldest kids were all out working on the boat or the farm or whatever and she was alone with the youngest that had a sore foot. Anyways she is looking for the skin, she must have known there was something wrong, she must have suspected over the years because she was looking but she could never find it, maybe he had changed in his manner to her. Anyway the child says, 'What are you looking for?' and she replies, 'For something soft to make a shoe for your sore foot.' 'Why don't you use the old skin that Daddy keeps behind the stone above the fire?' She asks her daughter, 'Which stone?' And the wee girl in her silliness points to one just above the lintel that is loose and there in the space behind it is the skin, oiled and smooth and supple.'

He really wanted a cigarette but it was not allowed.

'She kisses the bairn on her head and runs out of the door and as she is running to the shore she is stripping off her clothes. The neighbours are watching, they are always watching and they see her running into the sea and becoming something else and diving and she feels the water against her softness and her pelt and she is stretching the old muscles and moving with the water grace and is free. Her bairn is crying but no one who can hear cares, the wee girl is bawling for all her worth. She knows fine that she is always going to be alone now.'

The nurse looked at him and said, 'That story obviously means a lot to you.'

He did not reply.

His time was up.

CHAPTER 39

McGillivray had agreed to meet his Father in one of the many Kirkwall cafes but he had far more time than he anticipated. He stepped out of the clinic into the rain, not a polite or gentle rain but a sombre drenching. The Town was as cheerless as ever, always depressing to people from Hamnavoe. Needing to get out from under the weather, he went into the silence of the red Cathedral raised almost nine hundred years ago by the Vikings. To the Southerner, raised on the tales of their monkish enemies they seem to be murderers and villains, but to us they are mighty scholars and adventurers who travelled in longships to Jerusalem, Greenland and Byzantium. Kol, father of Rognavald raised the Minster in memory of Magnus, Jarl, Saint and Martyr. From all over the North the pilgrims came here to his shrine to hear mass and seek healing for diseases of perspective distorted by poor sight or madness.

Sigurd of Dale, the son of old Tandri went mad. His kind neighbours sewed him into an ox hide and carried him south; a long voyage he had but worthwhile for when he was laid on the tomb he got back both his wit and his health sufficient to him much to the relief of his friends. How on earth could they have got him back home if he had stayed mad? Could they have faced another journey?

Whilst healing despair often, he was not above inflicting it on those who slighted him. A thief who stole gold from his shrine lost his wits as did poor Sigrid from Unst who did not desist from her sewing on his feast day. Both were only restored to sanity after promises and pilgrimage.

Somehow or other the bones survived both the greed of the relic seeker and the purifying zeal of the Reformer by being sealed in one of the vast stone pillars near what had once been the high altar. There they had been found a century or so ago, re-interred and a plaque hung to mark the site.

McGillivray did pilgrimage in his turn. In his madness he sat before the tomb on one of the hard rush-seated chairs and rocking slightly, hugging himself, he began to pray repetitively, rhythmically the old words, *Magnus Orcadiensis, Ora Pro Nobis, Magnus of Orkney pray for us,* again and again and always the rocking, *Magnus Orcadiensis Ora Pro Nobis*. But he got the words wrong, around him the Presence changed, became unwelcoming. He shivered and went back out into the still falling rain.

That night McGillivray slept. He stands in a chapel of undressed stone. A type of lead tracery covers the walls in Celtic design. Light pours in through great windows and he sensed the sea and its music. He was happy.

Through the door, he could see in the distance the shape of a man amongst the shadows of the marshalled poplar trees. Is this the man he has come looking for? The man turns and looks at McGillivray silently through the veils of the evening. His breathing is quiet but his heart rejoices. The man stands by a lake and moves around towards him. The shadow smiles.

McGillivray becomes aware of the hills around him, the black valley and the stony water. As he moves nearer the man changes his form. He is now on a horse that is not a horse but a thing of the sea. His clothes are archaic and dank, hair like kelp. But the worst is that he and his Steed have no skin. McGillivray can see all their bones and sinews, the blood coursing through veins and arteries. It is McGillivray's death that is on their minds.

McGillivray turns and runs and his breathing is heavy and the fear is holding his feet to the ground and them moving towards him their breath on his neck. He is sweating, his breathing laboured short pains, sharp. He is running and the running is all that he is. His mind is begging for prayers to call out to God but his lips and mind are both frozen me mercy, me mercy.

McGillivray awoke and still the fear was upon him; he was afraid to sleep but despite his protesting it claimed him and threw him again into the Sabbath; the local Brethren are gathering at the pier head, God Willing, Weather permitting.

They had chosen to leave their perfectly small meeting place, their little tin tabernacle, to stand and sing together near Sunday sinners in the Hamnavoe Hotel. Their little pink faces, gleaming and well scrubbed, give testimony to the cleansing power of the blood of the lamb. McGillivray, dreaming, is full of good will. He decides to go down to the pier to bear public testimony with them to the Cause before the assembled town drunks. Catcalls are never pleasant. 'However, duty cannot be shirked and six days shalt thou slumber.'

He goes upstairs to get ready. There is no need to change out of the simple grey green suit he had worn at the morning service. He brushes his red hair out fully over his collar. He checks his reflection in the cracked mirror and feels quite pleased at the over all effect, of both confidence and modesty. Nothing was either too elaborate or too fancy. 'One,' his mother used to say, 'must always dress as if about to be summoned before the judgement seat. Remember!' she would continue, 'that which is whispered shall be shouted from the rooftops.' Underwear must be clean.

He fusses over his choice of shoes. Heels are probably a tad too much. Stilettos tut over the flagstones and leave a trail of disapproval in their wake. He would have to wear flats again no matter how unflattering they were to his calves.

He pays a little visit to the smallest room to wash his hands.

The pink edged Bible, AV, good enough for Paul, was collected from the bedside. He runs his manicured finger, plain varnish of course, along the living room bookcase for the Sankey. It resisted coming out.

He glances in the mirror above the bureau to check his lipstick. A backsliding hair is firmly tucked in place. It was five minutes before the hour. The time had come.

They are blessed, the rain holds off despite the luminous clouds. Although the year is wearing on and the autumn equinox was close, there is no wind. His hair will stay fine.

McGillivray walks through the town briskly. He turns left towards the pier and acknowledges curious glances with a nod or a quiet smile. He is able to hear the public address system crackling into life over the words of the opening prayer. He is late but not too late. They would not really miss him. His footsteps quicken slightly until he reaches his firm place beside the preacher. He opens the clutch bag with a click to let out the reluctant book. The hymn begins. His loud voice boomed out over the quieter voices of the rest of the elect. The angels were singing, eagerly anticipating the one sinner who should repent. Just as he was, he was coming, with no plea to thee, O Lord, he comes.

He woke.

CHAPTER 40

On the second Sabbath day after his return, he felt himself well enough to go to the Kirk with his parents. They sat in their normal pew on the left hand side of the Kirk. Even the congregation was changing; he would never have gone back if the holy ministers were still in charge but now 'a lady minister' had answered the Call, she had been a lawyer and was far too pragmatic for many of the Evangelicals who had left to feast on the Word elsewhere. Praise Be.

Everything about the Kirk was familiar to him; the stained glass windows with their Nordic Messiah surrounded by swarthy coloured men, the blue of the carpet, names carved into the wood of the pews by generations of bored boys. The only thing strange was the lack of homophobia from the pulpit. He was not yet safe.

The minister was in the pulpit. She stood to give out the psalm, the Eighty Fourth, in the Scots metrical. The first verse was wonderful, that it was written by a shepherd king for the sons of Korah mattered not. It felt eternal.

> How lovely is thy dwelling-place,
> O Lord of hosts, to me!
> The tabernacles of thy grace
> how pleasant, Lord, they be.

He had no need to look at the book in his hand. He knew the words but had no memory of learning them. Even the sparrow was noticed and allowed to remain in the house of God to nurture her young under the protection of the Divine. He could see her in the eye of his mind, comfortable, happy, flying to and forth to bring food to their hungry young. What fools! They thrapple her, the three men, as soon as they come into the sacred space by the choir's door at the right of the pulpit. They leave her feathered corpse on the grey carpet and pay it no further attention. Neither minister nor people acknowledge their presence. Only McGillivray sees the Leader, Dan, he with the heavy eyelids and the pronounced Adam's apple, take the minister's high chair beneath the pulpit. His two accomplices sat one to his left, the other to his right.

The Leader glances at the Bible laid out open by the Beadle on the communion table. He gets bored and starts to tear out the pages one by one. He crumples them up in his large hand and throws them onto the floor, sheet by sheet, then chapter by chapter. The other two, they just sit and they stare at him, alone now, in his pew. The younger one, the one with the jacket, taps his hand with a juggling stick and begins to whistle. McGillivray felt the sweat on his palms, the clenching of his gut and the dread. He looks around at the other members of the congregation but they do not see the intruders or perhaps they don't mind them being there; it is a judgement; queer bashing is holy work.

McGillivray got to his feet and pushed past his father and mother who had to half stand to let him out. Embarrassed eyes watched him run to the front of the kirk; he stooped down to gently pick up what he thought was the broken sparrow and raised its trammelled corpse to his ear and listened in vain for a pulse. He fled with the little heap of feathers and blood in his hand through the blue double doors that lead out onto the little hill and down to the street. No one else saw the three young men stand up and follow him out into the brightness of the day. He took the turning to the right and headed along the street towards the Ness and beyond that to the West Shore. They were still there.

> For God the Lord's a sun and shield:
> he'll grace and glory give;
> And will withhold no good from them
> that uprightly do live.

In the past, whenever there had been need, it was out on the West Shore she had come to him, the *bat qol*, the daughter of the voice who spoke to the Prophet after the tempest through the mediums of salt, wind, rain and air. He went to meet her where he had always found himself to be waiting; where as a child he had learned the Numinous.

Just beyond the Ness, its campsite and the Old Lifeboat Slip are the Tender Tables. There, in the days before swimming pools, those children who learned to swim did so among its low cliffs and geos with their tiny patches of grey sand.

In his mind, it is not a bitter Sabbath morning but a Tuesday afternoon; unseasonably warm, perhaps in March, the early seventies. He sees himself, the wee McGillivray, immune to the cold, all knees, sandals and no breeks and a-straining from his mother's hand whilst he searches the patch of stippled sand looking for doubloons and diamonds.

The stone lies there waiting to be found; itself, an island in its own tiny ocean; a wee world where it has been left to rest by the morning's tide.

It has not been a short journey, a long space from its igneous cradle, a narrow shining seam in a far off cavern, earth fires cooling and then a persistent grinding in the fankle of oceans that bore it over the globe to that spot, that precise place, that child.

For the smallest moment the clouds change allowing a spit of light through that set everything on fire, a fallen star.

McGillivray sees it, then 'Treasure!' ran over screaming and crouched down, stroking it with sticky fingers.

'It's lovely Mammy. What is it? Can I keep it?'

The clouds move on. The light goes out.

'It's just a stone, Love. Don't be daft. Leave it. Throw it back.'

The memory faded. He inhaled sharply and continued to walk. Farther round the shore, the double rut track leads to the final harbour, the kirk yard where the Stromness dead have left our land in their stone ships for centuries. As he got nearer, he became consumed with powerlessness and his incredulity at what had happened. He tried to reason out the unreasonable and to accept the unacceptable. He could not. It was not fair. As a child, there is normally a rationale behind a punishment, a sanction, pain. Occasionally, there may be no obvious logic behind it, then the eternal cry of the angry child arises, 'It's not fair!' There was no justice behind the attack of the three men. It was not fair. There was no one to appeal too. It was not fair. In no sense had it been deserved, but the child inside needed to believe that the aggressors were in some sense in the right. The unprovoked, the disturbed, the bad and the mad are demons too wild to be heard by the civilizing fire. They must be kept out by the dark. There had to be a reason behind what was done, yet there was none and there could be none. No lessons were there to be learned, nor any higher purpose served. Shit happens. There is no destiny, fate, providence or Lady Luck. Santa left home with the Tooth Fairy and they went down to the Flattie bar for a drink. It was not fair.

Just on the shore side of the kirk yard's boundary wall, in the unconsecrated ground that belonged to no one, he began to dig, his sharp spade turning the sandy ground. The day wore on, people came and went but no one spoke to him. No one helped. He dug deeper and harder. He placed the sparrow in the hole and covered it over. That which was, went.

An epitaph on a Hamnavoe gravestone:

> *They lived happy and died peaceably.*
> *Blessed are they that die in the name of the Lord.*

He looked up from the bare shore to the naked emptiness of a slate sky that seemed to spread out forever, the sun lost behind thick clouds. The heavens held only the promise of rain. He knew that he would die with his birth name and no other, no longer any need now for protection or comfort. He had become broken as bread and no more redemptive. Justification was no gift of faith or through the death of another. His own pain and his blood were not salvation, for there was nothing to be saved from, no reconciliation needed. He was alone with the mallimaks, mallards, and the smallest of the sand hoppers; they were sufficient for him, but he felt very alone.

CHAPTER 41

McGillivray could not hide from the eyes of the seagulls looking down from the chimney pots or from the cats skulking along the main street forever. He could not keep away from the eyes and the tongues. No one there knew how to respond. His very presence invited questions from loud children. The violence written on his face demanded the kind of answers from their little parents that contaminate innocence; their pleading eyes would beg him not to make things worse, not to bring up the bad South; to understand that unpleasantness is best confined over the water, on the other side of the Jordan, outside Eden. An Angel with a fiery sword stands on the pier and keeps the damned far away to protect us. Nothing bad has ever walked through these streets or haunted. There are no ghosts here and never will be.

But there are and he was one; a presentiment transformed McGillivray into something other, something fey, but without the common decency to be one of the dear departed in their stone boats down on the west shore. No, he had come back to haunt the Street and now stood in their way. With those who were brave enough to approach, who did not nip into the lanes and closes when they saw him, the interactions were always difficult.

Donny came up the lane as he went down, Donny whom he had fancied in Primary 7 with his blond hair and lanky legs, who now worked on a farm with muscles as majestic as a Clydesdale but his brain no faster.

'Whit happened to you beuy? Whit happened tae the ither chap? I bet he came off worse.'

McGillivray laughed, 'I cannot stop, I have to pick up my prescription before the surgery closes.' He longed to say, 'I want to tell you the truth, to have your arms around me but your wife would not like it.'

Then, Old Dougie of Foss drawing on a fag outside the bar of the Royal Hotel, 'Man – I wis in the war but I nivver saw a face like yours.'

Then Mrs. Cumlaquoy, lovely Mrs Cumlaquoy with her felt hat of cerise that made the grey street bright whom he loved on account of her toffee tart she had made for him when he was seven. She was good friends with his mother but he did not know what she had been told.

'I heard aboot your accident; it's made me afeared to go sooth.'

He wanted to stop her distress and her memory of the boy he once was, the laughing boy now all bruised, to her distress he wanted to say, 'I would not alarm you, Mrs. Cumlaquoy. I would have your world lovely and your peace intact, do not make me make you think on sorrows your goodness cannot change.'

So all he said was, 'I am fine, we are coping.'

'You are brave beuy, I dinnea ken hoo you dae it.'

He smiled and tried to look heroic. To him the word didn't fit. He had been unlucky to be in the wrong place, too stupid to heed advice to get out and then fortunate to survive. She held his hand for a moment. She was a widow. Her bright young man had not returned from a beach soaked with blood in Normandy.

To David he told the truth. They had had pints together, David had stood by him when the tongues had wagged, and he deserved honesty.

'I was attacked.'

'Really, beuy?'

'No, they were trying to drive me off the estate or to kill me,'

'Kill you?' The shock on his kind face, this was his friend.

'Yeah,' McGillivray replied working hard to keep the fear out of his voice. If the attack had continued, I would be dead.'

'Are you all right talking about it? How are you now?'

He replied, 'Yeah OK, but still a bit shaky,' or 'Still alive,' but not the truth, never the truth, not even to David the truth, *I was crippled with psychic pain earlier on the way back from the shop. I thought about screaming in the street. I thought I could see Them in the corner of my eye. I thought They were coming for me although I know that They are far away and will never be on this street or any other in Orkney. But they are etched on my eye and are with me.*

'Let me know,' David said, 'if there is anything I can do.'

McGillivray smiled and thanked him.

In the old days, the Town had employed a bellman whose task it was to walk up and down the street to make announcements about the activities of the Council and also publicise commercial opportunities, that such and such a cargo had landed, that seed corn was now available. Newspapers with their classified ads had made his services unnecessary as had the activities of the woman known to all as Peggie Gabb, her real name long since forgotten. She smelt out news in the air and her blunt nose pulled her as fast as her varicose legs would bear her towards McGillivray whose conversation with David was coming to an end. The latter, alerted by the tapping of her stick, looked up with pale eyes and fled. She placed herself in front of McGillivray and there was no escape, her walking stick and shopping bag as effective as any set of shackles.

'I am so sorry to hear what happened to you, was it a car accident?'

'No, I was attacked.'

'No,' she muttered. 'Wicked people in the South, they would have been after your money.'

Her mouth savoured every word. There was information here that was perhaps not yet known at the Eventide Club.

'How much did they get?'

He did not want his attackers tainted by the foul mouth of Peggie Gabb; their intention had been pure, their calling honourable in its strange way. They were better than her.

'They were not thieves, it was not money they were after.'

Peggy was as thrilled as if the sainted Queen Mother, God bless her, had given birth to Beelzebub right in front of her. 'No, what on earth can they have been wanting?'

The whole Town would know whatever McGillivray said to her within twenty minutes. It was no longer time to hide. He had not seen his good blood shed, he had not survived to hide now. Gossip, Peggie and be damned.

'They were not wanting anything, Mrs Gabb, they were queer bashers and they wanted rid of me. I am a homosexual, you may have heard it mentioned.'

That was enough for her, she picked up her bag and scampered off, her only dilemma the choice of shop to go in to spend her news. Andro Huip, whom he had never liked, came out of the Bank and saw him. McGillivray saw him consider nipping back in but deciding not to, to accept the challenge from the Lord and do his work gladly. McGillivray considered him to be the kind of fascist, then common but now so much more rare, who believed that there had never been any joy south of the Pentland Firth. All conversations with him degenerated into comments on the iniquities of incomers and the horrors of places further away than the south end of Hoy. Andro put on his best holy smile composed of a slight lean forward and a set of dentures, newly polished. The sun glinted off the top left molar. It had been commented, by Peggy and others, that this religious stoop meant that his eyes were constantly at breast height. Mrs Cumlaquoy had no time for him.

'I was so sorry to hear about what happened to you. I am remembering you in my prayers.'

McGillivray did not say to him in the middle of the street the speech he had prepared, 'Andro, you wrote that letter to the paper on the marriage of people with similar genitalia, I will not have your prayers. If you accept, Andro, that queer bashing is wicked, you will have to challenge your idea that lesbians, gay men and others whom you consider deviant have the right to respect and life. The inerrant word of Scripture is wrong, your attitudes fallacious and if there is a hell, it is where you and the other hypocrites will surely go, and hopefully quite soon.'

He kept his silence for Elspeth was approaching with her hand extended.

She was from South, but you would not know it, she gave him a sorrowing look and said, as if regretting his survival, 'You were mentioned in the gathering on Sunday, you and your parents.' She did not need to explain why she considered his parents were so impoverished. To her, homosexuality was like drink, an affliction that infected certain families. It's discovery always explained a lot.

Neither Andro nor Elspeth were as crude as the clerics of hell in their fine Latin churches who deplored the attacking of homosexuals but were not surprised that otherwise decent folk responded in outrageous ways when they saw two men kissing or women holding hands and so undermining the values of society. He saw it in their eyes though. He knew that they would ask for prayers for him at the midweek meetings. In over heated front rooms they would bow their heads and just asked the Lord to help him repent and return home to the fold. There would be great rejoicing for does Scripture not say, *As we know God works always for the benefit of those who love him, who have been named to his will.*

CHAPTER 42

As in those days the morning mail only reached the Island in the early afternoon, mornings were not distressing. After lunch the tension would grow in his guts and reach its peak at about 2.30pm. For about an hour he would listen out until he was certain that nothing would arrive for him. Each day the same pattern for several weeks until eventually the Postman came down his path and delivered not one but three envelopes. The first contained a vast card with a gold rim. He opened it and saw that it was from 'all at the Cathedral'; they had chosen the 'Haywain' by Constable and sent it with true love. It would have been laid on the desk by the door beside the rack with the shoddy booklets produced by the Catholic Truth Society. The priest must have made an announcement after the Mass; a straight man making a stand; a priest condemning sin. He would have known that their families were there in front of him with their heads bowed; he knew that they knew. He would have watched their responses as they shook his hand and went out to the left and into the Street or turned to the right and picked up a pen. They signed.

The second letter was from the Inhumane Resources Department of the Council. Dear McGillivray was informed with regret that policy decreed that after a lengthy period of sickness he would have to be declared fit for work before taking annual leave. He was expected at the office a week on Tuesday or his pay would cease. The signatory, a Squiggle, Miss, invited him to call her at his convenience on her direct line if he had any queries.

McGillivray decided to avail himself of this kind invitation and rang La Squiggle. He dialled the phone, his breathing fast and his stomach on fire. There was a click, he inhaled, and it went to answerphone. 'I am away from my desk...' He rang again, twice, and gave up. The next morning, after a night of dreams filled with car parks and express trains, he tried again and with success. She informed him, that yes, the letter was quite correct and the policy of the Council was clear. He explained to Squiggle, Miss, twice that his circumstances were exceptional, that Jerome had told him to remain in the north for as long as necessary, that he had no issue with the running together of sick and annual leave. La Squiggle sighed inaudibly. This was a routine disinformatory and placation situation of the kind covered in Module Three of the course she had recently attended re: the handling of difficult members of staff hoodwinked by incompetent managers. She had got the two star pass certificate and a special letter of commendation. It would be wrong to say that she enjoyed this kind of call, it was all so familiar; a chance to use her new skills was not to be sniffed at. She glanced at the postcard pinned to her noticeboard and tried not to envy her colleague in Tenerife. To ensure that her voice had the right level of bright warmth, she smiled into the handbag mirror kept purposely beside the phone. She pushed her chair back and got to her feet. This simple call handling technique enabled her to sound assertive and indicated to others around that she had a Difficult Client. Her colleague understood the signal. She nodded gravely across the desk and switched on the tape recorder to monitor the conversation for training and quality purposes. She was ready to be supportive and hoped to learn something. Squiggle always did these things so well.

Squiggle's voice was pitch perfect, exactly the levels of warmth and assertion that had so impressed the level three assessor. The effect on McGillivray was precisely the one intended. He did not argue. He accepted her sympathy at his unfortunate accident, and unable to intervene, continued to listen. He agreed it was such a shame that his manager had not apprised him of the full implications of the situation; however as he had seen the staff handbook, he knew very well that his pay would reduce and eventually stop unless he returned to work and passed the physical. He thanked her for her time and she hung up. Her colleague put on the kettle and took through some tea in her favourite mug alongside two iced biscuits. She deserved them.

The third letter was from the bank. It said that because he had given the attackers his pin number, policy forbade his money being refunded. McGillivray phoned Middleton who laughed. All he said was, 'Tell me the name of the Manager.'

An hour later the unfortunate financier himself was on the phone to tell McGillivray that they were making him an ex-gratia payment due to 'special circumstances' and to pass on his best benevolences for the future. He was horrified that so regrettable a misunderstanding had occurred. McGillivray accepted the apology and promised to say no more about it. He rang Middleton immediately who seemed unsurprised. 'I am sure he was very polite,' he said. 'I asked him if he looked forward to reading the headlines, 'Mugging victim robbed again by bank manager.'

After all of this excitement, McGillivray made himself a cup of tea, opened a packet of fudge brownies, and put two on a plate. He went through into the living room, sat down, and decided to 'move on,' to 'put the past behind' and 'live in the present' and to consider having positive thoughts. He knew the latter was risky; the only positive thinker known in Orkney had been moved for his own safety to the public asylum in Aberdeen where his attitude was adjusted on an electrical apparatus.

Feeling the lack of anyone to talk to McGillivray began to write down what had happened to him. He was terrified of forgetting information needed by the Court. His memories were his weapons that he would use to avenge himself on his enemies. They had to be burnished, polished so that when the time came for them to be seen in public they would shine like the sun. He had no computer so wrote in long hand, his preferred notebooks the hard backed cash books used by local shopkeepers to calculate profit, profitability and loss.

CHAPTER 43

A few days later, Middleton rang back; they were close to arrests and needed to speak to him before they could take place. Could he return to Grimsbrough as soon as possible?

He wanted to go and the crossing was smooth, travelling easier now; the bruises were less clear on his face and his hair had been washed. The most visible evidence of the trauma was his stookie and there are many innocent ways in which an arm can be broken.

The train skimmed the Caithness coast then cut through the Northern Highlands of Sutherland towards the Moray Firth and Inverness. McGillivray had books with him and found a little verse calming. From high above the railway track, the old stone Duke looked down upon him passing through the landscapes that wasted for his own gain. His desolations called up to him with the empty voice of the ruined land, his name never blessed. McGillivray did not hear, did not notice, having no ear for the misery of others. At Helmsdale some deer came near the line; near Carbisdale, a buzzard sat stereotypically on top of a stunted tree.

After seven hours travel, he was only in Inverness where, as everyone knows, the best English is spoken but smiles are never returned free of charge. He gritted his teeth in time to the music; the voices of Celtic women made tinny by speakers singing over and over 'The Road to the Isles', 'The Skye Boat Song' and 'Mairi's Wedding' for tourists. *Ceud mille failte,* indeed.

He had booked a window seat on the direct train to Darlington. Opposite him there was a lovely young man wearing a t-shirt advertising the Immaculate Conception Primary School. They did not speak. McGillivray read a book of Queer Verse assertively.

The train bore him over the running waters, the Tay and the Tweed, inexorably South, down down into the other Country and into his fear. At Newcastle, he examined the faces of those who got on dreading their recognition; the bored, the indolent; those in need of a seat clambered on but no one knew him. The fear of the newborn, the lamb ever startled, filled him with coldness and crushed down on his shoulders. He put his book away to grip the edge of his seat in more comfort. At Darlington, he disembarked; it was cold.

He went over to platform one and boarded the glorified bus waiting there. It was night by the time it pulled him east through the chemical plants and wastelands where there was no accidental beauty. He thought he recognised a man, something about the breadth of his face, sitting a couple of seats away and bowed his head to focus better on his book. It was upside down.

People's response in Grimsbrough was different to those in Stromness. Unlike islanders, these people were well used to violence. Although everyone knew intellectually that he had done nothing to deserve the marks on his face, yet it seemed that the folk belief of 'what goes around comes around' meant that he had in some way to be guilty.

Some casual acquaintances thought that his behaviour was responsible: he had either been offensively camp or cruising. Others blamed his and others political activity. 'We live quiet lives; keep ourselves to ourselves, no one knows. If you had done the same, hadn't trumpeted your sexuality to the whole world, then you'd be OK.' One politico, a colleague, had him up against the wall, his left hand gesticulating, 'It was because of what you represented, they knew you worked for the Council.' His mate contradicted him, 'Nah, he was just earning too much money, legally.'

For the first few times, he'd argue, try to set them straight, tell his truth. But this would always take a lot of time and involve argument. He would get angry; they wouldn't know what they'd said. He couldn't explain. Another invisible barrier would grow; his internal isolation would increase. On the whole it was easier to smile, mutter nothing, allow the collusion and assumption of agreement to take place. There are many kinds of trials.

Jerome arranged for McGillivray to be taken to a house belonging to Abe, a friend of Adam's. 'You know,' he said, 'those men who attacked you are the kind of men I'd fancy.' McGillivray smiled as one does and especially if there is no where else to go. 'I know,' he said, 'what you mean.' Indeed he did. Scott was very cute.

CHAPTER 44

Jerome knew too many people for McGillivray to remain homeless long. He pulled strings that enabled him to jump the housing queue and move into a flat about one physical mile from the Border. A mile was enough.

His new sanctuary was the top flat in a house that had just been renovated. Mrs. Brodie who lived on the ground floor had once owned the whole building. In return for her practical flat she gave the place to a housing association who converted the rest – and it was wonderful. He had a nest under the eaves with such low ceilings he developed a stoop. It was beautifully done with a bedroom, a living room, a kitchen and a bathroom. The sense of being high up gave a sense of security; no one could climb in the window uninvited to hurt him. The two solid front doors were not able to be battered down. The front room had a window seat with a view over a park. Lowry had never been anywhere near.

The flat was let bare and so furniture had to be obtained before he could move in, the perfect excuse to repeatedly visit the Gateshead Ikea. The insurance money arrived from the first crime just as he was heading South and so there was enough in the bank for his fridge, chairs and table. He bought a futon. He slept on the proceeds of crime.

Adam and Maeve were with him in the coffee area when two men from the bar in Grimsbrough came over and asked if they could join them. They had been eating meatballs and so did not mind. They started the questions before they sat down.

'We heard what happened to you, it's terrible, have they got them yet?'

'Yes,' he answered, 'they have.'

'What will happen to them now?'

'The police tell me, that if they are found guilty they will go to prison for about six years.'

The two men were indignant. 'But that means with time off for good behaviour they will get out in in about three years. Me, I would throw away the key after what they did to you.'

McGillivray sighed. These were the people he found hardest to bear, those who assumed that his politics would have changed because of what had happened to him. He learned that nothing above or beneath the good earth could silence the flow of a Daily Mail reader.

'Aah, but you forget the victim. In these cases it is always the victim I think of.'

'But I was the victim. And three years seems a long time to me.'

They went tight-lipped.

He emphasised his point; 'Three years is a long time to a young man. It is as long as a university degree.'

They never spoke to him again. They did not finish their coffee. Life is hard.

The truth was that he knew too much about these three men with sticks, about their homes and their lives. He had lived on their street and used the same shop. He understood the laws they obeyed and the ones he had transgressed.

A holocaust survivor wrote that it is always a mistake to try and understand why one is being persecuted. To succeed in understanding is to take the side of men with sticks, to collude with one's damnation. He was right then and he is right now. All that the persecuted ever need is for the bastards to stop the kicking. Nothing else. No excuses. No need to explain. Just stop being a bastard. McGillivray had taken their side.

CHAPTER 45

The State wanted its day in court; to set the boundary lines between innocence and guilt, all would be tested and a judgement given. McGillivray had imagined that as the wronged one he would have certain rights over the criminal justice process. He found out that he didn't; it wasn't up to him to press charges. The Police and the Crown Prosecution Service when they decided that there was enough evidence for a case decided to proceed and allocated him the role of victim. They sent him a letter just in case he was in doubt. The Clerk to the Teesside Justices used fine stationary and had a pretty turn of phrase.

> The case against the above named in which you made a statement to the police, has now been sent to the Crown Court sitting at Teesside. This letter is to give you some information about what will happen now.
>
> A date for the trial has not yet been fixed and it may take some time before this is done. However, the defendant(s) have indicated an indication to contest the case and the solicitors representing the defendant(s) have indicated which witnesses they require.
>
> At this stage you have not been required to attend but the position may change. For this reason the court has made a conditional witness order in your name. This is the court's formal

> request to you and it is enclosed with this letter...
>
> Because of the way in which a listing of cases is done at the Crown Court, it may not be possible to give you much notice of the trial date. If you are required to attend you will be advised (or "warned" as it is formally called) by the police. Once you have been "warned", you are legally required to attend as a witness. The court has power to take action against witnesses who do not attend without a good reason. If you have difficulties in attending on the date fixed for trial you must contact the police witness liaison officer or the officer in charge of the case...
>
> Thank you for your co-operation.

If he did not co-operate he would go to prison again and be fined. They really should have saved their threats. They didn't need to warn him; no way was he going to miss this performance.

Processes worked themselves through. More letters were sent. The likely date was set, and as days do, drew closer; the attitude of Work to the whole process became stranger and stranger. He became aware of looks; discussions had taken place in rooms forbidden to him. Jobs in the public sector in the days pre-internet were advertised in the Guardian on a Wednesday, the only day that many ever bought it. Indeed the prime measure of the health of a team was the number of copies in the waste bins. He saw a job in London and applied. He went down for the interview and was successful. He should be able to get away the week after the trial. His non interventionist God was looking after him.

On the last Friday, in the afternoon, Jerome called McGillivray over to his desk, now devoid of photographs and said that his manager had passed on instructions and they were to have a conversation.

He pushed back his chair, placed his manicured hands on the desk and stood up. 'We will go into the Counselling Room.' Jerome led the way down the corridor and opened the door. Inside he sat down as on a throne and inclined his head graciously at McGillivray to sit.

'We,' the royal 'we', he declaimed, the speech was rehearsed, 'have no objection to granting you special permission to attend the trial as you are a prosecution witness.' McGillivray looked at him blankly and retorted. It took some effort to keep the contempt out of his voice. 'It's not annual leave, I have no choice in going,' he said. He did not wait for dismissal but got up and walked out of the room, the door slamming behind on Jerome, alone with his box of empathic tissues and view of the chemical plant.

CHAPTER 46

On that peculiar Monday he arose early. The women who loved him had made sure he was not alone. Grace O'Malley sent up a bouquet through Interflora. Rüthe travelled down from the islands on the preceding Saturday to sleep on the blue futon purchased for £49 from Ikea. Maeve moved down for the whole week. Martha kept them forewarned about what was happening on the estate. There had been little sleep for any of them and so they were in need of the dark, Teutonic coffee that Rüthe brewed on the stove. They drank it solemnly, sacramentally, held hands for a moment, and stared in each others eyes. At the same moment they all exhaled, shrugged their shoulders and walked out of the flat into the coldness of the morning. Rüthe looked up; she tugged at McGillivray's arm and pointed to the park, 'Geese,' she said, 'wild geese, and they're leaving.'

They walked along the long road through the town down to the police station. McGillivray gave his name at the counter and all of them were bustled together and into a small interview room where they waited. Middleton and Clark came in quickly and chatted about nothing whilst an escort of CID officers gathered to accompany them over to the Court. The walk was quite short, just over a small green and round a corner. McGillivray knew from his previous experience that there was probably an underground tunnel that they could have used. The Police were clearly panicky themselves and kept dealing with their anxiety by trying to reassure them that nothing was going to happen. Naturally, this made them more nervous. They tried not to speculate. Three musicians were rehearsing on a make shift platform in the square; one of them was testing out her amplified fiddle. McGillivray thought he recognised the tune.

The escort party did not make an entrance through the front

door; rather they skulked in a deliberately nondescript entrance at the near side of the building and down a carpeted corridor to 'The Special Protection Room', an enclosure where witnesses thought to be potentially under threat could be kept private and comfortable out of sight of the Defence team. It was official, windowless. Someone had made an attempt to normalise the place by turning it into a kind of parlour. The effort had been made with kindly intentions but the results were unsettling. Two brown Parker Knoll chairs faced each other across a red veneer bookcase. On its top shelf there was a little plant pot that contained two knitted woollen daffodils with green leaves covered in dust. There were no books; instead a few old doctors' surgery magazines and some jigsaws lay on the shelves. Walls were white or maybe cream and decorated with framed prints of old Grimsbrough and hunting scenes in which it was impossible to see who was the prey.

Central catering had been booked and placed on a pine table, institutional coffee in a vacuum flask with a plate of biscuits of the kind known as 'assorted'.

They settled in to wait and made small talk. One of the CID officers came into the room looking over his shoulder anxiously; he spoke rapidly to all three of them.

'There is a mob in the building. About forty of them and their children have gathered in the corridor outside the courtroom.'

McGillivray asked, 'What are they here for?'

The Police man explained breathlessly but took the time to make sure they understood. 'They want to support their friends and intimidate you. They don't want you to give evidence.'

Another, a more senior officer arrived. He was even more anxious and had been speaking to court officials.

'It's not safe for you or for Maeve to leave this room. If you need to go out for any reason an officer will accompany you.'

Maeve went pale.

'Even for me?'

'Yes, it's obvious that they know who you are. We think that they are trying to get to you as well.'

Maeve and McGillivray hugged each other. They were in a decorated cell locked up with artificial flowers and a jigsaw puzzle of the transporter bridge, that engineering marvel over the river Tees; pieces were missing.

Middleton and Clark left them alone whilst the barristers were engaged happily in their pre-trial discussions. McGillivray learned later that the defence was debating the legality of the arrests and the identity parades in an attempt to stop the trial there and then. McGillivray was not that bothered; in his mind there was no doubt about their guilt but he acknowledged that they had the right to the best defence they could muster.

Gradually the atmosphere in the room changed from tension to boredom. There was nothing to do, nothing to think of that could be diverting. The only entertainment was the experience of being brought to the toilet by several armed policemen. When it was McGillivray's turn, he was bunched into the middle of a delicious CID group; they came round a corner and he was suddenly face to face with them all again, whole families come together to watch his demise. Public hangings must have been similar. A pleasant day out for all; some had taken flasks and cakes. Children would reminisce to theirs in coming years about having been taken that day. He was outside again, out on the steps on a Wednesday and the door of the cathedral locked. All around him there were cries, the herring gulls screaming, fulmars boking; 'There he is.' 'It's the queer.' McGillivray felt alone with the panic in his arms and shoulders returning. He said to the policemen, 'What can we do?'

'Keep walking, don't let them see that they are getting to you.'

The officers clustered more tightly making him feel trapped rather than safe. They stood outside the cubicle and tried not to listen. He was unable to piss. Waste.

After that, the police decided that it was too dangerous to walk through the public areas of the building. Instead, they gained special permission from whomever to use the private passageways that were the secret domain of the judges.

At about 2.30pm, the CID returned to the room and told McGillivray that he would not be needed that day.

'Would you mind returning at about 9.30am tomorrow?'

'Of course.' And that was that. Anticlimax.

They were escorted to the back exit of the Court and then left to fend for themselves. As quickly as possible they hurried into the anonymity of the main shopping area, the pedestrian precinct at the foot of Linthorpe Road.

They started looking in shop windows, their responses exaggerated by adrenaline. They fell about with laughter at some of the more ridiculous clothes. McGillivray saw some baggy white trousers with olive green stripes.

'I'd like to get those for tonight but I haven't any cash on me.'

Rüthe laughed.

'Don't worry; I'll put them on my plastic. They can be a present. I think you need something to cheer you up.'

By the time they had bought the pantaloons, it had dawned on them that they were too close to the Border for comfort; anxiety was evident on all their faces. The road felt unsafe and so they got a taxi back to the flat. At about six o'clock the phone rang. They all jumped. It was Jerome.

'How did it go today?' he demanded.

McGillivray spoke quietly, 'Nothing really happened. The lawyers spent the whole day arguing.'

'Did you give any evidence?'

'No,' a definite irritation, McGillivray felt he shouldn't have to deal with this. 'The trial hasn't even begun.'

'How long do they think it's going to take now?' Jerome demanded.

'They're not really sure. They think it should be over by Wednesday.'

The Boss spoke quietly as if he was making a special concession to a spoiled child, as if the Trial was a special treat, an indulgence he rather resented giving, 'We still need you to come in after it is all over. You can have a day to recover but then you must turn up for work.'

'That seems all right. I'll keep you informed of what is happening.' He paused and rather reluctantly added, 'Are you coming to the Leaving Do tonight?'

The Boss replied, 'I hope so, I'll see how things work out.'

He rang off. He didn't attend and the evening was sweeter far for that.

CHAPTER 47

War, someone told McGillivray, is mostly boring. People wait for long periods for the worst to happen and when it does and they are not dead yet, they have to start again, just where they were and then face it again, and again, each time more tired, more bored, more weary until it stops at a time over which they have no control. Tedium does not make good prose. Events are needed to carry the plot along. On the second day there were no events. The Court officials were terribly apologetic, the Special Witness Protection Room was occupied by a murder case, one that was more important, and so they were confined in the long room that barristers used for robing and disrobing. It resembled the peg hall in a primary school, long rows of empty hooks. No one trusted either enough to leave their garments there. There was no other furniture apart from the kind of table bought from an office catalogue and a full-length mirror. There were no chairs. So they sat on the floor and started reading poetry to each other. McGillivray and Maeve were both fond of earnest verse, the joyless kind with an intensity to match their current experience. His favourite,

> A naked hand crawls over a red road on
> sand
> to be reunited with its wrist.
> Vanity is hope.
> In dry water, a star turns into stone
> before it is drowned.
> Under the black sun, ashes are dug high
> into the uncaring sky.

They were not left alone, a CID chaperone whose name they never learned stood at the door half listening for disturbance all the time and periodically left for a couple of minutes for more coffee. Whilst his back was turned Maeve and McGillivray giggled like naughty children and chanted dirty poems to each other whilst Rüthe smiled and looked on indulgently. The laughter passed and the tensions returned more cruelly whilst they waited. Lunch was brought to them and yet more coffee but they didn't eat. They were released early again; Martha who had stood outside the courtroom all day and gone in whenever she was allowed told them that the barristers were still fighting and would not go into details about the nature of the battle.

The third day, they were returned to the parlour cell; it felt familiar and they were glad to be there. Maeve maintained that the daffodil had grown. They sat around it and drank their institutional coffee and were cheered by its cheering colour and comforting texture; artifice always improves on nature. In the mid-afternoon cheering broke out in another part of the building, there was singing and swearing; Maeve dropped a cup, terrified. Events here were not good. They stared at each other, not knowing what had happened. The noise got closer to them and reached a crescendo. The door opened.

Middleton and Clark came in and sat down on the two empty chairs. One was red eyed. They were both shaking. Rüthe moved closer to them, protective. Strong, she was always strong. 'Two of them have been acquitted, the lawyers said that we mishandled the evidence, we should not have shown you the pictures before the ID parade, it contaminated your memory.'

Middleton put his head in his hands. Maeve knelt beside him and put her hand on his knee.

'Those two we arrested first, there was a tip off from someone at the Church. That's why we got you down from the islands. We caught the third one later. We had a phone call in the middle of the night. Someone had seen a beautiful man standing in the middle of a field patting a white horse. It was raining that night; and it seemed odd. We sent a car over as soon as and there we found him, filthy. Alone. He had been running for weeks. His clothes were almost gone.'

They stared at each other. No one could speak.

Middleton asked McGillivray, 'What are you going to do when

all this is over?'

He replied, 'I'm going home for a bit.' Middleton went ashen faced and Clark was about to speak but McGillivray quickly reassured them. 'No, no, not across The Frontier but to Scotland for a week or two then I have plans.'

Clark swore, 'Thank fuck for that, they'll be looking for you.'

Middleton cut over him, 'It's not fair but you have to leave here as soon as you can. We don't think they know where you are tonight. You should be safe.' They looked at him and he continued, 'If you hear anything at your door, call us. We're on alert.'

Maeve and he held hands. They looked at each other and went home. This time there was no nonsense about shopping or being seen in public; the Police took them in the back of an unmarked red car and watched until they were safe inside. At about 5 o'clock the phone rang. It was Jerome with his persistent 'How is the trial going?'

McGillivray told him what had happened in a matter of fact way.

'Badly, two of them – including the ringleader – were acquitted today on a technicality. The trial of the third will continue. The Police mishandled the evidence but the point of law was so fine that it wasn't their fault.'

'How long is it going to take now?' he asked.

'They don't know.'

McGillivray heard a sharp inhalation of breath, 'We still need you to come back to work. Come in on Monday.'

McGillivray burst out laughing, there was nothing else to do. Alas, poor Jerome. This pathetic Manager who had frightened him so much had turned himself into a clown digging graves outside Hamlet's castle in Elsinore. His formality simply made him more foolish. After a few moments delight, he pulled himself together and managed to reply in an almost level tone. 'The Police have told me to leave town as soon as possible. I'm more or less under house arrest, not allowed to go outside at all.'

Jerome snorted like a bull. 'You still work for us. I don't think you understand the pressure that I'm under.'

McGillivray was fluthert. 'I don't think you understand what is happening to me,' he said, then repeated himself, surprised at having to think like this. 'I don't think you understand what is happening to me. You have no idea what I am going through.'

Jerome lost his temper and shouted down the phone, 'How dare you try to define my experience! We need you in the office to round things off.'

Trying very hard to keep calm, his words very clipped and precise, McGillivray asked, 'Can you guarantee my safety?'

Jerome replied, 'I think you're exaggerating.'

McGillivray lost the effort. All the anger, all he had been holding in came out and he yelled down the receiver at the underweight bastard, 'Fuck off!'

He slammed the phone down. The phone rang immediately but he didn't answer it. Panic came into the room and took him hard by the shoulders and the breath. He knew that Jerome would harm him if he could; he had gone too far. He remembered that as part of its personnel procedures the Council operated what it called a "grandparent" scheme. If a worker had a dispute with his or her line manager they could take it to their boss's boss. The point of this was to try to prevent disputes escalating and act as a mediation service. There had been a session about it at the departmental away day.

This seemed like a good time to see if the system worked. McGillivray immediately rang his grandparent. They had a brief telephone conversation that he assumed was covered by confidentiality. He really should have known better by then. Nevertheless, management came to the conclusion that it would be unwise for him to go against police advice and put his life at risk to come into the office. He would be free to leave the town as soon as the case was finished. However, they did agree that McGillivray should first meet Jerome in order to debrief him.

The Boss of the Boss finished by reiterating policy.

'The council always places the safety of its workers at the top of its priorities.'

The conversation ended on a good note. McGillivray hung up and breathed more easily but the respite did not last long. Again, the phone rang. McGillivray answered to Jerome himself angrier than ever, trying to control his voice, his temper not very far away. He informed McGillivray that he would come around to collect council property as soon as possible, probably within half an hour. McGillivray downloaded his files quickly from the laptop on to a floppy disk. He went through his bookcase and rooted out the relevant ones. None were that interesting. The doorbell rang. Rüthe answered it, and she, not a small woman, was almost shoved aside by the explosion of Jerome into the living space. Nothing was going to get in his way. She stood outside the door and listened with a notebook in hand. Just in case.

Jerome began with threats, the cuckold who has at last got the upper hand whom no one can condemn: 'I have to tell you that what you said to me is going to be placed on your personnel file.'

McGillivray had no idea what this would do for his future employment, for all he knew, the files followed the worker from Council to Council. He started to smile and placate. It worked. By the time he got Jerome to the door and out of his life, his anger had been dissipated. The persecutor had turned into the 'please love me – I will always be your friend' type. Most importantly, he had revoked and even forgotten his threat. As soon as the door closed, McGillivray started to swear. When he ran out of English, he continued in Gaelic and German. He had enough vocabulary to work on for fully ten minutes without repetition. When he was spent he went into the bathroom and rinsed his mouth out with Listerine.

All this time, Rüthe had been listening in the kitchen. Now, she came out pale and shaking and embraced McGillivray in a huge hug. They stood for the longest time, silence, apart from the wailing of the sirens, rich in their ears.

CHAPTER 48

On the 4th day, Middleton and Clark were both fairly certain that McGillivray would be called to give his evidence. For the final time they returned to the court and the special witness protection room.

This time there was not such a long wait. McGillivray was summoned to the court. He was taken up through the secret carpeted corridors and staircases to the courtroom. He entered it through a side door.

McGillivray's impressions of the judicial system in England were entirely formed by 'Crown Court'. This television series had filled his school lunch breaks throughout the seventies. The oak panelled set was always the same, a dock at the back of the room, high up. The public was seated in a gallery overlooking the whole room. The different parties neatly segregated themselves into appropriate groups; witnesses who had testified and were now watching the rest of the action, family and friends of both parties. Even the most complex cases always took three half-hour hour sessions with time for an advert break. Members of the public acted as the jury.

However, television is not real life. Books create a false empathy; the assumption is that through drama and documentary a vicarious offering of the lives of others is made. All stories are partial truths. Authors interpret, even historians. Most are liars. Eliding, smoothing things out; perfectly good characters who deserve their own sub-plots are destroyed. Even stories based on a truth are only an approximation. Nothing happened like that. There never was a god mother who said to Cinderella, 'You shall go to the ball,' and McGillivray was not ready.

The court was not a large room. The wooden furnishings were light and modern looking as if they had been provided by some discount furniture warehouse – beech effect. There was no separate gallery. The jury took up about a fifth of the available floor space. About twenty-five chairs were ordered in rows of five seats. These were full. A glass screen separated them from the empty press box.

McGillivray was shot straight into the witness box. The sole remaining accused was directly opposite him and on a level. There was no doubt at all in McGillivray's mind that he was pretty boy, Scott, the middle one, he who had felled him with the devil stick. They had the right man. He was going to send him down. He was going to make him pay.

There was no differentiation amongst the people in the public gallery. They were all jumbled up together through lack of space. Rüthe sat by herself in the back row. Directly in front of her Dan, the Leader, sat alone. She could have strangled him or slit his Adam's apple open. She could have borrowed a brick and cracked open his skull but she didn't. He was allowed to spectate and smile. He had won the battle he thought and could almost taste his ultimate vindication. In any case, no matter what happened to Scott, he was free and nothing could touch him. He knew and McGillivray knew that nothing could touch him.

Dan was innocent. His innocence must be upheld. He was a freeman and his eyes were upon McGillivray. Now in the dock it was McGillivray standing and the jury consisted of three men with sticks. They had heard all the evidence and the foreman, this good man, this free man, announced the verdict. A black cap. He has been asked and agreed to carry out sentence. Maybe he was wrong though. Maybe McGillivray was wrong, maybe the whole book has been wrong and the CID had tainted his memory. Maybe the one they had arrested was not the Gargoyle. If it was, he should be free and compensated. If these are slanders then no one can apologise enough; two wrongs do not make a right. Yet someone had hit him. And there were three of them.

McGillivray stood up straight in the witness box and took the oath. He swore on the Brownie Law to tell the truth, the whole truth and nothing but the truth. His mouth was dry and he was so nervous that he had to repeat some of the words over. He turned and faced the Leader, Dan and got ready. He was going to make him pay. He was going to send him down but it was not Dan who was on trial, he was free, and he was waiting. Perhaps he is still waiting.

The prosecution barrister asked him to tell his story, what had happened on that Wednesday night.

He drew breath and began, 'It is night and I am alone again. The inevitability of the walk home. The short walk to the empty house through the quiet streets, the dark streets. In cities it is always the night that I have preferred, the silent night when the cars and the shoppers are gone and it is only the others, those who have no good reason, who are there...'

He was asked to describe his injuries. He recited the list that he had had to recite many times before.

Ribs suspected broken
Right arm fractured
Three teeth broken
Several wounds to the head
Severe bruising to the left side of the body
Face unrecognisable,
Severe shock,

Suspected but later dismissed – damage to vision and hearing.

The barrister then said, 'We have photographs we would like to show you. Can you confirm that this is you?'

He had expected these pictures but thought that they would be presented in some kind of dramatic way, large black and white prints with borders; these were more like holiday snaps. The form seemed to magnify the content. McGillivray had not seen himself in the injured state. Of course, he had looked in the mirror but by the time he was ready to do this, he had been able to adjust to how his face would be. Now, he was unprepared completely. Memory had dulled and blotted out the bruises. As his past half-closed eyes met his present ones, he almost fainted. His knees went weak beneath him. He had to use the sides of the witness box to keep himself erect. He was going to make him pay. He was going to send him down.

He affirmed that it was indeed him. There were a few more

questions. The Defence tried to make a case and failed. Then they were done with him. That was that. He left the witness box. There was movement in the court.

Crisis broke over him and there was motion and fear eddying around him and his friends. They were alone and the mob was screaming and knew he was at bay. They knew he was at bay and that he was prey. They knew the law, had experience that he did not. He was alone. The police were no longer there to protect him. Their obligation under the special witness protection scheme was to ensure that he was able to give evidence. Now he had done so, their responsibility had finished That's it. Job done, hands shook and so on. He was alone.

In the eye of McGillivray's mind he was caught up in the mob and they were around him and the panic was hard stones. They were triumphant with hot screams and yells. Two of their own were now free and immune. They could do anything they liked. The State had held up their rights to govern their enclave by their own laws. They were going to make him pay. They were going to send him down.

Rüthe pleaded, 'You can't do this. You have to get him out of here in one piece.'

The Police saw there was sense in this. Perhaps as they conferred they imagined the headlines. A decision was made to provide an escort to get them past the mob and down to the court back door, where a taxi was summoned. This was a privilege. He was meant to feel honoured.

All the way down to the exit, advice was being offered.

'You must not go out by yourself. Don't leave your flat unless you have to. Are you intending to come to the case tomorrow?'

'I would like to hear what he has to say, to defend himself. I want to be here for the verdict.' It had never crossed his mind to do anything else.

They were insistent. Panic in their voices, they had no illusions. 'You must not do this; as soon as it is over we will telephone you and let you know what happened. We really can't guarantee your safety.'

CHAPTER 49

The fifth day of the trial was the strangest. They spent the whole morning in the living room of the little flat with nothing to do but look at the phone waiting, willing it to ring. And it didn't. And then all that interminable afternoon the same until they were past drinking coffee and had nothing left to say to each other. At about 4.30, when they were not right in their heads with the boredom, the phone rang at last. Maeve took the call. She listened intently. They waited.

'Six years,' she screamed.

The Word of the Judgement spread fast and gathered a few people to celebrate the Good News. Someone produced a bottle of champagne. A colleague rolled a joyous spliff and they all talked, laughed, and giggled.

And that was that.

Except it wasn't. The story should end but it didn't. All the main characters in one room having a party, the Manager hugs McGillivray in a thin and chaste fashion. Adam throws Maeve into the air. Fade to credits. McGillivray in one of his few adventures amongst the London culturati heard a teller from Armenia finish her story with their traditional formula: 'three golden apples fell from heaven, one for the teller of the tale, one for the listener and the third for the person who understands'. Very tidy, he thought, he felt a sense of completion in an appropriate ending and a little bit flattered; the third extra apple would be theirs.

Perhaps no one can ever get the apple because there is nothing to understand. A story has no meaning other than the joy of telling and the pleasure of listening. To expect much more is a mistake. George, inventor of Hamnavoe, our poet, he recommended silence at the end, be content with that, he said, after the runes have been carved. It's written there, over his head, where he lies now, himself quiet, amongst our beloved dead. He was wise and never a talkative man; everyone knows that in real life there are no happy endings. Love stories end in death or divorce; there is no third way. So silence. Enough. Know when to stop.

The doorbell rang. It was CID. They pretended not to notice the smell of weed as they had other matters on their mind. McGillivray, they said, should get away from town as soon as possible. 'They will be looking for you', they said, 'and this time they won't make any mistakes.' That ended the Party.

They all dispersed that night.

McGillivray left Grimsbrough that evening and returned only to pack his things for the deliverymen. The second home lost. About half way through the last morning Jerome arrived with his colleagues to say goodbye. Perhaps there was some kind of reconciliation. So that was that. Nothing for him to do but go well escorted to the station, towards but not across The Frontier. Another leaving, everything he had in a suitcase, a train.

Boat journeys divide up the lives of islanders. When he got into the new house, rented on his behalf by the kindness of his parents, he unpacked. At the bottom of his case were the clothes he had worn on the night of the attack; a smart black jacket made of wool and a white polo shirt with the red ribbon printed on it. They had not been washed. Maeve had preserved them for him just as they were and placed them in an IKEA bag. Tucked in with them a wooden necklace in a native American style bought in Camden a year or so before the attack that had been meant to bring luck. He stuffed the bag under his bed and left it to moulder.

Various friends talked to him of closure, of the need to put the past behind them. This he wanted to do. One spring evening he pulled the bag out from under the bed and unwrapped it carefully. He took out the shirt and turned it over and around in his hands, caressing it and smoothing out the creases. He was surprised that the blood had almost lost its redness and taken on a range of oranges and brown. He hugged it to himself and wept, the tears flowing from him in huge convulsions that swept through his body.

He carried the shirt into the kitchen and placed it gently on the sink unit. He took candles, votive lights and arranged them around the room. He lit lavender to cleanse the air and so transformed the space. He put the shirt in the basin and added detergent and turned on the taps.

He pushed the clean water over and through the fabric. Nothing seemed to change for a long time. Seven times he rinsed it. Brown water swirled in the sink down and through and out to the sea. The seven tears that are meant to call the seal man from the water but nothing happened inside him. No one came yet. There was no release, no removing the stain. Closure is an American lie used to justify revenge. Healing is getting used to the pain, learning to be damaged. It changes over years but past suffering does not inoculate against further calamity. When it occurs, as it must in every human life, another wave of damage breaks on the rocks and falls back onto itself and is gone taking a little more of the self, the identity with it until all is eroded, nothing left but the smooth surface of the sea.

CHAPTER 50

Whenever he closed his eyes, they were there, the three men with sticks and they were waiting for him, always. He had hoped that going back North would keep them away. That no one needed to lock the door on the Island and that he was safe would stop them, but no, they were still there and one of them, the tallest, always whistling the same three notes, the music that had punctuated his blows.

The pips of the BBC seven o'clock news rang the end of each restless night and signalled his attempt to engage with the day. On this particular morning, long before the brief light of the Winter Solstice, he pulled an unwashed woollen jumper over blue skin and found his socks and underpants behind the radiator. From the security of the mirror, his cracked reflection watched him sit on the mattress to put on his shoes. It was not impressed.

The stairs down to the kitchen were narrow but he coped. Breakfast consisted of instant coffee, black because the milk was stinking and medication, eight kinds. His favourite tablet was royal blue but he appreciated the orange ones as well. The other five were white and nondescript of various sizes. Each was consumed in turn with its ritual swig.

After these morning ablutions, he went to sit at his desk by the window. The curtains were open but the sun had not risen. The second cigarette of the day burned his fingers as his Apple tried to start up. The files had not closed down properly and so his poem of the previous night confronted him on the screen.

> I am in the Town missing the Island
>
>   and the sheep of my childhood.
>
> I was drunk but am sober now
>
>   Simply hung over and wistful

At what has happened so often
in the blessed New Year.
I want to go home, soon, but not yet.

He pressed delete and took another hit, another exile poem. Many whose claim and ability to write were greater than his had already done enough of them, but he, unlike the best of them, was not dead.

Movement drew his eye to the window; a mother and her two children, walking past on their way to school. The youngest child pointed and then said something to his mother. She shushed the boy and they hurried on. He felt the weight of their judgement. Their disapproval was heavy upon him. He knew for them he was the drunk who had never done anything for himself, had sponged off his mother, let her do his laundry. Now she was dead and they could see him looking out of his window, writing about them. They were wrong in this at least. He could not write but he did want his own back.

There was nowhere tangible to go for him now but island folklore.

McGillivray picked up his jacket from where it had been hung on the floor. The gods who cared for the drunk had been kind to him; his phone and wallet were in the pockets, but what he was really looking for was missing. Panic filled him until camouflaged by the dark, he touched the cold spine of the volume borrowed from the Orkney Library at the bottom of his satchel. He was right to be worried, it had a reputation for being elusive. In the ninety seventh archive box out of the hundred deposited after the death of Ernest Marwick, the great collector of island folk belief, he had found it in a heavy manilla envelope marked 'Not to be opened without the presence of three Ministers'. Clearly, that meeting had never taken place.

The Library trusted researchers to be ethical. McGillivray was not. He waited until the presiding officer was away from her desk and then concealed the paper in his coat pocket. He tried to walk calmly down to the toilet; once the door was secure he ripped the paper apart. It was as he hoped. There in his unbelieving hand was 'The Book of Black Arts,' the very same that had given Rachel Tulloch, now long dead, the power to bewitch the island of Sanday. Tammy Gibson had used it to become a cat. George Mackay Brown, the Stromness writer, had told of how the parish minister had destroyed it by burying it in the garden of the manse just across the road from where McGillivray sat. But George was wrong, the book had survived, or at least the copy from the island of Sanday had and it was in his hands. McGillivray turned the black pages slowly and tried to decipher the precise white handwriting reputed to be of the Devil himself. It was legible, in old Scots but the meanings were clear. He exhaled. There was hope. He put the book under his jacket, collected his stuff from upstairs, said goodbye, and ran to catch the bus back westaways to home. Only the fool says libraries are dull.

The time had come. He tucked his emergency half bottle into the bag beside his hope and left the house. And it was dark.

CHAPTER 51

Outside, the bitter cold of a day with no weather did nothing for his hangover. The sudden drop in temperature caused his chest to clench. Tightness briefly increased his anxiety. For the first time in years he felt a need to lock up the house but had no idea where the key was. Half a valuable hour was wasted searching but when found, at the bottom of a drawer in the bureau, it would not turn in the lock. There was nothing to do but trust to his luck.

He picked up his bike from where it had spent the night beside the wall. He knew his bones would not bear the sclatterring over cobblestones down the steep Kirk Road and so there was no alternative but to bear the humiliation of wheeling it past the cats looking down from the security of house windows. He did not dare to throw stones at them, and risk broken glass. The disapproval of the cats would have been enough but they were not alone, no, from above, from their perches on chimneys, the seagulls watched too, safe in their feathered smugness. He hated them with the same passion that he reserved for the believers who had abandoned the churches for which the road was named. They were dissipated, faith blown away on the wind.

At the bottom of the hill, he turned left and walked along to the combined bakery. He paused at the door and looked at the notice pinned up in the window, a death announcement for the late Emily Cumlaquoy of Inner Garth farm, her funeral to be held Thursday, this notice an intimation for family and friends.

A number of people stood gossiping at its till. He pretended to ignore them and their bright conversation. The biscuit packets held his fascination until the coast was clear enough to put his usual white cider down on the counter. The assistant, a woman who had known him all of his life, checked him over to ensure that he was concealing nothing.

'No credit,' she said, unasked.

He pretended not to hear and said, with the confidence of a man who knows his benefits are fresh in his pocket,

'A couple of brown rolls please with cheese and pickle.'

His first words of the day felt acidic to him in his dry mouth.

'Margarine?'

'Please, and a brownie.'

He stood back slightly and looked around in the vain hope that she would not be able to smell anything alcoholic on his breath. Without even looking at the cider, she said to him in the weary voice of someone who has had to say the same thing often before.

'We cannot sell you that yet. It's too early.'

He put the illicit drink back on the shelf and picked up some cola, diet, on account of his health.

He made the customary small talk, 'Not bad weather.'

She put twenty menthols down beside the food and made the standard reply.

'No place like Orkney on a fine day.'

He bit his lip slightly, put the purchases in his satchel and left.

School was about to go in. From the playground came the hurlygush of children reluctant to bow their heads in submission to the hated curricula. Mingled with their racket was something unexpected. At the Pier Head, by the memorial to Alexander Graham, three women were busking. McGillivray did not recognise any of them at all. 'Strangers,' he thought, 'from Kirkwall or further afield.' That there was no reason for them to be playing music on such a bitter morning meant that they were being extravagant, almost wanton, and heathen.

The oldest woman was about seventy. Her hair was immaculately set and rinsed blue. Over her tweed suit she had positioned some pearls and a brooch of the sort a grandchild would choose. Her instrument was a bodhran, the firm and meticulous beat made with a marvellously carved knucklebone. She did not appear to be enjoying herself.

The fiddler was younger, perhaps her daughter; she swayed with the music, her eyes closed, her blonde hair heavy in the wind that was not blowing. There was nothing else strange about her.

The third was little more than a child. Her dress was green and of some sort of archaic cut. She made the mouth music for her dancing but performed in a way that made little sense of either rhythm or beat. McGillivray thought she was probably on drugs.

He dropped a coin onto the empty, flat bunnet in front of them.

'Fine day.'

The drummer looked him full in the eyes and said quietly,

'You'll pay.'

CHAPTER 52

McGillivray mounted his cycle and did not fall off. The saddle felt unfamiliar to him. It had been long enough since there had been a space between the winds and sufficient certainty of sun for a spin. With just a few turns he left behind the pier without drawing attention from any of the small fishing boats that had been placed there, the paper had said, for the new documentary on island sustainability. The statue of the small explorer, John Rae, watched him along the flat Ferry Road out of the Town into words he knew very well, the words in the book he would use. They gave him the tune he did not know and it burned into ear and into his memory

O, Mester King o' a' that's ill,
Come fill me wi' the warlock skill,
An' I sail serve wi' all me will.
Trow tak' me gin I sinno!
Trow tak' me gin I winno!
Trow tak' me whin I cinno!
Come tak' me noo, an' tak' me a',
Tak' lights an' liver, pluck an' ga',
Tak' me, tak' me, noo, I say,
Fae de how o' de head tae de tip of de
tae;
Tak' a' dat's oot an' in o' me,
Tak' hide an' hair an' a' tae thee,
Tak' hert an' hams, flesh, bleud, an'
biins,
Tak' a' atween de seeven stiins
I de name o' de muckle black Wallawa!

Trows were 'the other people', 'the good people' whose names should not be used in case they took offence. They had haunted the cairns and howes that covered the islands. One of the first witch trials in the islands had involved poor Elspeth Reoch who had left her baby to them. A knight, transformed into a fairy after his earthly remains were left behind on a red field, had taught her the dark arts. 'Wallawa' was assumed the Devil himself, he always took the form of a tall black man on his all too frequent visits to the islands.

Irritability, that contemptible emotion, gave him a spurt of energy that carried him up the Cairston Bray and away from home. He peched a bit until he reached the top but was delighted that he did not need to get off. To celebrate his unexpected fitness he allowed himself a moment to have a cigarette to get his breath back. To his annoyance the words played in his head, their meaning opaque.

Trow tak' me gin I sinno!

He dismounted, rested his back against a concrete fence post, and lit up. As he inhaled, he allowed himself to look around. Beneath him the town, shrunken by distance, breathed slowly and quietly. Smoke rose, a car moved along the pier. An old three-master, a training ship, cut through the Sound beyond the Kame. McGillivray felt a small disappointment that it was not in full sail. He had seen one years before and the beauty and the splendour of it had taken away his breath, the living vessel riding the salt fields, triumphant into Haven Bay. He turned round. To his right was a poet's house, its blue shed with its grass roof, and a view, wide over the bay of Eyrland and along to the Orphir hills. Far beneath, he could make out the reef where the seals often lay, bloated, maggot like in the morning sun.
More words from the song,

Trow tak' me gin I winno!

He turned to face the way he would go. His eyes rested over the landscape heavy with the winter sky; in the medium distance lay his destination between the two lochs and the long straight road that headed eastaways to Kirkwall, the other side of the island.

McGillivray took a small sensation from the bottle in his knapsack, remounted the bike, and freewheeled down the hill. Speed began to disentangle his brain, made him sentimental. It was strong to him, the illusion that nothing substantial here had ever changed. There were no cattle to watch from the farm of Howe. They were warm in the byre. Their field had once held a mound. When opened by the archaeologists a cairn was found that was at least five millennia old. When its builders, these first people went under the grass, their distant descendants built a round fortress with hollow walls, a broch that in its turn they surrounded by a small village. These were cosmopolitan people who travelled and traded afar. Someone brought home a Roman ring, bright with carnelian carved with an emperor. It is now in the museum in Kirkwall. For generations they prospered until they too went down, this time under newcomers from the North with bright steel and broad sails. Perhaps no one buried them. Two hundred and fifty generations all told, a long time.

The momentum from the downward slope carried him as far as the Brig O'Waithe. He grunted and began to pedal up the kind of annoying, slow gradient that motorists never notice. He rode past the former 'Golden Slipper' and Unstan Tomb with its memories of Isa's baking. Half-forgotten tastes took him over the hillock, around the long bend and then again freewheeling down into Stenness village. A hare, out of season, cavorted unnoticed by him in the field. The cold made his face red and sore. He dismounted, used an asthma inhaler, and continued until just past Corrigall farm he took the road to the left, to the Neolithic, towards Brodgar and the stone circles. Every time he saw them, he could hear an old man, a friend of his father's say, 'No wan kens who raised them. Mind this on beuy: when King David wis a bairn the newest of these stanes wis already aulder than the auldest kirk.'

The road took him past what was left of the circle of the Stenness Stones by a 19th century farmer who thought them inconvenient. Tradition associated them with things female and the Moon. As such they were of no use to him. Where the lochs almost met, the Watch Stone guarded the path to the Great Circle dance of Brodgar. Twenty-seven of its great stones still stood out of sixty. Legend, too often repeated in these days salted with heritage, says that these are the last remains of the giants, children of Lilith, she who refused Adam his desires and was given up as a punishment. On the longest night of every year they were in the habit of holding a party here, drinking and stumbling around under the moon until one last fatal solstice they got too quarrelsome and careless to notice the time; not one got home before sunrise. All were petrified where they stood or lay, drunk, their faces frozen forever by morning light. Typical men.

He tried to remember the next set of words to the tune birling around the cavity of his head. When he had them at last he yelled out in triumph at the blue Volkswagen passing,

> Trow tak' me gin I winno!
> Trow tak' me whin I cinno!
> Come tak' me noo, an' tak' me a',
> Tak' lights an' liver, pluck an' ga',

CHAPTER 53

An owl rose suddenly from a fence post and into McGillivray's face. He swerved and fell off into the ditch at the roadside. Disentangling himself, he left it where it fell. No one would take it from there, not in Orkney.

Rather than taking the authorized gate into the monument he clambered over the barbed wire fence near to where the Comet stone stands; the petrified fiddler, forever alone, outside the circle, controlling it, making the malformed giants dance and delight in their doom. The fence snagged McGillivray's breeks. He had to tug them to get free. The wire stung him. A red flower blossomed on the blue fabric.

As the Season proper had not yet begun, the Circle was free of its modern pilgrims in their unnatural colours and glass eyes. He felt relieved at being able to work his work in peace. He also hoped that no one who knew him saw him. There was no need to give anyone more evidence.

He sat himself down in the deep ditch that men had hewed from the earth five thousand years ago. Its steep bank served to ward off the gaze of any early morning tourists and gave him the chance to steady his nerve. He looked into the satchel and was relieved that the book had not managed to escape. The white words danced before his eyes, making it hard to see clearly. When he found the right place, he rehearsed the text to himself several times without moving his lips. It would not be good to make a mistake. Although he knew nothing would happen, it still felt safest to remember his manners. Just in case. Years before, with a lad from the school, he had made this trip to do this same thing. They had heard the stories and wanted to see what they could see but after three circuits of the stone they became feartied and pedalled back as fast as they could towards home and Cremola Foam. This time, there was no turning back.

He took a deep breath and began to walk. The living text set free from the page by his arrogant mouth hung heavy in the air on his breath. Three times three he walked around against the sun; each circuit three hundred and ninety two megalithic yards precisely, nine circuits, two miles.

'Tak a atween the seven stanes'

The walk took a long time and was not interesting, one foot after another and then the same again, around and around and another foot. When he was done, nothing had changed apart from the pain in his feet. He sat down behind the Comet stone facing away from the circle. It's cold became part of him but he did not dare to move. The weight of the vast light above him began to change, shadows to lengthen. Stillness crushed him.

A chord of music caused him to turn around. There was nothing there. He laughed at his own surprise. Nothing was going to happen now, it was time to leave. He stood up and gathered his belongings to him. As he stood up he saw a crow staring at him with blank eyes from the sign that warned the passer-by that the monument was protected by the Secretary of State, to damage it, an offence. He threw a stone at it angrily and settled back down, hugged himself, white hands clinging to the Book he had already begun to hate. The bird made no move.

He heard another noise, much louder, much. He peeked around the stone and saw a horse champing its hooves on the ground. From each of the plaits on her mane a multitude of silver bells hung. He shuddered and tried to hide. Against hope a shadow moved over the sun. For a moment things seemed very dark, but when it passed, his hands were empty. The Book had come home. A third time he heard a noise, this time a voice and it was calling his name. No defence was left. He got to his feet and stepped out.

CHAPTER 54

The voice was that of a woman, whose grey eyes held him motionless like prey. Her clothing in that peculiar context seemed normal, a light circlet of silver held down her black hair. A cloak of shadows hung loosely over a dress made out of green and silver light but she was no Walliwa, no Devil. He had got something wrong. That she was not real and had no existence apart from in his mind was no comfort or protection. Delusions have their own veracity and work according to their own laws; scars sear dreams and return each night until the sleeper begs for wakefulness. He knew that all too well.

She could be anyone from his subconscious, Isis, Azraiel, Lilith, Jezebel, Diana, Hecate, names of unpleasant women who had strong views on the role of men filled his mind, all of them frightening. Best to flatter, he thought, call her the Virgin. Whoever this phantasm was, she would not be offended by being confused with the Mother of the Christian God, meek and mild. He began to pray quickly. Although Presbyterian by training, he had spent enough time with monks to know a little Latin. The first words, 'Ave Maria' came quickly to his mind but before he reached the 'Dominus tecum' she laughed. He was relieved she sounded amused. There was mirth in her eyes. The crow flew off.

'Well,' she said, 'I have never been called the Queen of Heaven before. I was not who you expected to see.' She laughed. 'I am not Him either. My country is elsewhere. As I am amused, you can live, but tell me, why am I here?'

He told the truth. If this woman were in his mind she would know his lie and punish him. 'I am stuck,' he stuttered. 'I want to write things and everything has been done before. There are too many plough men and dancing stones, I cannot, I thought you would be...'

Mistake. She was not pleased. Her brow darkening reminded McGillivray of various unpleasant encounters that now seemed horribly plausible. With horror, he knew who she was. He had strayed into the wrong tale. Warning stories flashed across his mind. The good people took one man walking in a field. Never again by day was he seen, but at night he could be heard from under the nearby hill imploring, in blank verse, to be released. Then there was the story of the fiddlers, one of them caught for fifty years, but he did not want to think about that.

McGillivray gulped and stopped speaking abruptly. He could feel himself becoming unsubstantial, shrinking. His hands felt different. He looked down at them as he saw toad skin spreading over them, his body shifting into something vile. He squatted down on his knees.

She continued, 'Nothing is ever new. All stories have happened before. Inky men come and creep here to me, their Queen. Dust covers failure. Nothing changes.'

'You will pay,' she continued, 'with a kiss. It is always a kiss,' her eyes seemed to recollect something or someone long ago, 'and then I must have you for the seven years learning times four. It is the rule.'

Twenty-eight years seemed a long time to spend with this woman, any woman. His knees went weak under him. This was far more than he had bargained for. He asked time to consider, to weigh up the odds, 'It is not every day that such an opportunity presents, er, your Majesty. I am very grateful', he croaked, 'that your Grace would favour me so but...'

He had said too much. She took his pleading words as consent. To break the spell, she clapped her hands twice and let him get up from his knees. He was laid bare with a clean knife, gutted. No mutuality exists between mortal and immortal. Although flesh fails and turns into ash on the hill, he was not burned. He did not die. She became sure of him.

Naked as a newborn, she took him up on to the horse behind her. He had never ridden before and although the ground seemed far away and the horse very much alive there was no time for fear. McGillivray held on to the woman's waist tightly yet she did not seem to notice his presence. The speed of the air against his face felt as if his very flesh was being pulled off.

The pain caused him to scream but no one heard, there was only the race and the running, the familiar country left far behind. After a time, they came to rest in a bland vastness without features where even the horizon was not.

They dismounted. She said imperiously, 'I would have you rest a moment. You may lay your head on my lap. I would stroke your hair.'

He thought it best to do as he was told in the hope that she would confuse alacrity to obey with enthusiasm. He had no need to worry. He was nothing to her. When she stroked his hair it was as one would a new puppy not a lover. She began to point out the lie of the land, making sure he was spared no detail. Under her reluctant direction his eyes began to focus on a long road stretching out from the North towards a distant South. He smiled and made a bland comment. She showed her displeasure by drawing in her breath sharply. 'That is no way to talk to me.'

Her dragon appeared. She smiled at it and patted its muzzle with her hand. It fixed him in its gaze for a moment and then was gone in a blue lowe. McGillivray swallowed and became very respectful. He had no escape.

'The road leading southwards is easy. Many are those who take it and none return.'

'And that way,' she pointed with her ring finger, 'is the hard and narrow road that leads to the North, to the place some call Heaven. There are broken stones. No shelter from wind and rain. Few take it.'

He felt despair. He knew enough of the North already and had no desire for more. He wanted heat.

'There is another road, one not described in the Book. We shall take a third way,' her tone changed into something soft, a pleasant song almost legible in the air. 'We are going westaways to the youthful land.'

She spurred the horse on to the crossroad. At first their way seemed delightful, a country lane through a meadow that meandered pleasantly around the darker metaphysics and avoided speculation. The wind was no more that a breeze to delight the heart and sharpen the wit. He wanted to drink from the shallow brook that accompanied the road. She saw that he was thirsty and helped him down from the horse. He lay down on the soft grass and reached out his hand almost to the water but it was dry.

They rode on again. Before long they came to a dark country where it seemed that the sun had flickered out and there was no moon. All that could be heard in the mirk was the hallyoch of the ocean pulling back through many pale stones on white sand as it set them yammering and howling against each other. He clutched at the woman's waist, terrified lest he should be disseminated, a ghoul.

'This is the first and final shore', she said, in a voice he did not recognise at all, 'out of these waves, all life in the land and air crawled and to this beach it will one day return. All bones grind small.'

They crossed some great river; the spray raised by the hooves drenched him but it was not clean water that filled his mouth and eyes, no, they were crossing the wound of the earth where the blood spilt runs. All of it flows there, the blood from the battle, the knife of the surgeon, the life of the murdered child, the blood of the moon and the womb. She talked about the good world bleeding, yet, amongst all the grief her white horse rode on. There is always another wave on that shore.

In the half-light of that other day, that wrong day, the horse came to a standstill in front of a small hill in a wind blasted field. Nearby, they could hear the scream of corn being crushed in the mill. The Woman's voice made his humanity strain.

'Look at the hill; tell me what you see.'

He was puzzled; there was nothing to describe.

'I see a hill, barley under the sky.'

'Look again. What see you now?'

He stared at the smooth turf and saw something change. The wind sighed.

'I see a crack in the earth, a small fissure.'

A corncrake made its dreadful noise. Again she made him turn around and look at the hillside. This time there was no doubt.

'I see a door. It has opened for us. A lintel stone leads to a cold bed.'

He knew exactly where he was. Logres would have been better, or Arabia, or Avalon or almost anywhere else. In all of their riding they had come no more than a mile or so. They stood on the threshold of Maeshowe, the home and the hall of the night where every year, the light dies.

The woman spoke, 'Obey, and you will return. Once we go in you will be silent and listen. If you speak, you stay here until Judgement, the Day when the sea gives up its dead.'

In this wise, her seal was placed on him and she took away his words. She urged her horse on. It stepped forward slowly, each hoof falling delicately on the yielding turf towards the shadow of the door, the smell of stone upon dead earth.

They entered.

CHAPTER 55

Maeshowe lies just off the main road from Stromness to Kirkwall on the other side of the village of Stenness – grid reference 58° 59' 56" N, 3° 11' 20" E. Archaeologists call it a passage grave, and it is considered to be the finest of its kind, New Grange in Ireland the only comparison. It is very dark inside. Natural light only penetrates the long passageway one has to crawl through to enter around the Winter Solstice. In photographs produced for websites on the wonders of the ancients it looks like a dramatic beam illuminating. The only time McGillivray had seen it, the light felt dirty, unwashed, intruding where it was not wanted. The passage can be blocked by a pivot stone of colossal weight that can be moved with very little effort, but only from the inside.

Our wise men and women today fight over who the people who built Maeshowe were. It has been argued that they had clans and totems, perhaps even Shamans; some were the People of the Dog, others the Otter, still others the Eagle. From the small houses and villages over a millennium structures emerged that were colossal in scope, whose scale implies hierarchies of power and religion. There, chieftains and priests may have held sway at Brodgar where the waters meet. There, they raised the stone circles, built a ceremonial city and dug vast henges, the first to do so in all of Britain. Rocks were brought, each district dragging and pushing their own megalith over the low hills to the site of the temple of the Sun. Close by their village, stone houses were raised for their dead to inhabit. The greatest of these began with a vast ditch encircled by an earth barrier. In the centre they erected four stones. Later, these were entombed in a stone chamber made from megaliths corbelled and capped, no one knows how. These places mattered over a far greater breadth than just the islands; messengers went down to Anglesey, and to the great centres of worship in England.

There are legends aplenty about the place. Trows are said to have lived there. The Rip Van Winkle story originated there; islanders make claims, sometimes they are true. Vikings redug the ditch and may have used it for burials. There is no doubt that they went in.

Section 93 of the Orkneyinga Saga, the accounts of the Norsemen in the Isles, in its account of one thirteenth day of Christmas recounts how Earl Harald of Orkney went in pursuit of Svein Asleifarson. A snowstorm forced the men marching on foot to take bitter shelter in this grave. To show that they were literate and unafraid they covered the walls with runes. No blessings. No answers. No great statements about Time and Space, no. They did what young men do. They bragged, boasted and lied. The Guide translates what they left behind in an age appropriate way: 'My Sword is bigger than your sword,' 'I am bloody good at doing this,' and 'These runes are high up,' but only 'We fucked here for three days' if no children are present. This is the first description of gay sex in the islands. Two of the men went mad. We are not told why.

Amongst the graffiti, there is an image of a dragon; carved and curled it sleeps, lost in reptilian dreams. When McGillivray was a child, the custodian allowed him to trace its line with his finger and listen for its breathing. That is when he realised it was alive, its life a secret that must not be shared and only he knew. It was, it still is. One day, he thought, it would awaken like Arthur and drive Orkney's enemies into the Firth. Soon.

The custodian lifted him up so that he could crawl into the side chambers where the dead bodies had been and lie on his back to look at the mighty stone roof. Not any more, and no more playing housies in the Neolithic village of Skara Brae either. The Heritage has made sure of that. Everything is conserved. Admission by tour under protection of a guide. So many enter now that their breath is eroding the dragon. Soon, no one will sleep under the Howe. There will be peace.

CHAPTER 56

McGillivray blinked. Nothing was right. This was no corridor leading into the centre of a tomb. He was indeed in a bitter place but he was outside and from the colour of the bitter air at a time between day and night or night and day. He was confused by lights flashing across an orange sky in steady procession, bewildered by the sound of many waters rushing in and over themselves. Only the air smelled of the grave. Its stench made him cough so much that a small creature, furious at being disturbed started up and was gone. He clung to his fear, it was all that was tangible, comfortable for him. It was strong as the night and as welcome as an old friend whose stories one has grown to know all too well. He was home. This was Hell. This was where they had said he would come and they were right.

The Woman laughed at him, 'No,' she said, 'you are not dead yet. We will go further in and further down.' He got up behind her pillion style and they rode down into what took form as a town.

She was proud of it, this was her capital and she wanted him to appreciate everything he saw, her achievements. She pointed out the sights with pride. Bound to silence he could only listen and nod. This was just as well for everywhere he looked he saw people with what seemed to be badly drawn faces with pencil eyes. The buildings were not quite right, as if their designers had not quite understood perspective. There were no right angles. In the centre of the place, overlooking a plain of pox marked tarmac, the steeple of an old red kirk gave its figure to a marred sky. It was on fire. A young woman danced in the light of it flames to the sound of a fiddler and a bodhran.

On they went, down roads, through traffic and past the closed windows until a red light stopped them near a shelter made of shattered glass. A youngster with coloured hair was leaning against it. She pointed at McGillivray, nudged her two neighbours to get them to look. All three threw back their heads and cackled uproariously. One of them got out her phone and started to take pictures – he didn't have any idea what was so funny until he looked down and realised that for all this time he had been naked; his clothes had all perished in the riding and he was as he would be when the time comes, as it will for all of us, for the winding sheet.

To his shame, she said, 'You are not fit to be seen. We must get you new clothes.'

CHAPTER 57

The woman started her bike up again. She turned down a coffin-wide lane, parked, and bade him dismount. At midnight he knew that this kind of passage between warehouses would be full of dancers, drinkers and those who should know better, but in the grey light it was derelict. Evidence of a good night out, the fast food boxes, bottles and fag ends covered the pavements. A heap of what could be rags lay in the shelter of an open skip. This was clearly the wrong turning, but no, she was not the kind of person who made mistakes. She pressed a bell hidden behind a broken shutter and a door opened. They ascended stairs and entered a shop of the kind that is too expensive to have stock and where nothing has prices. Perhaps nothing is sold.

A young man, clearly the person in charge, formed himself from behind a counter, his head already inclined to the polite position; he was very thin and wearing cologne.

'Madam has a problem?'

The woman stood back and left McGillivray standing naked in the middle of the floor. The Manager looked him up and down for a long moment. He drew air in sharply between his teeth and clapped his hands to summon his assistant. A young man, Ralph, foreign by his speech, came up with his arms full of almost androgynous clothes to lay on the counter. The woman examined them closely. Most she dismissed as inappropriate although she lingered over the fanciest; he wondered if she was considering a dress. His unspoken thought clearly amused her, 'That may come,' she said, 'but not yet. We'll have something more familiar to you.' With a sharp heart stab he realised both that he was being teased and his mind was still open to her.

As there was no changing room, and as he no longer had any

shame to protect, he had to put on the clothes in front of them all. The man in the mirror, highly delighted, preened back at him. The gorgeous reflection was glad indeed to be clothed. He stroked the strange fabrics theatrically and revelled in the glorious skill that had coloured them in the shades of all grasses, turning to get the best angles on how the cuts flattered his figure. McGillivray watched and waited until the apparition was done. The Manager grabbed back his attention with an overly polite 'ahem'. He was smiling and clearly proud of the achievements of his establishment.

'Sir looks so good. They will do you well. How is the fit?'

McGillivray, pleased at the effect his errant reflection achieved by pulling in its stomach was beginning to feel thin. His pleasure was so great that he was about to give the highest praise known in all Orkney. As the words, 'Just fine,' formed in his mouth, for once, discretion stopped him in the nick of time. The Manager blinked with irritation; he smiled through clenched arse and said 'Indeed Sir.'

They left.

She did not pay.

CHAPTER 58

The Woman with McGillivray riding pillion behind her rode down another long street, turned a couple of corners then stopped in front of one of many nondescript entrances. She went in first, he followed quickly, the anxiety of separation speeding him through the heavy doors before they could close, leaving him cold on the street.

The room was a club, something special clearly as despite the ambiguous time of day the place was very full. A live band was playing on stage, a trio of women singing some kind of rock. It really was not his kind of thing. In his youth he had been too pious for music with satanic rhythms. Now he was too snobbish. He clenched his teeth thinking that the older one should really know better.

To block the music out, he turned his focus to the crowd, who seemed to be a little bit of everything. No one, irrespective of shape, was embarrassed to be on the dance floor.

A toned and slippery young man danced towards McGillivray from out of the crowd. He pressed himself against the new jacket. One of his eyebrows was dyed pink. He seemed to be Continental.

'Well, Handsome, can I get you a drink?'

McGillivray looked up to the Woman, who nodded her permission. Two shots glasses instantly appeared in the Lad's hand. McGillivray took one but as he raised it to his lips he heard the cautionary voice of an honorary auntie, 'Mind this on; if ever you meet the Good People avoid the food you are offered. Think what happened to that fiddler and that Greek lassie, Persephone.'

Her husband, Manus, cut across her, 'Aye and there was Jimmock in Evie, your grandfather's cousin. He was kept under the hill for a hundred years or more in payment for a stoup of ale. And he never even liked it.'

McGillivray dropped the glass. The Woman shrugged silently and dismissed the pretty one with a slight movement of her little finger, the emerald on her ring glinting sharply. The dancers picked up again and she disappeared in a blue lowe. He waited. Nothing happened. He lingered at the side of the room as it was gradually emptied, the broken glasses cleared up with the remaining customers who had not scored.

He went up to the man at the door to explain; just as he was about to speak he remembered the words of the Queen. One word, one request for help and he would never be free, he would never get home. McGillivray shrugged, and went to put his hands in his pockets. There was nothing to do but go out into the non comprehending dark. As he left, something atmospheric shifted high above the clouds and forced rain to fall in drops that smelt disgusting and seemed almost to burn where they fell on his hair. His clothes offered him some protection but nothing seemed to keep out the acid for long. He started to walk along the street, the same street, always the same street and no end to the city, the light unchanging.

CHAPTER 59

After much walking he came to a square building that stood in the middle of some kind of plaza lined with small trees. Thin black ribbons hung festooned from the branches, remnants of some kind of celebration that moved almost imperceptibly in the chemical stained air. It had a large porch. On either side of it were arched windows that looked as if they had been boarded up for some time but something about the place did not seem quite dead. The door was ajar. He walked over to it, kicking through an accumulation of leaves and rubbish. If he had been breathing he would have held his breath but there was no need. He pushed at the open door and went in, so many thresholds, so many crossings but never a homecoming.

In front of another set of double doors a seated man studied a large book with a green binding. He turned the pages slowly and with great care. They were blank.

McGillivray recognised him, the main proprietor of the shop, at once. 'I am,' he said, ' the Curator, the Archivist, the Right Hand Man. I am also the Manager. You are welcome.' McGillivray inclined his head slightly but did not accept the proffered hand; something about it was revolting. 'Walk in front of me.'

The doors opened onto a long chamber lit by a light from no obvious source. Rows of males and females of all ages sat, their heads bowed in concentration at individual tables, each writing in another of the large green books. The only noise was the scratching of pens and now and again, a small short scream. No one paid attention. Everyone wrote.

The Manager stopped, 'Sit here,' he said. 'Work.'

McGillivray pulled the chair back, and sat down. He opened the green book, dipped the pen in the ink well and began to write on the empty pages. The ink was white. No marks were visible. He dipped the nib in again and tried to make another mark, the same. He touched the nib with his hand. It burned and left a white mark. He tried to get to his feet and ask for help. The Manager looked at him, one eyebrow arched. McGillivray slumped. He could not speak. He picked up the pen and began to make words.

He wrote lots of lies. All writing is lies. Nothing is fact. Pages filled, hands stained white. If he slowed, the book screamed. When the last page was filled, the assistant came, the man with the coloured eyebrow took it to the shelves that covered the walls and put it in place amongst all the others, no title on the binding, the white words of his life, lost amongst all the others, meaningless.

The assistant placed another volume in front of McGillivray. He opened the cover and began at the top of the first page. Of the making of these books there was no end, and his soul grew weary. Every now and again he stroked his aching right hand with the left, noticed the lines on it growing, liver spots appearing, his skin itself paper. He was becoming old. He was becoming very old and he had what he wanted. She had given him his gift and his doom. He had his desire, he was the writer who asked not for readers. He was happy.

CHAPTER 60

The Manager came and stood by his desk. 'Come,' he commanded. McGillivray had atrophied. The assistant helped him to his feet and guided him out through both sets of doors and onto the street. Nothing had changed. The air was as bitter. They walked slowly on and further along the empty streets. At the far end, they halted before the entrance of some kind of park. It had great railings of silver; there had been majesty here once. A cinder path lead to its centre. On either side of him, in the shadows he could see shapes of people moving, writhing, restricted. One man reared up in front of them, his trousers down around his ankles, he pushed a needle into the vein in his groin and was gone.

In the centre the Woman stood amidst four trees. She made address to him, her tone high, impersonal.

'I will give you a gift for the contribution you have made, a small token for all the work you have done with me.'

McGillivray went down stiffly on one knee taking his cap from his head. He could taste the gold, fame, contracts and an agent; it would almost be worth his aching knees.

'I have thought long and decided. Truth would suit you, I think. You shall have a tongue that will never lie.'

It took a moment or so for the full impact of his doom to dawn on him. He gabbled out his first words breaking the silence of the peaceable years; his own voice sounded unfamiliar. The vowels hurt.

'No,' he panicked 'no, your Ladyship. I've got a living to make, I want to write, and poetic license is needed. How can I speak of my neighbours and work mates with honesty? I would rather not. If it's all the same to you and as it's been such a pleasure to serve you I'll just be on my way.'

'Peace,' she said. 'What must be, must be.'

The Manager plucked a burnished apple from one of the trees; it sighed gently at its sudden loss. A lilt moved through the leaves, their newest sorrow. The red apple was passed to McGillivray with a polite nod and an unspoken demand.

McGillivray looked at the fruit for the longest moment. Eventually, he shrugged his shoulders, raised it and felt the texture of skin against his lips and teeth. He bit into the sharp flesh and chewed. It tasted of nothing but apple. He felt unaltered and shrugged, relieved.

The Woman laughed. 'Should a liar feel different to an honest man? Do you expect to be a saint? Now go, before I change my mind and keep you here!'

As he walked through the huge silver gates he heard her voice calling after him, 'Remember McGillivray, my man, you can still interpret.'

CHAPTER 61

He blinked and found himself on the grass at Maeshowe, his back flat to the hill at the far side from the entrance. In the distance he could see a herd of tourists moving across the field; to the fore a blond tour guide pedalled in his direction with an officious manner. He looked down at himself and saw he was still wearing the outlandish garb given to him by the Queen. He had to get away before they arrived, saw him in this getup. He did not know how, was not ready yet, to explain anything. He climbed over a barbed wire fence, ran over the grass and over the next field onto the road. He walked back towards the Stones: his bike was where it had been left, unrusted; the satchel by the Comet stone appeared undamaged by dew. He cycled back to the town the way he had come. He was no longer surprised that the three women were still playing at the pier, a few more coppers in their bunnet. He risked the main street and pushed the bike back up the hill past judgemental birds and laconic cats until he got back to his house and opened the unlocked door. The arrangements of dust with which he decorated the floor of the hall were undisturbed and so it was clear to him that no one had been in, but then no one ever came in.

Safe now, he took the satchel off his shoulder and emptied its contents into the kitchen bin. He went up the narrow stairs to his bedroom and stood in front off the mirror. The clothes from the shop under the hill were all gone. He stripped himself of his island habit and saw himself there soul-naked and ugly. Nothing had changed. Exhausted by drink and exercise, he fell on his bed and slept. For the first time in years, he slept.

All that night the south easterly wind, the worst for the Town, threw hail, hard as words sharp at his window. Despite the clamouring, he slept soundly till eight. After showering and dressing he went down to the shop to get bread, honey and milk.

Just that, nothing more. No comment was made. When he got back, he made coffee, ate some of the food and took his medication.

It was time to start. He went through to his writing room and opened the curtains. The world outside was covered with a thin dust of white that would last mere moments after the rise of the cold sun, too bright for delusions. He looked out at incongruous palm trees in his garden, the one his mother had planted and the houses opposite, below. Beyond them the grey sea, and the shapes of the other islands, the edge of Hoy, Flotta with its oil terminal and Cava, now abandoned. From his window, there was little sign of plough and fishermen, hawk rise, and voe. These symbols that have gone away in their stone ships, the pure and impure alike, are all dead. McGillivray picked up a pen, a sharp edged one he had used for calligraphy and wrote in huge letters on sheets of newspaper, 'I hated this place.' He paused, exhaled, and then wrote 'Fucking Hamnavoe.' With sticky tape he attached the sheets to the front of the framed paintings of Hoy and the town on the wall and he laughed.

END

Afterword and Acknowledgements

The quote on page 110 is from the 23rd Psalm in the version contained in the Scots Metrical Psalter of 1650 and sung at most respectable funerals to the tune *Crimmond.* It won't be at mine. I much prefer 'Highland Cathedral'. Psalm 84 vvs 1 and 11 are quoted much later.

Whilst the author asserts his rights and so on, this piece took on shape on a creative writing course taught by Carl MacDougall. The experience of hearing it discussed by the other students and Carl's acute insights were formative to its production. Without their encouragement the text would not have been committed. Thanks to them is gladly acknowledged. The editor, Seonaid Francis, then licked me into shape, a process for which I am very grateful.

Adam, Rüthe, Maeve, the Manager and Martha are all composite characters with elements drawn from the various men and women who were strongly supportive in McGillivray's life. The actions attributed to them are distorted through perspective and should not be thought of as accurate. They all, the Manager included, kept McGillivray alive. If he were real he would be glad.

The late Dave Johns of the real Middlesbrough made up about 20% of the Adam character. He died in 1994; he was loved and is missed daily. This book is dedicated to him. With every job change he took his salary went down. May his name live forever.

More Books From ThunderPoint Publishing Ltd.

Mule Train

by Huw Francis

ISBN: 978-0-9575689-0-7 (eBook)
ISBN: 978-0-9575689-1-4 (Paperback)

Four lives come together in the remote and spectacular mountains bordering Afghanistan and explode in a deadly cocktail of treachery, betrayal and violence.

Written with a deep love of Pakistan and the Pakistani people, Mule Train will sweep you from Karachi in the south to the Shandur Pass in the north, through the dangerous borderland alongside Afghanistan, in an adventure that will keep you gripped throughout.

'Stunningly captures the feel of Pakistan, from Karachi to the hills' – tripfiction.com

A Good Death

by Helen Davis

ISBN: 978-0-9575689-7-6 (eBook)
ISBN: 978-0-9575689-6-9 (Paperback)

'A good death is better than a bad conscience,' said Sophie.

1983 – Georgie, Theo, Sophie and Helena, four disparate young Cambridge undergraduates, set out to scale Ausangate, one of the highest and most sacred peaks in the Andes.

Seduced into employing the handsome and enigmatic Wamani as a guide, the four women are initiated into the mystically dangerous side of Peru, Wamani and themselves as they travel from Cuzco to the mountain, a journey that will shape their lives forever.

2013 – though the women are still close, the secrets and betrayals of Ausangate chafe at the friendship.

A girls' weekend at a lonely Fenland farmhouse descends into conflict with the insensitive inclusion of an overbearing young academic toyboy brought along by Theo. Sparked by his unexpected presence, pent up petty jealousies, recriminations and bitterness finally explode the truth of Ausangate, setting the women on a new and dangerous path.

Sharply observant and darkly comic, Helen Davis's début novel is an elegant tale of murder, seduction, vengeance, and the value of a good friendship.

'The prose is crisp, adept, and emotionally evocative' – Lesbrary.com

The Birds That Never Flew

by Margot McCuaig

Shortlisted for the Dundee International Book Prize 2012

Longlisted for the Polari First Book Prize 2014

ISBN: 978-0-9929768-5-9 (eBook)
ISBN: 978-0-9929768-4-2 (Paperback)

'Have you got a light hen? I'm totally gaspin.'

Battered and bruised, Elizabeth has taken her daughter and left her abusive husband Patrick. Again. In the bleak and impersonal Glasgow housing office Elizabeth meets the provocatively intriguing drug addict Sadie, who is desperate to get her own life back on track.

The two women forge a fierce and interdependent relationship as they try to rebuild their shattered lives, but despite their bold, and sometimes illegal attempts it seems impossible to escape from the abuse they have always known, and tragedy strikes.

More than a decade later Elizabeth has started to implement her perfect revenge – until a surreal Glaswegian Virgin Mary steps in with imperfect timing and a less than divine attitude to stick a spoke in the wheel of retribution.

Tragic, darkly funny and irreverent, *The Birds That Never Flew* ushers in a new and vibrant voice in Scottish literature.

'...dark, beautiful and moving, I wholeheartedly recommend' scanoir.co.uk

Toxic

by Jackie McLean
Shortlisted for the Yeovil Book Prize 2011
ISBN: 978-0-9575689-8-3 (eBook)
ISBN: 978-0-9575689-9-0 (Paperback)

The recklessly brilliant DI Donna Davenport, struggling to hide a secret from police colleagues and get over the break-up with her partner, has been suspended from duty for a fiery and inappropriate outburst to the press.

DI Evanton, an old-fashioned, hard-living misogynistic copper has been newly demoted for thumping a suspect, and transferred to Dundee with a final warning ringing in his ears and a reputation that precedes him.

And in the peaceful, rolling Tayside farmland a deadly store of MIC, the toxin that devastated Bhopal, is being illegally stored by a criminal gang smuggling the valuable substance necessary for making cheap pesticides.

An anonymous tip-off starts a desperate search for the MIC that is complicated by the uneasy partnership between Davenport and Evanton and their growing mistrust of each others actions.

Compelling and authentic, Toxic is a tense and fast paced crime thriller.

'...a humdinger of a plot that is as realistic as it is frightening' – crimefictionlover.com

In The Shadow Of The Hill

by Helen Forbes

ISBN: 978-0-9929768-1-1 (eBook)
ISBN: 978-0-9929768-0-4 (Paperback)

An elderly woman is found battered to death in the common stairwell of an Inverness block of flats.

Detective Sergeant Joe Galbraith starts what seems like one more depressing investigation of the untimely death of a poor unfortunate who was in the wrong place, at the wrong time.

As the investigation spreads across Scotland it reaches into a past that Joe has tried to forget, and takes him back to the Hebridean island of Harris, where he spent his childhood.

Among the mountains and the stunning landscape of religiously conservative Harris, in the shadow of Ceapabhal, long buried events and a tragic story are slowly uncovered, and the investigation takes on an altogether more sinister aspect.

In The Shadow Of The Hill skilfully captures the intricacies and malevolence of the underbelly of Highland and Island life, bringing tragedy and vengeance to the magical beauty of the Outer Hebrides.

'...our first real home-grown sample of modern Highland noir' – Roger Hutchison; West Highland Free Press

Over Here

by Jane Taylor

ISBN: 978-0-9929768-3-5 (eBook)
ISBN: 978-0-9929768-2-8 (Paperback)

'It's coming up to twenty-four hours since the boy stepped down from the big passenger liner – it must be, he reckons foggily – because morning has come around once more with the awful irrevocability of time destined to lead nowhere in this worrying new situation. His temporary minder on board – last spotted heading for the bar some while before the lumbering process of docking got underway – seems to have vanished for good. Where does that leave him now? All on his own in a new country: that's where it leaves him. He is just nine years old.'

An eloquently written novel tracing the social transformations of a century where possibilities were opened up by two world wars that saw millions of men move around the world to fight, and mass migration to the new worlds of Canada and Australia by tens of thousands of people looking for a better life.

Through the eyes of three generations of women, the tragic story of the nine year old boy on Liverpool docks is brought to life in saddeningly evocative prose.

'...a sweeping haunting first novel that spans four generations and two continents...' Cristina Odone/Catholic Herald

The Bonnie Road

by Suzanne d'Corsey

ISBN: 978-1-910946-01-5 (eBook)
ISBN: 978-0-9929768-6-6 (Paperback)

My grandmother passed me in transit. She was leaving, I was coming into this world, our spirits meeting at the door to my mother's womb, as she bent over the bed to close the thin crinkled lids of her own mother's eyes.

The women of Morag's family have been the keepers of tradition for generations, their skills and knowledge passed down from woman to woman, kept close and hidden from public view, official condemnation and religious suppression.

In late 1970s St. Andrews, demand for Morag's services are still there, but requested as stealthily as ever, for even in 20th century Scotland witchcraft is a dangerous Art to practise.

When newly widowed Rosalind arrives from California to tend her ailing uncle, she is drawn unsuspecting into a new world she never knew existed, one in which everyone seems to have a secret, but that offers greater opportunities than she dreamt of – if she only has the courage to open her heart to it.

Richly detailed, dark and compelling, d'Corsey magically transposes the old ways of Scotland into the 20th Century and brings to life the ancient traditions and beliefs that still dance just below the surface of the modern world.

'...successfully portrays rich characters in compelling plots, interwoven with atmospheric Scottish settings & history and coloured with witchcraft & romance' – poppypeacockpens.com

The House with the Lilac Shutters: and other stories

by Gabrielle Barnby

ISBN: 978-1-910946-02-2 (eBook)
ISBN: 978-0-9929768-8-0 (Paperback)

Irma Lagrasse has taught piano to three generations of villagers, whilst slowly twisting the knife of vengeance; Nico knows a secret; and M. Lenoir has discovered a suppressed and dangerous passion.

Revolving around the Café Rose, opposite The House with the Lilac Shutters, this collection of contemporary short stories links a small town in France with a small town in England, traces the unexpected connections between the people of both places and explores the unpredictable influences that the past can have on the present.

Characters weave in and out of each other's stories, secrets are concealed and new connections are made.

With a keenly observant eye, Barnby illustrates the everyday tragedies, sorrows, hopes and joys of ordinary people in this vividly understated and unsentimental collection.

'The more I read, and the more descriptions I encountered, the more I was put in mind of one of my all time favourite texts – Dylan Thomas' *Under Milk Wood*' – lindasbookbag.com

Talk of the Toun

by Helen MacKinven

ISBN: 978-1-910946-00-8 (eBook)
ISBN: 978-0-9929768-7-3 (Paperback)

'She was greetin' again. But there's no need for Lorraine to be feart, since the first day of primary school, Angela has always been there to mop up her tears and snotters.'

An uplifting black comedy of love, family life and friendship, Talk of the Toun is a bittersweet coming-of-age tale set in the summer of 1985, in working class, central belt Scotland.

Lifelong friends Angela and Lorraine are two very different girls, with a growing divide in their aspirations and ambitions putting their friendship under increasing strain.

Artistically gifted Angela has her sights set on art school, but lassies like Angela, from a small town council scheme, are expected to settle for a nice wee secretarial job at the local factory. Her only ally is her gallus gran, Senga, the pet psychic, who firmly believes that her granddaughter can be whatever she wants.

Though Lorraine's ambitions are focused closer to home Angela has plans for her too, and a caravan holiday to Filey with Angela's family tests the dynamics of their relationship and has lifelong consequences for them both.

Effortlessly capturing the religious and social intricacies of 1980s Scotland, Talk of the Toun is the perfect mix of pathos and humour as the two girls wrestle with the complications of growing up and exploring who they really are.

'Fresh, fierce and funny...a sharp and poignant study of growing up in 1980s Scotland. You'll laugh, you'll cry...you'll cringe' – KAREN CAMPBELL

About Tim Morrison

Tim grew up in Orkney then attended Aberdeen University to study Divinity with the intention of being ordained into the Church of Scotland. He subsequently worked in training and development in Health and Social Care.

He is an active political campaigner, blogs as the OrkneyVole and is the the lead applicant in the 'Orkney Four' case brought against Alistair Carmichael MP under the Representation of the People Act.

Outside of Scotland Tim has lived in London and Middlesbrough, but is now back home in Stromness.

He has written poetry and short prose published locally, and completed his M.Litt. with the University of the Highlands and Islands, gaining the Post-graduate Student of Year Award.

Tim is the third member of the Stromness writers group to have signed with ThunderPoint Publishing.